When Rafe cl...
door behind ...
at the ceiling,
she would ha... ...
kissed her.

For a moment, she'd thought he was about to. And, God help her, she'd wanted him to, with the same deep longing she'd harbored for the past nine years.

Despite everything, the spark between them had never died.

Guilt churned inside her. She owed him so much. Besides what he'd done for her since her accident, he'd given her the most precious gift she'd ever received. And he didn't even know it.

She owed him the truth. But if she told him, would he hate her? It didn't matter. She had no choice.

She squeezed her eyes shut, a tear tracing a damp path down her cheek. How could she ever tell Rafe that the little boy sleeping in the room down the hall was his son?

Dear Reader,

A new year has begun, and in its honor we bring you
six new—and wonderful!—Intimate Moments novels. First
up is *A Marriage-Minded Man?* Linda Turner returns to
THE LONE STAR SOCIAL CLUB for this scintillating tale of
a cop faced with a gorgeous witness who's offering him lots of
evidence—about a crime that has yet to be committed! What's
her game? Is she involved? Is she completely crazy? Or is she
totally on the level—and also the perfect woman for him?

Then there's Beverly Barton's *Gabriel Hawk's Lady,* the newest
of THE PROTECTORS. Rorie Dean needs help rescuing her
young nephew from the jungles of San Miguel, and Gabriel is
the only man with the know-how to help. But what neither of
them has counted on is the attraction that simmers between
them, making their already dangerous mission a threat on not
just one level but two!

Welcome Suzanne Brockmann back with *Love with the Proper
Stranger,* a steamy tale of deceptions, false identities and
overwhelming passion. In *Ryan's Rescue,* Karen Leabo matches
a socialite on the run with a reporter hot on the trail of a story
that starts looking very much like a romance. *Wife on Demand* is
an intensely emotional marriage-of-convenience story from the
pen of Alexandra Sellers. And finally, welcome historical author
Barbara Ankrum, who debuts in the line with *To Love a Cowboy.*

Enjoy them all, then come back next month for more excitement
and passion—right here in Silhouette Intimate Moments.

Yours,

Leslie J. Wainger
Senior Editor and Editorial Coordinator

Please address questions and book requests to:
Silhouette Reader Service
U.S.: 3010 Walden Ave., P.O. Box 1325, Buffalo, NY 14269
Canadian: P.O. Box 609, Fort Erie, Ont. L2A 5X3

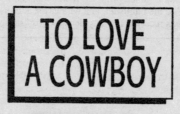

TO LOVE A COWBOY

BARBARA ANKRUM

Published by Silhouette Books

America's Publisher of Contemporary Romance

SILHOUETTE BOOKS

ISBN: 0-373-07834-X

TO LOVE A COWBOY

Copyright © 1998 by Barbara Ankrum

BARBARA ANKRUM

says she's always been an incurable romantic, with a passion for books and stories about the healing power of love. It never occurred to her to write seriously until her husband, David, discovered a box full of her unfinished stories and insisted that she pursue her dream. Need she say more about why she believes in love?

With a successful career as a commercial actress behind her, Barbara decided she had plenty of eccentric characters to people the stories that inhabited her imagination. She wrote her first novel in between auditions and she's never looked back. Her historicals have won the prestigious Reviewer's Choice and K.I.S.S. Awards from *Romantic Times*, and she's been nominated for a RITA Award from RWA. Barbara lives in Southern California with her actor/writer/hero-husband, and their two perfect children.

To Barbara Joel, my soul sister and best friend, who always knows when I need a kick in the pants and when I just need to whine. This one's for you.

With special thanks to my agent, Irene Goodman, for keeping the faith. You're the best.

Chapter 1

The phone shrieked on the bedside table, wrenching him from the shadowy nightmare of plunging hooves and the white-eyed fury of an angry bull. Disoriented, he jerked upright in bed, blinking at the yellow pool of moonlight spilling through his naked bedroom window and onto his glistening arms. In the utter stillness of night, his heart battered the wall of his chest and echoed in his ears. A familiar pain shot through his right side and knee at his sudden movement. He sucked in a breath between clenched teeth and cursed.

For the briefest of moments, he wondered whether the ringing had been part of his dream—a judge's timer buzzer signaling the end of his ride, the scream of the ambulance that had come to pick up the pieces that day.

The phone jangled again.

Damn. Rafe's glare went from the phone to the clock as he raked the hair from his eyes with one hand. One-forty-five a.m. Who the hell would call him in the middle of the night? Probably a wrong number. All the same, some darker instinct made him reach for the receiver.

"Yeah?"

"Uh..." came a tentative female voice, "Mr. Kellard? Mr. Rafe Kellard?"

So much for a wrong number. "Yeah? Who's this?"

"Uh, Mr. Kellard, my name is Nancy Kowalski. You don't know me, but..."

Annoyance bunched the muscles of his shoulders, and Rafe sent up a silent prayer that she wasn't some glittery-eyed rodeo groupie who'd waited until the dead of night to track him down. The novelty of that had worn off years ago. He shot a look at the clock again. Exactly three hours before he had to roll out of bed and head for the fence line. Mentally he calculated how long it would take him to fall back asleep, if he even could.

"...I'm a trauma volunteer at Reno General, in Reno, Nevada," the voice on the other end went on.

That got his attention. "Reno?" he repeated, trying to get a grip on who she was.

"Yes...Nevada. I'm sorry, I know it's late."

"It's the middle of the night. Look, if this is some kind of prank call—"

"No, sir. Nothing like that. Uh...if you'll just bear with me for a moment..."

Something prickled the back of his neck. Her voice sounded a little shaky, uncertain, as if she were trying to say something difficult. That realization cleared the cobwebs from his brain. What had she said? Reno General? *Hospital?* The word settled into Rafe's consciousness like a cold, flat stone.

Reno. Reno. That was seven hundred miles away. Hell, he didn't even know anybody in Reno. Did he? He realized the woman was talking again.

"...just brought a patient in to emergency, and going through her things, all we found was a newspaper clipping about you in her purse. It had a note written on it with your address in case of an emergency. I know this is a long shot, but—''

His heartbeat slowed to a standstill and his throat went dry. ''A woman?''

''Yes. Mr. Kellard, do you know someone named Cara Lynn Jamison?''

If the woman on the phone had reached through the wire and sucker punched him, she couldn't have more effectively driven the breath from his lungs. The room seemed to shift as Rafe swung his bare legs over the side of the bed, switched the phone to his other ear and braced his right hand on the bedside table.

Carly.

''Mr. Kellard?'' the woman asked. ''Are you still there?''

He cleared the sudden tightness in his throat. ''How is she?''

The woman hesitated. ''At the moment, her condition is listed as serious.''

He squeezed his eyes shut. *Carly. After all these years.* ''Serious. What the hell does that mean?''

''Are you...her husband, Mr. Kellard?''

Another time, he might have laughed at that question. But not tonight. ''No.''

''A relative?''

''No.''

''I see.'' An uncomfortable silence stretched on the wire between them.

''What happened to her?'' he asked in a hollow voice.

''She was involved in a motor vehicle accident on the Truckee Pass. There was an unexpected storm here, and the roads are very icy tonight. Ms. Jamison is unconscious, and has been since she was brought in. There are a few other minor injuries, but that's all I'm at liberty to tell you.

Would you happen to know where we might contact her husband?''

Rafe's hand tightened on the receiver. "I..." He cleared his suddenly clogged throat. "I couldn't tell you anything about that, except...I knew she married."

"Well," the woman went on, "there's no ring on her left hand, but we assumed...because of the child..."

He sat up straighter. "She has a kid?"

"Yes. A little boy. He was in the car with her. He's doing fine. Only a few minor cuts and bruises. But he's pretty scared, and we can't seem to get much out of him."

Rafe put his hand over the mouthpiece and cursed softly. He took three deep breaths, then spoke again. "Listen, I don't know anything about her husband, Miss—?"

"Kowalski."

"Yeah, Kowalski. I...uh, haven't seen Carly for some time. Years, in fact. We used to be... That is, we're old friends. That's all."

"Oh." The single syllable betrayed her disappointment.

"Her home phone number in Los Angeles was disconnected, and her car is full of her things, as if she were moving. We're kind of at a loss. Does she have other family we can contact?"

Rafe thought of her parents, who'd died when Carly was seven, and her maiden great-aunt Katherine, who'd practically raised her. He'd heard she'd passed away in L.A. only last spring. "No," he answered at last. "There's no one I know of."

"I see."

Rafe listened to Kowalski breathing on the other end of the line. She was waiting. For what? For him to say he'd come for Carly, for her son? For him to throw away years of trying to forget what had happened between them? To forget her? Hell, he couldn't do it. He wasn't responsible for Carly or her kid. Just because she carried around some dog-eared newspaper clipping about him from better days.

Just because once he would have done anything...*anything* to keep her from walking away from him.

Winter seeped against his bare feet through the cold planked floorboards of his bedroom. Outside the window, what he hoped would be the last snowflakes of the year struck against the pane and melted.

Through the dark shimmer of glass, he could almost see Carly, with a mane of silver-blond hair that framed her face, the single dimple that dented her left cheek when she smiled, the special light that had shone in her golden-brown eyes—until those last days they were together. It had gone out then, like a wind-sucked flame.

He'd spent the past nine years trying to blot the picture of her from his memory. Now a slippery road and an out-of-the-blue phone call had resurrected it. He ground his teeth together. She wasn't his problem, dammit, even if she—

"Listen, I—I'm sorry to have bothered you," Kowalski mumbled on the other end. "We'll do our best to work something out for the boy. Social services has provisions for this sort of thing."

The iciness of the cold floor crept up through his legs. "Provisions?"

"Well, yes. You see, his mother's in no shape to care for him, and because of his age..."

A thought crept into his consciousness as the woman mumbled on. One that startled him with its swiftness. A child. Carly's child. She'd talked of having children. With him. What if—?

"...temporary foster care. With no relative or close family friend willing to claim him...take responsibility—"

"How old is he?" Rafe asked sharply.

"What?" Kowalski stammered.

"How old?"

"Uh...seven...maybe eight. We're not sure. He won't really talk."

Seven or eight. Rafe's mind tripped backward over the years, counting summers come and gone. He'd last seen Carly nine years ago. His hand, which had gone suddenly cold, tightened involuntarily around the phone. She would have told him if— Wouldn't she?

"Of course," Kowalski went on, "the courts will have to appoint some sort of a guardian—"

"No." The word was out before he could stop it.

"I—I beg your pardon?" Kowalski stammered.

He rubbed his temple. "I said no. Listen, how do I get there?"

"You mean—?"

"Yeah. How do I get to you from the Reno airport?" He flipped on the bedside lamp and scribbled the directions on a scrap of paper by the phone. "I'll be there as soon as I can."

"Mr. Kellard," Kowalski began when he'd finished, "I'm really…very sorry about all this. He's a cute kid. Scared, but sweet. I'm glad he won't have to be shuffled off into…you know…"

"Yeah," Rafe agreed. Foster care was something he did know about, and something he wouldn't wish on any kid.

"I just wanted to say," Kowalski continued, "that, well, I'm a big fan of yours, Mr. Kellard. Have been for years. I sure hope everything works out all right."

Rafe hung up and stared out into the inky, snowswept night. "So do I, lady," he muttered to the empty room. "But I wouldn't lay good money on it."

Rafe's uneven footsteps echoed in the lonely hospital corridor. Ignoring the wintery ache in his right leg brought on by the cramped flight and the cold night air, he headed for the third-floor nurse's station.

The night-shift nurse sat alone behind the desk, haloed in the harsh light of a halogen lamp, her gray head bent over the charts she was working on. She looked up as he approached. She was small, and wiry, with a face he supposed simply scared the illness right out of most of her patients. Her name tag read Nursing Supervisor Rawlins.

"Yes?" she demanded in a smoke-graveled voice.

With one hand, Rafe brushed the snow from the shoulders of his sheepskin coat. "Cara Lynn Jamison? They told me downstairs she was on this floor."

He felt the professional coolness of Rawlins's scan—from the dark shadow that stubbled his jaw to the damp tangle of hair revealed when he pulled off his battered Stetson.

Her deep brown eyes darted back to the cluttered top of her desk. "Ah…let's see…Jamison. The car accident?"

Rafe's jaw tightened. After a sleepless night on a pitching express-cargo plane out of Durango, he was sorely tempted to remind her Carly's life counted for more than the sum of a few broken automobile parts in some snowstorm, but he bit back the retort.

"She was brought in last night," he answered, meeting her stare. "A Miss Kowalski called me."

The woman's demeanor warmed slightly. "Oh, Nancy. Of course. You must be—" she looked at a note on her desk "—Mr. Kellard?"

"Right." With still-numb fingers, he fumbled with the buttons on his sheared-sheepskin jacket and shrugged it off.

"Nancy said you were on your way." The nurse pushed her chair back from the desk and stood. "She didn't think you'd be here so soon."

Soon? It felt like days since he'd gotten the phone call, but it had only been a little over five hours. He ran a chilled hand down his face. "How is Carly…Ms. Jamison?"

The nurse stood and came around the desk with a squeak of rubber heels. "I'm afraid you'll have to speak with the attending physician about that, but I'm sure you'll want to see the boy—''

He reached for her elbow as she brushed past him. "Not until I get a straight answer from you. How *is* she?"

She glared back at him, lips pursed and cheeks hollowed. Then, inexplicably, her face softened. "She's still in ICU. She's stable, but there's been no change in her condition. She hasn't regained consciousness. I'm sorry."

The knot that had curled in Rafe's belly since the phone call cinched inexorably tighter.

Another, younger nurse took Rawlin's place at the nurses' station, staring wide-eyed at Rafe's hand on Rawlin's arm. "You all right, Marge?" the new one asked.

"Fine," Rawlins replied tartly, not taking her eyes off Rafe. "Mr. Kellard is upset, that's all."

Slowly, he released the woman, then, on a deep breath, followed her to the elevator. They disembarked on a floor marked Pediatrics.

The dimly lit hallway, the antiseptic smell, the soft hum and beep of machinery in the rooms he passed, disquieted Rafe more than he wanted to admit. God, he hated hospitals. After he left the last one, he'd sworn they'd have to kill him before getting him near another one.

They stopped at a room marked 217.

"He's finally asleep," Rawlins announced in a surprisingly gentle voice. "It took nearly the whole night, because he insisted on seeing his mother. But of course..." She pushed the door open silently.

An arc of light fell upon the huddled form of a boy, nearly lost in the too-large bed. He looked more like seven than eight. But hell, Rafe was no expert at guessing kids' ages. Straw-colored hair peeked out from beneath the covers, and as he drew closer, a face appeared, too. Except for the small bandage across the forehead, it was the face of a cherub.

Swallowing hard, Rafe felt his heart thud heavily in his

chest. Carly's child. Her son. He looks just like her, he thought. Same mouth—naturally curved up at the corners; same nose—small, straight. The jawline was different—squarer.

Something in the kid's hand caught Rafe's eye. He pulled the cover down slightly to reveal a photograph one of the nurses must have given him to hold. Rafe slipped it out of the boy's small hand and stared at it in the dim light. Carly, the boy and a blond-haired, slightly built man smiled back at him. They were standing on the deck of a sailboat. One of those thirty-five-foot jobs that slept six and could sail to a tropical paradise on a moment's notice.

Impressive. But not altogether surprising. He's always known Carly would land on her feet. In money.

The boy in the picture was holding up his prize catch—a fat six-inch fish, still wriggling on its hook.

Rafe's gaze traveled back to the man in the picture—and the protective embrace he had around Carly and the boy. They were a family. Any fool could see that. The kid belonged to this stranger to whom Rafe had once lost Carly. Not to him.

Definitely not to him.

A strange kind of disappointment disguised as relief skittered through him. Not that he'd really wanted to believe the boy was his. More than that, he would never have believed Carly capable of keeping such a thing as his own child from him.

Rafe slammed his eyes shut. He had never wanted to believe she'd left him for another man, either.

Carly had even denied it. But a woman didn't just run out on a man she claimed to love—or a man who loved her—without a damn good reason. *Well,* he thought bitterly, looking at her child, *some reasons are better than others.* She'd wasted no time marrying that law professor of hers and starting a family. *The family she'd said she wanted with him.* As he looked at the flesh-and-blood ev-

idence of Carly's union with another man, the hurt cut
more deeply than Rafe had expected. Not for the first time,
he wondered how different his life would have turned out
if he hadn't been so shortsighted.

He stared at the child, transfixed, feeling more acutely
aware of the impassable rift that had grown between him
and Carly than he had in all the years that had passed. The
boy made everything somehow more concrete. Final.

He turned to Rawlins. "What's his name?"

"He said it was Evan," she answered. "That's about
all we could get out of him." Rawlins smoothed the blanket at the foot of the boy's bed. "Shall I wake him?"

Rafe tore his gaze from the kid and started for the door.
"No. I want to see his mother first."

A herd of horses was stampeding through her head.

That was the only explanation that made any sense to
Carly's muddled brain. Eyes closed tightly against the
thundering pain, she risked a slight movement of her head,
toward the sound that had brought her up from that dark
abyss of blessed nothingness.

The Voice.

More specifically, the man's voice. She couldn't make
out any real words. Only the soothing baritone that seemed
as familiar as the heartbeat thudding inside her head. Instinctively she leaned toward the sound.

Instantly she regretted the movement. Pain exploded
through her head, as if some very large monster were rattling the bars of its cage. Nausea crept up her throat, and
fear pumped through her like a stab of cold air.

Blackness threatened the hint of light behind her lids
once more. It ebbed and flowed with the current of pain,
like the slow sweep of a raven's wing. Darkness had always scared her, yet she fought it off now, only for the
sake of that voice....

Open your eyes.

Had the thought been her own, or had the Voice demanded it? Her thought process rebelled. Too muddled to think... But it seemed a reasonable request. Her eyes refused to cooperate. Why? Something heavy was...pressing on her. If only she could shift out from under it—

A chill of sweat broke out on her skin. *Big* mistake, she thought, swallowing hard and stilling instantly. The burning pain, she realized, was definitely in, but not limited to, her aching head. It was, in point of fact, everywhere. She felt broken, like a china doll.

Some high-pitched metronome echoed the rapid tripping of her heart.

Okay. Okay. Don't move. Just...just lie here.

But where's here?

Frankly, my dear, I don't—

"Open your eyes, Carly. You can hear me. I know you can," came the Voice again, clearly this time. Something prickled her foggy mind. It sounded familiar, like the voice that had haunted her dreams for years.

Dreams.

Relief poured through her. That was it! It was all a dream, she reasoned. If she opened her eyes, she'd wake up and see it was all an illusion—the pain, the voice, the darkness.

"Carly—"

Do it! she told herself. She'd never been a coward— except, she amended, maybe once. Pushing back the darkness, she forced her eyes open.

She found herself flat on her back in a...bed. Not *her* bed, she noted with a frown. Not even her bedroom. The partially curtained-off room—awash with shadowy shapes—seemed dimly lit and stark, the dimness relieved only by the daylight spilling from a nearby window. Sunlight glinted off some steel contraption above her.... What was the word? *Pulleys.*

Below that, her leg—swathed in white—hung like an ungainly ballast on a scale. Her ankle throbbed.

Broken?

She tried to wiggle her toes, then sucked in a sharp breath. *Definitely.* Swallowing down a wave of nausea, she sent up a silent prayer that all this was still just a dream. But on a scale of one to ten, this open-eyed dream had the other one beat hands down.

The shadowy figure of a man swam into focus as he got to his feet beside her. At first, he wasn't much more than a blob of darkness against the light behind him. He mumbled something that sounded like a prayer as the blotchy shadows fell away from him.

Her heartbeat stalled in her chest. Now she knew she was dreaming. Rafe Kellard was ancient history and wishful thinking all rolled into one. Despite her best attempts to banish him from her subconscious, he'd inhabited her dreams for years now. It shouldn't surprise her that he was here in this one. Only he seemed…real…standing beside her here—wherever the heck here was.

A crooked, familiar smile lifted one side of his mouth. "Welcome back."

She stared at him for a long moment, half expecting the apparition to vanish. It didn't.

"Rafe?" The word came out in a croaking whisper.

His expression grew guarded even as she watched it. "Hi, Carly."

She sucked in a breath. *Rafe.* Dear God, he was real. She drank in the sight of him for a long, confused moment. He looked bigger than she remembered. Stronger. The years had honed his already muscular frame like a fine weapon, forged by flame to steely perfection. His broad shoulders strained the seams of his denim workshirt. A day's growth and then some of dark beard stubbled his chin, highlighting a thin white scar along his jawline. She didn't remember that being there before.

Silver threaded the coal-black hair that cut carelessly across his eyes. She remembered those the most—the bluest eyes she'd ever seen on a human being, they could be cool as the deepest ice, or warm as a sun-baked Colorado sky. Now, they seemed hooded by some emotion she couldn't name.

Her voice sounded hoarse when she mumbled, "I don't understand."

A small breath of laughter escaped his lips. "Hey, that makes two of us, darlin'."

Carly squinted at the room. "Where...where am I?"

"In a hospital. In Reno. ICU, to be specific."

The room revolved in a slow, sickening spin. "Hospital?"

"You had a car accident near here. Do you remember?"

She stared blankly at him, trying to get a grip. Accident? If she'd had an accident, surely she'd remember. Wouldn't she? She tried hard to clear her thoughts...to think. Her head ached.

"Not really. I remember...driving," she began haltingly. "And...the snow..." Her mind went blank. Nothing. Think. Think!

Then, images flashed through her mind: snow, swirling and driving against the vanishing blacktop; suitcases crammed in beside an overgrown ficus tree and Evan's Super-Nintendo in the back seat of her Accord.

Oh, my God! She lunged up off the pillow.

"Evan!" Pain knifed through her as Rafe's strong hands pressed her back against the pillow.

"Take it easy, Carly."

"My son—"

"He's doing fine. He's sleeping right down the stairs."

"Where?" she demanded. "I—I have to see him— I have to make sure—"

"Calm down. Just settle on down. He's fine. I swear, I

saw him with my own eyes. He's sleeping. Got a few bumps and bruises, nothing serious.''

Shock settled her against the pillow. "Y-you saw him?''

"Yeah. Just a little while ago.''

"Are-are you sure?''

"Yeah, I'm sure.''

She moistened her lips with the tip of her tongue. "But…y-you don't even know him. You could be wrong.''

Rafe's eyes grew dark, and an odd smile lifted his mouth. "Nobody had to tell me who he belonged to. I recognized him the minute I saw him.''

Her breath froze in her throat, and she watched Rafe, hardly daring to breathe. "You did?''

"Yeah. He looks just like you, Carly.''

A terrible mixture of relief and guilt sapped what little strength she'd mustered. She sank back into the pillow. People had told her Evan looked like her. He had her color eyes, her color hair. But she'd always thought him a perfect little clone of his father.

The ache in Carly's head grew worse, and she reached up to find a bandage protecting the left side of her forehead and a tender swelling around her left eye and cheek.

Rafe's hand covered hers, pulling her probing fingers away from the bandage. His hands felt rougher, stronger than they had nine years ago, the last time she shared a touch with him. There was no disguising the way he made her heartbeat jump. The monitor beside her bed announced it unrepentantly.

Withdrawing his hand, he kindly ignored the erratic beep. "You banged yourself up pretty good. They said you were wearing your seat belt. That was lucky. You're gonna be okay now. It could have been a lot worse.''

Her whole body hurt, her ankle throbbed, and her head felt like an overripe melon. But he was right. Evan was safe. Nothing else really mattered. She looked back at Rafe. "How long have I been here?"

"Since last night." His eyes left hers and trailed down to her jacked-up ankle. "You've been out all this time. What in the devil were you doing driving in that storm, Carly?"

Something hovered below the surface of his even expression—frustration, maybe anger—but she was too exhausted to sort it out. Raw emotions tumbled through her, and she tamped them down. She didn't want to make a fool of herself in front of him. Not now. Not after all these years.

"Carly?"

"I—" She closed her eyes to push back the throbbing ache. She felt what little strength she'd mustered seeping out of her. Trying to remember what he'd just asked her seemed to take all her concentration. "The motel had overbooked because of the storm. I…had to keep going. I don't remember much else." Her eyes widened with sudden alarm. "Oh, Rafe, was anyone else hurt in the accident?"

Rafe's expression softened for only a moment. "No. Drunks have this miraculous habit of coming out without a scratch and turning other people's lives upside down."

He didn't say "including mine," but the words hung between them anyway. *A drunk driver.* Anger seeped past the sheer relief of being alive. Damn whoever it was for risking her life and her son's with their carelessness. She *had* been lucky. It could have been worse. Much, much worse.

A chubby nurse garbed in green scrubs cruised into Carly's line of vision with a smile on her face.

"Ah, we're finally awake, are we?" She pressed the backs of her fingers quickly to Carly's forehead and cheeks, then felt the pulse at her wrist.

"Is she lucid?" the woman asked Rafe, as if Carly weren't even in the room.

"My name is Cara Lynn Jamison," she replied testily before he could answer, "and Bill Clinton currently occupies the White House. Except for a headache the size of the Rock of Gibraltar, a sore ankle, and a few unaccounted-for minutes, I'm quite all here, thank you."

The nurse gave Carly a quick smile, checked the tape on the heart monitor and wrote something down on a metal chart. Apparently, cranky patients were nothing new to her.

She looked at Rafe. "It's important not to tire her just now. You have three minutes. Then you'll have to go."

Rafe nodded as the nurse glided away, then rubbed a hand down his face, erasing all trace of emotion. "Look, they, uh…they said your phone was disconnected down in L.A. Nobody knows you're here, except me. Is there somebody I can call for you? A friend?" He paused. "Your husband?"

She stared at him for a moment, then shook her head.

Rafe frowned. He wanted to press her, find out if that meant no, she didn't want him to call the guy, or no, she wasn't married anymore. And why had she kept her maiden name? But all at once she seemed pale and terribly fragile. He walked to the window and pushed aside the thin green drape. Sunlight poured through the glass, but the cold seeped through the barrier as surely as it did into his heart.

She wasn't the girl she'd been all those years ago. She'd grown into a woman. Gone was the glorious mane of long hair that had been her trademark. In its stead, a short cap of silver-blond framed her face and made her look every inch the professional he suspected she was. She was still slender as a willow, but from what he could see, she'd filled out some, in all the right places. Places his gaze deliberately avoided. Places once as familiar to him as his own hand. A curse slid silently past his lips.

"Rafe?"

Carly's voice made him jump. He turned back to her.

"Yeah?"

"Why are you here?"

Hell if I know, he wanted to say. But he didn't. The truth was, he'd asked himself that same question a hundred times since getting on the plane in Durango. He still had no answer for it, except that he'd had no choice. Halfway across Nevada, he'd stopped kidding himself that he was coming for the kid's sake alone. He'd come for her. For some kind of resolution with Carly, whatever that meant. A finish to what they'd once had. In truth, he'd come as much for himself as for her.

Now, staring at her in the half-light of morning, with bruises darkening her cheek and jaw, her leg swathed in plaster and her eyes dark with fear, he wondered at the wisdom of that choice. Seeing her like this made him want to protect her from all of it. Some foolish impulse told him to hold her in his arms until she stopped looking so scared and that erratic little blip on the heart monitor beside her bed grew slow and steady and calm.

His hand curled into a fist at his side. He might be an idiot for coming, but he wasn't a fool. He wasn't going to be suckered into that trap one more time. She needed help, and for the sake of her son, he'd help until she could handle things on her own. Then he'd be outa here so fast she'd have to look twice to see his dust.

"Rafe?" she repeated. "I have to know. Why did you come?"

He walked over to her side and straightened the blanket beneath her arm. "Don't worry about any of that now, okay? We'll talk about it later. Right now, you need to get some rest."

Her hand found his. Despite the exhaustion that drained her, she held on tight. "Evan—my son—he must be scared."

"I'll take care of him."

She stared at him, her eyes glassy and bright. "But

why? You're not—I mean, we're not...your problem, Rafe.''

He gave a little snort of laughter. ''In a perfect world, you'd be right. But life's far from perfect, ain't it, darlin'?'' Disengaging her hand from his, he reached for the sheepskin coat he'd draped over the foot of her bed. ''So don't worry about it. Try to get some sleep. I'll try to get Evan in to see you later.'' Fitting his Stetson on his head, he made for the door.

''Rafe?''

''Yeah?''

''Thanks.''

''Sure.''

The ICU door closed silently behind him.

Chapter 2

The child sat Indian-style amid the tangle of sheets on the bed, ignoring both the Saturday-morning cartoons blaring from the ceiling-hung television and the woman who stood by the window, dressed in a severe navy blue suit. Instead, the boy stared wide-eyed at Rafe as he came through the door. Enormous brown eyes, fringed by thick, dark lashes, met Rafe's surprised gaze, and he stopped two strides into the room.

Once more, the boy's uncanny likeness to Carly hitched some emotion deep in Rafe's chest. The kid's chin went up with a defiant tilt, but there was no disguising the fear etched on his face. Rafe's heart went out to him, remembering all the times he'd been confronted with strangers as Evan was about to be now. All the times an imperfect system had set him up for yet another disappointment.

The stiff-backed woman looked Rafe up and down through Coke-bottle-thick glasses before walking toward him with her hand extended. She put him immediately in mind of Gunga Din.

"Mr. Kellard?"

"Miss—?"

"Blackwell. Rosalind Blackwell, child services. I was beginning to wonder if you were really here." She glanced at her watch. "Evan and I have been having a nice little chat, haven't we, Evan?" The boy nodded his head barely, but looked like a scared, bridle-shy foal about to bolt.

"He's a little nervous," Blackwell went on.

"That's understandable. Many of our children, when they come to us, are—"

Rafe cut in. "Excuse me, but I doubt Evan's mother would take kindly to your calling her son one of *your* children."

"I was hoping, Mr. Kellard," Blackwell continued tightly, "that we could talk about—"

Rafe looked at Evan, who sat frozen to his spot on the bed. "Miss Blackwell," Rafe said, "I'd rather we postpone this discussion for a few minutes. I'd like a chance to talk to the boy. Alone."

Rosalind Blackwell's smile hitched a condescending inch, and she looked at her watch. "I have two more cases before eleven, and I'm quite pressed for time."

Rafe narrowed his eyes at the woman. "So am I." He glanced at Evan. "So's he. So we'll talk as soon as I'm finished here. All right?"

She cleared her throat and pushed her oversize glasses up the bridge of her nose with one finger. "Well...I suppose it *could* wait...for a few minutes." She checked her watch again and picked up her brown attaché case on the way out the door. "I have another appointment at ten."

The door eased closed behind her. Rafe turned to Evan and lifted his eyebrows in a conspiratorial smile.

"I don't like her," Evan said in a small voice.

"That makes two of us." Rafe set his coat down on the chair near the bed.

"You a doctor? You're not gonna gimme another shot,

are you?'' The kid folded his arms across his chest and puffed himself up.

"Do I look like a doctor to you?"

Evan's eyes narrowed assessingly as he gave Rafe a once-over, landing finally on the heavy silver championship buckle at Rafe's waist. "Well…" he observed thoughtfully, "the other doctors don't have belt buckles like that."

Rafe glanced down at the buckle and grinned. "No, I don't guess they would at that." He reached down and ran a thumb over the shiny metal. "Like it?"

Interest sparked in Evan's eyes, but his tone was deliberately disenchanted. "That a cow?"

Rafe shook his head with a grin. "Ol' Tornado here'd be mighty insulted to hear you call him that. He's a bull, through and through. Mean as a cuss, and twice as ornery."

"You know him?" Evan asked.

"Well, you might say we're…uh, acquainted."

The boy's arms relaxed to his sides as fascination overcame aloofness. "You a cowboy, mister?"

"Shore am, partner," he replied in his best cowboy drawl.

Evan's mouth fell open in unabashed awe. "Awesome!"

Rafe relaxed a fraction. He hadn't impressed anyone in a long time. Not since he left the rodeo far behind him.

"I met a cowboy once," Evan said. "Cowboy Jake, at Buddy Felder's birthday party. But his guns were fake and he tripped over the rope he tried to spin. Can you?"

Rafe grinned. "Trip over a rope?"

Evan giggled. "Naw. Make it spin."

"In my sleep."

"Really?"

"I prefer to do it awake though."

"Will ya teach me sometime?"

Rafe hesitated. He wasn't likely to be around the kid long enough to teach him anything, but he didn't say that. "Maybe sometime. My name's Rafe." He held his hand out to the boy. Evan's felt small and smooth and tentative against his palm.

"I'm Evan. I know karate," he announced proudly, throwing his hands up in a karate stance.

Rafe's eyebrows went up in surprise. "Really?"

He dropped his hands. "Yeah, I'm only a red belt though. Jason and Daniel are almost green belts."

"Friends of yours?"

Evan nodded slowly, staring at the blanket tangled around his legs. "Back home. But I had to say goodbye to 'em on accounta we're movin'."

"Where to?"

"Sassinitti."

A frown pulled at Rafe's brow and he concentrated on the boy's pouting lower lip. "Sassinitti?"

"Yeah. Mom says it's on a big river in—" he frowned in concentration "—O...*Ohio.* She said we can go fishing sometime."

A light went on. Cincinnati? Ohio? Why in the hell was she moving to Ohio?

"Me an' Mom and Dad went ocean fishing once," Evan went on. "Mom wouldn't bait the hooks, so Daddy did. Only I could tell he didn't like it much, either. But I caught a baby shark. It was so cool. But Mom said I had to throw it back."

"Good idea." Rafe's gaze traveled over the boy's small face. "Where's, uh, where's your dad now?"

Refusing to answer, Evan looked out the window.

Taking a new tack, he began, "You know, your mom said—"

Evan swiveled a look at him.

"My mom? You saw her?"

"Sure did."

"Is—" Evan's throat bobbled "—is she a angel?"

"What?"

His eyes filled, and his lower lip quivered. "They wouldn't let me in her room. So I thought…they wouldn't tell me she went to heaven, like my dad."

Rafe's gut tightened. So the kid's father was gone. A twinge of jealousy and sadness for Carly shimmied through him. He sat down on the bed, but didn't touch the boy for fear of making him bolt. "No, Evan. She's very much alive. In fact, I just saw her. She's okay. She's just banged herself up a little in the accident. She asked about you. She wants to see you very much."

"You know my mom?"

Rafe nodded. "We're…old friends. I thought maybe you and I could sneak in together. Pay her a surprise visit. Whattaya think?"

His eyes widened. "Swear? Double-Dutch-cross-your-heart?"

"Absolutely," he replied solemnly, drawing an X across his chest.

"I wanna go now." Evan leaped out of bed and headed for the door.

"Whoa, whoa," Rafe called, stopping him halfway across the room. "First, you get your britches on. You can't go see your mom bare-bottom-naked, now can ya?"

Considering that, Evan pulled the split back of the too-large hospital gown together. "Oh, yeah…"

"Yeah." Rafe ruffled his hair. "Need any help?"

Looking slightly offended, Evan, already heading to the closet for his pants, replied, "I'm too old for that stuff!"

"Oh. Well, in that case, I'll wait outside for you and have my talk with Gunga Din."

"Who?"

"Never mind. I'll see you outside when you're ready."

Scribbling in a small red notebook full of notes, Rosalind Blackwell waited stiffly at the nurses' station, just outside Evan's room. Rafe didn't waste time with preliminaries. He got straight to the point.

"The boy's staying with me."

Blackwell glanced up. "I'm afraid it's not quite that simple, Mr. Kellard."

"Sure it is. The boy needs someone to watch out for him until Carly's on her feet. That's what I came to do."

"I appreciate that, but there are procedures we must adhere to."

"Fine. So tell me where to sign."

The woman sighed heavily. "You must know we have only the boy's best interests at heart…"

"Naturally."

"…and, since you're not a relative, we require the mother's permission."

"You'll get it."

The woman's smile flattened her face. "It's my understanding that you're not even a particularly close family friend. In fact, you've never met Evan until today. Is that true?"

"So? What difference does that make?"

"In cases such as these, where there is no close relative, it's customary that the child be placed in institutional care until a proper replacement can be found."

Rafe's jaw tightened. "And I'm not proper." It wasn't a question, but a statement.

Blackwell smiled. "You're not married, are you, Mr. Kellard?"

"No."

She scratched that little fact down in her book.

"What's that got to do with anything?"

"I have to ask myself," Miss Blackwell replied, "why a single man like yourself would want to take on the enormous responsibility of a young child like Evan, when you have no real ties to Ms. Jamison or her son."

A muscle jumped in Rafe's cheek. When he spoke, it was with barely leashed anger. "Patience has always been my strong suit, Miss Blackwell. Right now, that patience is running mighty thin. The fact is, my relationship to Ms. Jamison and her son are none of your damn business, nor are my reasons for being here.

"And as far as the boy's concerned, Carly woke up a little while ago. You can ask her yourself if she wants me to take care of Evan, or if she wants him consigned to one of your...institutions. Personally, I've seen 'em all first-hand, and I wouldn't wish it on any child, stranger or kin. And you can write *that* down in your little red book and—"

Evan burst through his door, nearly colliding with Rafe. His shirt was buttoned wrong and tucked half in and half out of his small jeans. But he was decent. "Can we go see my mom now? I'm all ready."

Rafe shook off his anger and ruffled Evan's sleep-tousled hair. "You bet, pard." He glanced at Miss Blackwell, who looked as if she'd sucked on something sour. "Miss Blackwell and I were just finished, weren't we?"

She snapped her book shut and forced a smile. "I...uh... Yes, we were. Goodbye, Evan."

Unexpectedly Evan slipped his small hand into Rafe's and pressed his body against him. A surge of protectiveness as foreign as the feeling of a child's hand in his welled in Rafe. It felt good and flat-out terrifying in the same moment. "Let's go," he said.

"Mr Kellard—?" Blackwell called before he'd gone two steps. He looked back at her. "Tell Ms. Jamison that I'll be speaking with her shortly," she added, tucking her little book under her arm.

"I'll be sure to do that, Miss Blackwell. I surely will."

Carly woke with the distinct feeling that she was being watched over like an incubating egg. She felt, in fact, overly warm, and insulated by the cottony feeling between her ears. Slowly she realized that the headache that had pounded there earlier had lessened.

Opening her eyes, she felt her heart give a little leap at the two very familiar shapes that came into focus at the foot of her bed: Evan, and behind him, Rafe. Like two versions of the same picture, one dark and one light, the pair of them grinned at her as she struggled to regain control of her thudding pulse.

"Mommy!" Evan wriggled across the bed, careful of her leg, and hugged her with all the tenderness he could manage.

"Hi, sweetie," she said weakly, inhaling the wonderful scent of him. "Let me look at you. Are you okay?"

"Yeah, 'cept this cut here," he said, pointing to the Band-Aid on his forehead, "and this one here," he said, holding up an all-but-invisible scratch on his little finger.

"You look...*perfect* to me," she answered, her voice thick with emotion.

Evan smiled tremulously, then blurted out, "I was really scared and I thought you were an angel and they put me in a room and wouldn't let me see you last night and I promised I wouldn't cry and I didn't...much. Aren't you proud of me?"

"Sure am, big guy," she said, pressing her lips to his cheek and hugging him as tightly as her sore wrist would allow. She looked up at Rafe. "I see you two have met."

"Yeah, and Rafe told me you were okay, and then we got done with Gunga Din, and then Nurse Rebecca—" he pointed to the amused nurse adjusting the curtains on the other side of the room "—she said she wouldn't tell if I came in here." He grinned conspiratorially up at Rafe, who winked back.

"Gunga Din?" Carly repeated, with a questioning look at Rafe.

He grinned and gave a little shrug. "You had to be there."

That smile. It reached all the way to her toes. Why had she thought after all these years she was really over it? "What else have I been missing while I was in La-La Land?" she asked.

Evan sat up and looked at her seriously. "Rafe's gonna take care of me until you get all better. He said he might even take me to his ranch. He's got horses an' cows an' everything!"

Carly felt the blood drain from her face as she looked at Rafe. *"What?"*

"Hey, partner," Rafe said, lifting Evan up off the bed. "Why don't you and Nurse Rebecca go find something to eat while I talk to your ma? You must be hungry by now."

"Awww...but—"

"Go on, now. We won't be long." He pulled ten dollars out of his pocket and handed it to Evan. "Maybe you two can find me some coffee down there."

The nurse nodded understandingly and ushered Evan out of the room after one last hug for Carly. When he was gone, Carly turned to Rafe.

For the first time she noticed the dark smudges bruising the skin below his eyes. He looked as tired as she felt, yet tension arched like an electric current in the silence that stretched between them. Finally, they both spoke at once.

"Rafe, I—"

"Carly—"

He bent his head and said, "Go on."

"Listen," she said, edging up onto her elbows, "I really appreciate everything you've done...coming here like this, but—"

"Just so there's no mistake, I didn't do it for you," he said bluntly. "I did it for Evan."

His words were like a slap, and she tried to keep the

disappointment out of her expression, but wasn't sure she succeeded. "You still haven't said why."

He hesitated a moment. "Because they told me they were going to have to let social services take care of Evan, since they didn't know who else to contact." He looked up at her, his jaw tight.

She didn't have to ask any more. She knew that Rafe had gone though hell as a boy, being shuffled from one foster family to the next after the death of his father. The idea that Evan could have fallen into a crack in the same system that had tossed Rafe's childhood around was too scary to contemplate. All she could seem to think of to say was "Thank you."

He exhaled sharply. "*Is* there someone to contact, Carly? Evan said his father was dead."

Panic fingered coldly up her neck. Deliberately she searched the morning light spilling through the distant window, so that she wouldn't have to look Rafe in the eye. "Tom died two years ago."

"I'm sorry," Rafe said at last. "I didn't mean to upset you."

She shook her head. "Rafe, I—"

"Look," he said, interrupting her. "Isn't there someone? A friend?"

Carly pressed two fingers against her temple. "There's my friend Chandra, but she's in Europe for the next two months, doing makeup on a film shoot. And—" She frowned, searching for the name that momentarily escaped her. "Oh—Jane, Aunt Katherine's friend. But she just moved into a retirement home near Laguna Niguel."

"There's no one else?"

Until Tom's estate was settled, she reflected grimly, her time had been spent in a headlong, often lonely rush toward sheer survival. Her hours with the P.D.'s office had been long and exhausting, leaving her with precious little time for anyone but her son. She'd never regretted that. It was what she'd had to do. Yet it was exactly why she'd left L.A. behind her. There had to be more to life, for both of them.

"There's just Evan and me," she said at last. "The dynamic duo."

The half smile that lifted the corner of his mouth sent warmth skittering unbidden down her spine. "Batman and Robin? Pancho and Cisco...?"

She smiled back. "Something like that. Actually, I'm sort of...at loose ends homewise. We, Evan and I, were on our way to—"

"Cincinnati."

"How did you know?"

"Evan told me. Do you have a place there?"

A frown pulled delicately at her brow as she looked up at him. "I—well, I've made arrangements with a Realtor to rent a condo there."

"Furnished?"

"No, my things are on a truck somewhere between L.A. and there. Why?"

"Have you given any thought to how you're going to get there? Your car is totaled."

A sound of disbelief issued from deep in her throat.

"Not," he added, looking pointedly at her dangling leg, "that you could drive it, anyway, with plaster wrapped around your lovely leg."

Color leaped into her cheeks. Her headache was back in spades. "I guess we'll fly, then."

"And once you get there, then what? You've got a bum ankle and wrist, not to mention a knock on the head that would have given a bighorn sheep a headache."

That earned him a groan. "Don't remind me."

"How will you settle in?" he demanded. "Unpack? Get to the grocery store?"

"I don't know! I suppose I'll have to hire someone. I have a job waiting for me. I— Oh...damn." Staring at the

blank pale green ceiling, she refused to let Rafe see the
tears that gathered behind her eyes. "I've really made a
mess of things again, haven't I?"

Again? Rafe doubted the ever-efficient Cara Lynn Jamison had ever screwed up her well-ordered plan for her life.
Certainly not when she left him behind and made a life
for herself in the big city. From the looks of her, she'd
done well, and a damn sight better than she ever would
have with him. Still, his heart twisted as he watched her
struggle not to cry.

Brushing at her eyes with the back of her fist, she
winced at the pain in her hand, then stared at it as if it
were a dog who'd just bitten her. The tears came then,
unchecked down her cheeks. "Damn! And I—I suppose
that's broken, too!"

Resisting the urge to reach out and touch her again, Rafe
shoved his hands in the back pockets of his jeans and said,
"Just sprained."

Her laugh came without a trace of humor. "I guess I
should be grateful for small favors."

"Carly—"

"Look..." she said, her small gesture begging for quiet,
"could you just... I really don't want to talk right now,
okay? I need some time alone to...sort through it all."

"That's not going to change things, and you know it."

"No?" she asked, more sharply than she'd intended.
"Well, maybe not, but I don't have a better idea right now.
Do you?"

"As a matter of fact, I do," he said, rolling the tension
from one shoulder. "You're comin' home with me."

"*What?*" She nearly choked. "You...you can't be serious."

"I'm fresh out of jokes, after a night like the last one."
With the same catlike grace she remembered, he prowled
to the window to stare out of it. "It's the only solution,
and you know it."

She swallowed hard. "It doesn't even have to be an option, Rafe, and *you* know it. You owe me nothing. And certainly not this."

He turned on her, almost fiercely, then bit back whatever he'd been about to say. A calming breath shuddered through him. "Look, you're not in any position to argue with my offer. It'll be a good month before you're healed enough to take care of yourself or Evan. I told the good Miss Blackwell of child services that I'd take care of your son until you were back on your feet. He gave me his vote, and unless you've got somebody else, you're stuck with me. But, you see, I've got this ranch to run, and it ain't gonna run itself from here. So, either both of you come with me, or I take Evan alone." He paused deliberately. "And I have the feeling you'd rather walk over hot coals than see that happen. Am I wrong?"

For a long moment, she could only stare at him, fighting off the bitter sting of his words. "No," she answered in a small voice. "You're not wrong." She started to add, "But not for the reason you think," but didn't get the chance.

"Good," he cut in with a singular lack of enthusiasm. "Then it's a deal."

"A deal is generally mutually beneficial to both parties," she pointed out. "What do you get out of all this?"

He shook his head, his hair falling carelessly over his forehead. "Tsk, tsk, Carly. L.A. is showing on you."

Her cheeks grew hot. "Tell me, or the deal's off."

His ice-blue eyes flared, vanquishing the flash of pain behind them. "You always were able to cut the chaff from the wheat, weren't you, Carly?" A cynical smile curled his lip as he gathered up his coat.

She stared at him, defiant, waiting.

"So, I tell you," he said, "and you'll come, right?"

It was absolutely unfair to ask that before he answered, and he knew it. But she nodded anyway. What choice did she have? Exactly none. And he knew that, too.

Her gaze followed him across the room as he retrieved his hat. She felt her stomach give a little tumble at her first full-length view of him. All six-foot-three of him. His stride was deliberate, and her gaze fell inexorably, if inappropriately, to the way his faded jeans hugged the lean, muscled contours of his thighs. He'd matured, changed. But to her dismay, her very physical reaction to him had changed not at all.

He turned back to her, hat tight in his fist, and approached her bed. "Let's see. What *do* I get?" he asked in a voice edged with steel. "Hell, I don't know, Carly. Maybe this time, I'll get the chance to say goodbye."

Closing her eyes, Carly tried to shut out the accusation in his eyes. "I don't blame you for hating me."

His footsteps approached the bed, and she heard him curse under his breath. "I don't hate you, Carly. Look, it doesn't have to be this hard." He shoved his fingers through his dark hair. "Hell, it can be whatever we make it."

She gave a mirthless chuckle. "You know that saying about being between a rock and a hard place?"

"Yeah. Which am I?" he asked, a grin in his voice. "The rock or the hard place?"

Her eyes met his in surrender. "You're both."

Chapter 3

"How much longer till we get to your ranch?" Evan demanded for the hundredth time. He bounced in the jump seat of Rafe's pickup as the truck navigated yet another cattle-crossing grate across the muddy, unpaved road.

The wide-open space was a relief from her days in the hospital and from the cramped flight from Reno to Durango. The last vestiges of winter were still gathered here and there against the spindly wire fence line, but most of the final snowfall of the year had melted. The air pouring through the partly opened window smelled wonderful to Carly—sharp and cold and sweet.

With a nod of his head, Rafe gestured toward the rich scrub pastureland around them, dotted with grazing cattle. "We've been on Rocking K property for the last ten minutes."

Carly blinked in disbelief at the rolling sweep of grazing land cradled in the lee of the San Juan Mountains. "When you said you owned a little spread outside of Durango, I pictured...well, a *little* spread." Her gaze took it in.

"There's nothing small about this place." She turned to stare at Rafe. "This is all yours?"

"Most of it," he admitted, glancing her way, his expression unguardedly proud. "What I don't own outright, I lease privately for graze." He pointed down the road, to a speck of a structure at the foot of the nearest mountain. "There's the house."

As they emerged from the mountain's shadow, Carly watched the steady approach of the ranch and its outbuildings. She rubbed sweaty palms along her denim-covered thighs, then toyed with the edges of the split seam that accommodated her cast. For the hundredth time in the past forty-eight hours, she questioned the wisdom of agreeing to this. Not once since their words that first day had Rafe allowed her a glimpse of his bitterness over what had passed between them so many years ago. In fact, he'd made every effort to be pleasant. But an effort was exactly what it seemed. The past loomed between them like a circling vulture, biding its time.

Loose gravel sprayed the bed of the truck as they pulled into the yard of the sprawling one-story log ranch house, bracketed by a pair of ancient pines. A covered porch, woven with the winter-bare vines of a climbing rose, ran the length of the front of the house. Hanging balefully at one end of the porch, a lone wooden swing rocked gently in the cool afternoon breeze. The house fit Rafe the way his clothes did—rough-hewn, without pretense, and utterly practical.

"Wow! A log cabin!" Evan exclaimed, his nose pressed against the truck window.

"Like it?" Rafe asked. "Gus and I built it a couple of years back."

"Gus?" Carly repeated.

As she spoke the name, a grizzled cowhand of about fifty, with a droopy mustache and legs as bowed as barrel staves, rounded the corner of the house, grinning broadly. He raised one hand in greeting.

"My foreman," Rafe explained as he threw the truck into park and climbed out.

The tricolored sheepdog walking beside the older man left his side and raced toward Rafe with happy, open-mouthed exuberance. Jumping four feet straight in the air, the dog gave Rafe a wet doggy greeting. Rafe ruffled the fur on its head affectionately, while fending off a full-fledged annointing.

"Hey, Mack! Did you miss me?"

The dog woofed in reply, tangling itself between Rafe's legs. Evan's eyes went wide at the possibilities. "Mom!" he said in a stage whisper. "He's got a dog!"

Carly nodded with a smile. Evan had wanted a dog for as long as he was able to talk. But they'd lived in a condo in L.A. with no space for one. Maybe things would work out here after all, she thought.

Rafe ducked his head back in the door. For a moment, she thought he'd forgotten what he was about to say. His gaze drifted, feature by feature, over her face until she felt color rise in her cheeks.

"Don't move," he told her, his voice suddenly hoarse. "I'll be right back to bring you in."

Watching him go, Carly lifted a hand to the bruise on her cheek, wondering how he could look at her without grimacing. She knew she must look awful. Yet his gaze had held something far from aversion. It had held, instead, a haunted look that acknowledged the history that stood between them. A look, she thought, that spoke volumes about the things neither of them had yet dared to discuss.

As he approached his foreman, Carly saw Rafe's wince of pain, and the way he favored his left leg for a few steps. She swallowed hard. Of course, she'd heard about the accident. It had only been a few years since Rafe was nearly killed by some bull.

Rafe had always imagined himself indestructible. Carly had always known he was not. For years she'd blamed the rodeo for their breakup, but she knew it had gone much, much deeper than that. Now, it gave her no comfort to know that she'd been right about what the rodeo would do to him. But looking at the ranch he'd carved out of the Colorado high desert, she suspected she'd also been wrong.

Rafe met Gus halfway to the truck. If she hadn't known better, Carly would have sworn he wanted to intercept the older man before he got too close.

The two talked for less than a minute. She saw Gus thumb a gesture toward the mountains and shake his head.

She was close enough to see Rafe's jaw tighten at whatever Gus had told him, but too far away to hear it. At last, Rafe crunched across the gravel drive toward the truck, his expression set and clouded. Gus followed close behind.

"Is something wrong?" she asked when he leaned in the door on the driver's side to get his hat.

He denied it with a quick shake of his head, but she caught a flash of frustration in his eyes.

"Carly, Evan," Rafe said, "this is Gus Toleranos. Gus, Carly and Evan Jamison. Oh, and this," he said holding the dog back from jumping in the cab, "is Mack."

Gus touched the brim of his battered hat. "How do, ma'am. Son?"

"Are you a real cowboy, too?" Evan asked, wide-eyed.

"Well, now, I reckon I am," Gus replied, with a grin and a wink at Rafe.

"Cool," Evan pronounced, but he wasn't distracted by that information for long. His excited gaze found the penned horses on the near side of the huge barn at the far end of the lane. "Horses! Oh, Mom, can we go see 'em?"

"Evan, for heaven's sake..." Carly scolded. "We haven't even—"

"Aw, heck," Gus said, brushing away her admonishment. "Ain't every day a city boy gets near real live horses who'll nibble carrots right outa his hand."

"Really?" Evan gasped. "You got any carrots?"

Carly shook her head. "Evan!"

"Shore I do," Gus told him, pulling a limp orange carrot from his pocket. "C'mon, I'll take ya. That is, if it's okay with your ma."

Evan's look pleaded with Carly. "Can I, Mom. Can I? Ple-ease?"

Rafe nodded at her, and she acquiesced. "Well, if you're sure you don't mind, Gus."

"Sure as ticks on a dog." Gus reached for Evan's hand and helped him from the truck. "Why don't you two go on in and get yerselves settled. The boy and me'll mosey on over and get him acquainted with a certain red roan colt I know."

"Can Macky come?" Evan asked Gus as he tumbled out of the cab, without so much as a goodbye.

"Try and stop him," Gus said with a grin.

Evan was off and running to the paddock, with Gus and Mack trailing at his heels.

A smile crept to Carly's mouth. She couldn't remember the last time she'd seen her son so excited...or so happy. Despite her uneasiness about coming here, she suspected this place was exactly what Evan needed. She wished she was as sure about herself.

"Don't worry," Rafe told her from the other side of the truck. "Gus is great with kids. He's had three of his own."

She smiled. "Oh...I wasn't worried about Gus. I'm just surprised Evan went with him. He's usually sort of shy with strangers." Rafe gave her an odd look, and she remembered that Evan hadn't been shy with him, either. But then, that shouldn't surprise her. Rafe had always had a way of putting people at ease.

Until they got too close.

Rafe came around the truck as she opened the door and

lowered herself gingerly to the gravel drive. She felt a twinge of dizziness, but knew it would pass. It always did. She reached for the crutches propped in the front seat.

"What the hell do you think you're doing?" he asked with a frown. He stopped in front of her, blocking the sun, his broad shoulders haloed with a light that belied their tension.

"I'm getting my crutches," she answered. "What does it look like?"

"I told you I'd carry you."

"That's not necessary." Or, for that matter, wise, she reflected. Physical contact with the man looming over her was something she thought it best to avoid altogether. Hanging on to the door for balance, she reached again into the truck cab for her crutches.

He shook his head with disbelief. "I say it *is* necessary. It's been a long day. You should be in bed. You can barely stand up, you're so tired. And you're pale as the snow on those mountains."

Carly caught her lip between her teeth. Her great-aunt Katherine's constant admonition rang in her memory: "There's no one to count on in this life but yourself. Remember that, Cara Lynn. Learn to paddle your own canoe and you'll be beholden to no one."

She wouldn't be a burden to him. She'd sworn she wouldn't!

Planting the crutches on the ground, she shook her head. "I'm fine." But even as she said it, a sharp pain shot up her sore hand as she braced it on the offending piece of foam-covered metal.

His eaglelike gaze missed nothing. "Dammit, Carly—"

"I can *do* it," she snapped, angry at herself. "I don't need—"

"My help," he finished for her, his voice laced with sarcasm. "Right. Hey, it's comforting to know some things never change.'' He swept a hand toward the house, then crossed his arms over his chest. "Be my guest.''

Carly gritted her teeth and planted the crutches ahead of her in the gravel. Without her right leg for balance, she found herself leaning back on the truck for support. Then, hopping on her left leg, she leaned into the crutches. But the second she put pressure on her right hand, her arm buckled in pain and she felt herself pitching forward like a felled tree.

Rafe swore and caught her by the shoulders, righting her against his chest. Then, pinning her there with one arm, he tore the crutches out of her hands and sent them sailing into the back of the pickup with a resounding *thunk!*

Ignoring her gasp of protest, he pushed her back against the truck, then gestured toward the house, a distant thirty feet away.

"Still gonna try it on your own? C'mon, Carly, I'm sure you can figure out some way to do it, even now, without asking me for help.''

She swallowed hard, angry at herself for her failure, and at him for taunting her with it.

His eyebrows went up mockingly. "No? Well, then I guess you'll just have to accept it.'' Reaching down, he scooped her into his arms, held her tight to his chest and started toward the house.

It didn't help that he was right, she fumed. He was, blast him! Clinging to the sheepskin coat covering his shoulders, Carly was all too aware of the angry heat their bodies shared and the heavy thud of his heart against her side. She tried to put a fractional amount of space between them, but it was useless. His hands dug into her flesh, inside the worn fabric of her slit-up-the-seam jeans, and beneath the down jacket at her waist.

Each point of contact was seared by the memory of what it had once been like to be held by this man. To be loved by him. Now there was nothing gentle or kind in the azure eyes that deliberately avoided hers. And only anger and long-buried bitterness remained in his embrace.

Tightening his hold on Carly, Rafe stalked to the house. The woman was stubborn, willful, and too damned independent for her own good. She'd never needed him all those years ago. Not really. Not the way a man needed to be needed. Not until this very minute. But even now, she couldn't accept his help without a fight.

Despite that, his traitorous body tightened with longing as he felt her womanly softness against him, as her hair brushed his neck and the sweet scent of her invaded his brain. Even as she fought his help, he wanted her.

Hell!

He wanted her even now.

Reaching the top of the steps, Rafe kicked at the partially opened door and eased through the entryway with Carly in his arms. With relief, he noted that the room was at least neat. Gus had seen to that. No newspapers lay strewn about, half-read and forgotten. No half-empty bottles of Jack Daniel's or ringed coffee mugs lay in testament to the sleepless nights of late. The ranch accounts Rafe had pored over night after night and left sprawled across the huge mahogany desk had been cleared out of sight, too.

Relief needled through him. Carly didn't need to know he was on the brink of going down in flames one more time. Be it ego or self-preservation, he didn't think he could take it if she knew and pitied him or, worse, realized she'd been right about him all along.

Late-afternoon sun poured through the high cathedral-shaped windows that looked out on the San Juans to the north, sending shafts of light across the colorful woven rugs scattered across the waxed pine floor. He carried Carly to the oversize forest-green sectional and deposited her there, where the sunlight played against the fabric. Her voice stopped him as he started toward the dying blaze burning in the fireplace.

"Rafe?"

He turned around as she slipped her arms out of her coat and peeled it off. His chest tightened at the sight of her. The sunlight streaked her silvery-blond hair almost white. The simple green T-shirt she wore outlined the womanly curves of her body and sent a sharp, unwanted pang of desire crashing through him. "Yeah?" he snapped.

"I'm sorry," she said in a small voice. "And...thank you."

"Well." He loosed a sharp breath. "That must have been hard to say."

"I can admit to being wrong."

A doubtful frown pulled at his brow. "Can you?"

She rubbed her leg just above the plaster that encased it. "I thought I could do it myself. I was wrong, okay? I didn't mean to make you angry. I just don't want to be a burden to you." A choked laugh escaped her. "Pretty dumb, huh? I mean, here I am, planted on your couch.... I can't even walk by myself." Her eyes grew bright, and she brushed at her cheek with the back of her braced hand.

Rafe's fist tightened at his side. "In a day or so, your hand will be able to take the pressure. But for now... Look, I brought you here to take care of you. You've gotta let me help you."

She nodded, staring at a colorful loomed pillow beside her. "I know. It's just...hard for me. It always has been."

With a shake of his head, he walked to the rock fireplace that encompassed nearly an entire wall. "That's old news, Carly. Hell, it wouldn't even make for a good editorial."

Stung, Carly hugged her arms. "It's not you, Rafe. It was never about us," she offered, bringing up the subject they had both been avoiding.

"Yeah?" He tossed a fresh log on the dying embers.

When he stirred it with the poker, a small flame burst to life. "Who was it about, then?"

"Me."

He slanted a look at her and gave a short laugh. "Right." Replacing the poker, he straightened. "There's no point in rehashing all that now. It's ancient history. Best to keep it that way."

She nodded silently.

Guilt crept through him as his gaze fell to the dark bruise beneath the fall of silver hair on her cheek. He felt like a heel. A first-class heel. As if she hadn't been through enough, without him starting up with her about things that couldn't be changed. "Hell," he mumbled, "I don't want to fight with you, Carly."

She looked up at him, her eyes hopeful. "Me either."

He spread his hands wide. "Truce?"

A small, grateful smile flickered at her mouth. "Truce."

For a long minute, silence stretched uncomfortably between them. Carly forced her gaze out the window, to where the sinking sun was gilding the edges of the mountains. She wondered how long the uneasy peace would last before the things that needed to be said between them found a voice.

It came as something of a surprise to find the old pain and bitterness so keenly in his eyes after all these years. She'd known she'd wounded him the day she walked out on him. But she'd never really known how much.

After that last phone call she made to him, a few weeks after she left, she'd never heard from him again. As the years went by and she heard about his exploits on the rodeo circuit, she'd assumed he'd forgotten about her and never looked back. Now, she wondered.

"It's beautiful here," she said simply, gazing out the window at the mountains, searching for a safe topic.

"Yeah, it is."

"How long have you been here?"

"About three years," he answered, absently rubbing his thigh.

"I heard you got out of rodeoing," she said, gazing at the rustic but comfortable room, with its log walls and its abstracts bearing the colors of Rafe's mountains. "But I never pictured you…settled like this."

He angled a look at her, the afternoon sun carving his sculpted cheeks with deep slashes. "Who told you I'd quit the circuit?"

Color crept up her cheeks. "No one had to. You were pretty big news for a while there. All-around-Cowboy…world champion bull rider and saddle-bronc rider. You had the media eating out of your hand, not to mention most of the female population of the western United States. I kind of half expected to see your face on the big screen someday."

He laughed—a sound she'd almost forgotten. It sent warmth careening up her spine.

"I think my nose has been broken too many times for that," he said. "Anyway, since when does rodeo news makes it all the way to the legal bastions of Los Angeles? I figured you'd be too busy counting your case settlements by your swimming pool, or—" he shrugged "—rubbing shoulders with celebrities, to be bothered with news about a bunch of cowboys."

The smile slipped from her face. "I worked for the P.D.'s office, Rafe. The only people I rubbed shoulders with were the gang members and drug dealers whom I plea-bargained, all in the name of a grossly overcrowded prison system." She paused, staring hard at her hand. "Believe me, I've heard all the lawyer jokes. But I won't defend myself or the way I make my living to you."

Rafe stared at her. Hell, what did he care? What she did with her life was her business. When she left, he didn't want to know any more about her than he had to.

"Sorry," he said at last. "Seems I'm not very good with

truces. Listen, are you hungry? I think I can dig something up in the kitchen.''

Rubbing her temple, she realized her headache had come back. ''Not very. I think I will take you up on the offer to lie down, though. I'm kind of tired.''

He nodded. ''I'll just go get your things out of the truck, then I'll settle you in. By the way, you'll be staying in my room.'' He started for the door.

''What?''

Turning back, he grinned at her stunned expression.

''I'll be taking the spare room down the hall. My room's bigger, easier to navigate with those crutches. Don't worry. You'll be perfectly safe.''

Carly rolled her eyes as he walked out the door, suspecting that that particular sentiment couldn't be farther from the truth.

The bottle of whiskey chinked against the rim of Rafe's glass as he refilled it for the third time. The amber liquor swirled like liquid fire in the sharp halogen light of the desk lamp. Rafe knocked the shot back in one quick gulp, gasping as the burn seared its way down his throat.

It had been a long day. Things had gone well, he decided...considering. They'd made it through the burned trout dinner Gus—and Evan—had made. Evan had kept up an animated dialogue about the days' discoveries and filled the room with laughter, while he and Carly had managed to avoid laying open any more veins, living up to their uneasy truce. Being comfortable around Carly, however, was something that made Rafe distinctly *un*comfortable.

Mack yawned loudly from his place on the rug beside Rafe's desk, then settled his head back between his paws.

''Yeah, I know just how you feel, Macky,'' Rafe murmured as he set the glass down precisely on the damp ring he'd already made on his desk blotter. He toyed with the glass and turned his attention back to the paperwork in front of him.

The numbers had long ago ceased to make any real sense to him. Not because he was drunk. He was a long way from drunk. No, they had ceased to make sense because no matter how many times he went over the accounts, they added up to only one thing—trouble.

Burying his face in his hands, Rafe pondered his alternative. Singular. There was only one way out of this mess that he could see. It was a gamble that could potentially cost him more than the ranch. A hell of a lot more.

He filled his glass again, took another swig of whiskey and stared at the sweater Carly had left draped over the back of the couch. The image called another to his mind—of another sweater, forgotten in her rush to leave him nine years ago. He'd come home after a long, exhausting weekend of rodeoing to find that was all that remained of their relationship. That and the note she'd written and propped against the mantel. A cliché, really. A Dear John letter. It had caught him off guard, like a blind-side punch, though later he'd realized he'd been expecting it for two years.

It hadn't been until three years—and a dozen worthless relationships, later—when he was laid up with nothing better to think about than his life—that he allowed the possibility that the blame for their relationship's demise might be as much his as hers.

Gus appeared at the doorway to the kitchen, a shadow in the darkness. Only the glowing tip of his cigarette announced him. "You gonna sit there all night?" he asked.

"Maybe."

Gus ambled into the room. "No point to that, son."

"No point to lying in bed when I can't sleep, either," Rafe answered tiredly, closing the ledger.

"You gonna meet with Stivers tomorrow?"

Rafe nodded. "I've got nothing to lose by giving it one last shot."

"He ain't gonna change his tune about that lease. Unless you can come up with the cash for that bottom land, it's going to Sunimoto Corp."

"I can't let that happen. He told me he wants to sell it to me first, if I can meet his price."

Gus exhaled a cloud of smoke. "You're still shy almost fifteen grand. An' the banks have turned you down, ain't they?"

"All but two. They don't look too promising, either." He fingered a green-and-brown rodeo pamphlet that lay on his desk.

A frown of sudden concern creased Gus's brow as he noticed the action. "Hey, you ain't actually thinkin' about—"

Rafe slid a wry look at him. "That's exactly what I'm thinking. The first pro rodeo in Durango is coming up soon."

"Hellfire," Gus grumbled, taking an agitated pull on his cigarette.

"If I take a couple of events, the prize money'll buy me that land."

"And a coffin, too, maybe."

Rafe stood and shoved his chair against the wall. "I rode for seven years with hardly a scratch. I can do it again. I know I can."

"That ain't what your doctor said, but, hell, you're the boss. You know as well as me, bulls like that devil's spawn Tornado can smell second thoughts a mile away. They eat 'em up for breakfast."

"There won't be any second thoughts. You should know me well enough to know that when I climb into the chute, I'm there one hundred and fifty percent. If you're thinking I'm afraid, Gus, you're wrong."

Flicking his cigarette into the fire still glowing in the

fireplace, Gus snorted. "You don't have to remind me
what kind of rider you were. I was there, remember? Hell,
I'd like to see the cowpoke who could accuse you of bein'
yellow. But courage and just plain stubborn bullheaded-
ness are two different things. Maybe a good dose of
healthy fear is just what you need. That, or another look
at that video of the last time you tangled with a bull."

Rafe turned and stared out the window into the darkness.
"A man with nothing to lose has nothing to fear. Without
this place, I'm nothing."

"That ain't what I see in the eyes of that gal down the
hall."

Rafe sent him an incredulous look. Then he laughed.
"You're seein' things, old man."

"Old!" Gus snorted. "I ain't so old I don't remember
a look when I see one."

"If you saw anything, it was surprise. She never thought
I'd amount to anything but a rodeo cowboy. That's why
she left, remember?"

Gus fixed his battered old hat on his head and looked
at him oddly. "I remember you was on the road more'n
you was home before she moved off. I remember that. I
don't know why she left ya, and I reckon you don't, neither." He paused meaningfully. "Why don't ya ask her?"

Rafe stared hard at his foreman. "We're friends, so I'm
gonna forget you said that. Good night, Gus."

Gus stared back, his face carefully blank. He scuffed his
worn boot against the floor. "All right. Night, Rafe. Pedro
an' me'll be on the north fence line at dawn."

Nodding tightly, Rafe watched Gus disappear out the
front door toward the bunkhouse. He ground his teeth together and cursed. *Why the hell don't people mind their
own business anymore?* Not, he reminded himself, that
Gus ever had.

He reached for the empty glass on the table, but before

he could refill it, a crash from the other room had him
sprinting down the hallway toward his bedroom.

He threw open the door to find Carly perched on one
foot near the bed, reaching precariously for the crutch
she'd dropped. It lay amid the ruins of a picture frame,
shattered on the floor. Her eyes looked red, as if she'd
been crying. More disturbing than that, except for her
jeans, all she wore was a bra.

"Oh, Rafe! I'm so sorry about the picture. It—"

Ignoring the mess, he stepped over the broken glass and
took her by her bare shoulders. She was trembling. "Never
mind that. Are you all right?"

"Yes. I got a little dizzy, but I'm fine now. I'm sorry."

Relief scuttled through him. "It's just glass. Jeez, Carly,
what are you doing up?" he demanded, forcing her to sit
on the edge of the bed. "I thought you'd be asleep by
now."

His gaze fell involuntarily to the soft swell of breast
cupped in lacy black. Unbidden came the thought that
childbearing had only enhanced the curves he remembered.
The curves that had once been his to hold. A bead of sweat
worked its way past his nape and slid down his back as
he watched an embarrassed flush creep up her neck.

Reaching for the T-shirt she'd left on the bed, she
clutched it to her chest. "I couldn't sleep—" she said, then
added "—in my clothes."

"So…why didn't you get undressed? Don't you have
something to sleep in?"

She swallowed hard and looked away. "I… Yes. That
wasn't the problem."

"What was the problem?"

Her gaze fell to the steel buttons on her button-fly jeans.
"The nurse helped me get these on today. I…I tried to
undo them, but my hand…"

The light went on. God, what an idiot he was, making
her sit there and explain. "Here, let me do it."

She clutched the T-shirt tighter as he reached for the buttons on her pants.

"I'm not gonna bite you, Carly. C'mon." He grinned uneasily. "It's not as if I've never done this before."

But that was a long time ago, Carly thought, and for an entirely different reason. Reluctantly she allowed him the access he demanded. Gently Rafe worked the first button until it popped free.

Carly stared at the top of Rafe's head as he knelt in front of her. His hair gleamed like jet in the lamplight, and she bit back the urge to reach up and run her fingers through it. The heady masculine scent that belonged only to him drifted to her, making her throat tighten.

He'd been drinking. She could smell that on him, too. Over her? she wondered with a pang of guilt. She'd thrown his life into chaos, and here she was asking for help again.

The second button popped free, then the third and fourth. The backs of his knuckles brushed the sensitive skin of her belly as he maneuvered for a hold on the last button. She sucked in a breath.

He hesitated and looked up at her. In that moment, she saw something she hadn't seen in his eyes since that first day in the hospital. Not anger, not bitterness, but a hot flash of desire.

The realization made her mouth go suddenly dry.

The last button popped free. For a moment too long, his eyes clung to hers and said what neither of them dared say. Tightening his jaw, his hands bracketed her waist. "Lie back."

She blinked at him. "What?"

"Lie back, Carly. I have to take off your jeans."

"Oh. Of course...I—" Feeling foolish, and as rigid as a fencepost, she did as he asked.

Rafe lifted her hips slightly off the bed, and tugged her jeans down until they puddled around her knees. Out of necessity, his palm touched the back of her thigh, her calf, her ankle, as he pulled the trouser leg free. It took all his control not to linger against the softness behind her knee, or let his eyes roam over the slip of silk panties covering her hips.

Gently he tugged the other pant leg free over the plaster cast. Her long, coltish legs, though bruised, were well muscled and strong. He remembered how much she'd loved to run. She was not now, nor had she ever been, as delicate as she seemed. Carly would heal well.

Then, he thought, she would go.

When he looked back at her, she was sitting up. The shirt lay forgotten in her lap. Her breath was coming fast, her gaze fastened to his. He swallowed heavily, then reached for the clasp at the front of her black lacy bra.

Covering his hand with hers, she stopped him. "*Don't.* I mean, I can do that. Thanks."

It wasn't disappointment, he told himself, but relief, that filtered through him like a hot wind. Or maybe it was the whiskey he'd drunk.

"You sure?" he asked. She nodded. He knew before he did it that it was a foolish impulse, but all the same, he didn't stop himself. It wasn't much. Only a brief brush of his thumb along the inside of her breast, but they both knew it was intentional.

He could kiss her if he chose. Tempted, he sensed that she wouldn't try to stop him. Only inches separated them, Rafe thought as his gaze roamed irreverently over her hair.

Inches…miles. A lifetime of mistakes.

Straightening, he stood, knowing it would be foolish not to. He'd been too damn long without a woman. It wasn't Carly he wanted, he told himself. Right now, any female would do. But even as the thought formed, he knew it was a lie.

"You need anything else?" he asked, more sharply than he'd intended.

Carly could hardly hear him for the thudding in her ears. She shook her head, not trusting her voice.

He reached for the newspaper that lay near her bed and spread it over the broken glass on the floor. "Stay away from that tonight. I'll clean it up in the morning. Get some sleep, Carly."

When the door shut behind him, Carly flopped back on the bed and touched the place Rafe's hand had caressed. She closed her eyes, wondering what she would have done if he kissed her. For a moment, she'd thought he was about to.

God help her, she'd wanted him to. Not sanely, not even wisely. But with the same deep longing she'd harbored for these past nine years.

Next door, she heard his door open and quietly shut, the creak of his bed as he sat on it, the thud of his boots as he pulled them off one at a time.

She stared at the ceiling. It wasn't for her to question why fate had brought them back together. Or why, despite everything, the spark between them had never died. She owed him so much. Besides what he'd done for her since her accident, he'd given her the most precious gift she'd ever received. And he didn't even know he'd given it.

Guilt churned inside her. She owed him at least the truth. But if she told him, would he hate her? It didn't matter. She had no choice. She'd put it off too long already.

Carly squeezed her eyes shut, a tear tracing a damp path down her cheek. But, heaven help her, how would she ever tell Rafe that the little boy sleeping in the room down the hall was his son?

Chapter 4

Late-morning sun poured through the gauzy-curtained six-paned windows of Rafe's bedroom, drilling Carly's closed eyelids with warmth and light. Rousing herself with guilty reluctance from a rest that had felt more like hibernation than sleep, Carly eased herself cautiously up in bed. In spite of a lingering stiffness almost everywhere, she actually felt human again. The dizziness had vanished, and the dull throb in her ankle had mutated into little more than an annoying ache.

She flexed her bruised right hand gingerly. Better. *Much* better, in fact. Able, she suspected, to take the weight of the crutches, if she was careful. That small bit of good news carried more weight than the rest of her problems combined. It meant independence. It meant that Rafe could get on with his work, without hovering over her as if she were some fallen baby bird. No more full-body contact with his hard chest, and no more of his scent filling her up with memories best forgotten.

She eased her plaster-encased lower leg over the edge

of the huge king-size bed. So far so good. Reaching for the crutches propped next to the bed, she stood and took a few wobbly circuits of the room. Rafe's bedroom seemed larger in the daylight. Furnished sparsely in oak, with beige carpeting to match the walls, the room was full of light. Two windows flanked the French doors that led onto a small outdoor patio with a wrought-iron table and chairs that stood gathering leaves around their legs. Unused.

Strangely, the bedroom felt the same. Utilitarian. He slept here, and nothing else. *Did that mean he rarely entertained women here?* No pictures adorned the walls, and she'd managed to break the only one he kept on his dresser. She bent down and picked it up. Predictably, it wasn't of Rafe in his rodeo days, but one of Gus, a pretty younger woman and two boys, standing near a smoking barbecue, making faces at the camera.

Carly wondered who she was. Gus's wife? Too young. Another possibility reared its ugly head—that she belonged to Rafe.

Now *that,* she thought, would be awkward.

No, not awkward. *Awful.* And it was too early to contemplate natural disasters.

As she returned the picture to the dresser, the scent of coffee seeped into her consciousness. Not the thick, dark, foreign kind that her too-hip-for-L.A. research assistant, Mara, used to bring her from the trendy coffee place down on Olympic. No, this coffee smelled like plain old garden-variety kick-you-in-the-pants coffee. The kind her great-aunt Katherine used to brew for her literary friends when their discussions meandered into the wee hours of the morning.

A smile lifted Carly's mouth at the memory. Katherine's approach to caffeine had been as pragmatic as her outlook on life. She used to say, "A good cup of coffee flushes out the mind of yesterday's trash and makes way for today's virtues."

Virtues.

Ha. She could use a few of those, Carly thought guiltily, recalling the wild, erotic fantasies that had possessed her last night, before sleep overtook her. Fantasies about Rafe and her, and what might have happened if he kissed her.

The way she'd wanted him to.

"Ohhh…Carly," she warned herself aloud. "Get a grip." Thoughts like that could only get her into deep, deep trouble here. What was once between her and Rafe had been over for years. If yesterday was any indication, the only thing they were likely to resurrect between them was animosity. He'd brought her here out of sheer…well…frankly, obligation. He'd come for Evan. As she suspected he might have done for any child in her son's situation.

Except Evan wasn't just any child. He was *Rafe's* child. Did he see any trace of himself in Evan? Did he suspect, even a little, that Evan could be his? Had that been his real reason for coming to Reno? If it was, why hadn't he asked her directly? If he had, she couldn't have lied. She would have been forced to tell him the truth—something she'd have to do very soon. A shiver went through her. She dreaded it.

With those dark thoughts still swirling in her brain, Carly managed to get herself ready for the day. What she craved was a long, hot, steamy shower. What she settled for was an awkward sponge bath. Her hair was hopeless, but she wet it and scrunched it into submission with her fingers.

Sometime today, she'd appropriate the kitchen sink for a serious shampoo.

Getting dressed was simpler now that her hand was on the mend. She pulled on a pair of slit-up-the-seam jeans and a pale yellow polo shirt, then stood in front of Rafe's full-length mirror, inspecting the damage. She raised a disgusted eyebrow over the bruise turning an interesting shade of green on her cheek and the ugly cut healing near her hairline.

Any notions she harbored that Rafe might still find her attractive crashed back to reality. She looked more like something her makeup-artist friend, Chandra, might have designed for a horror-film project—and then rejected.

The sound of her son's laughter drifted to Carly from outside, and she hobbled over to the window to look out through the morning glare.

What she saw made her heart lurch and her knuckles go white against the grips of her crutches.

Evan—her eight-year-old urban son, who until yesterday had only rarely laid eyes on real live livestock of any kind—and then it had been rabbits or 4-H pigs at the county fair—was gleefully bouncing around the paddock area on a trotting rawboned gelding, as if he owned the place. Of course, Rafe trotted along beside the horse, holding the reins.

She took a deep, calming breath and forced herself not to overreact. Rafe was with him. He was safe.

And he was *riding*.

Carly blinked at the sight of father and son together. A lump formed in her throat. The image was something she'd only conjured up in her mind over the years. And now here they were, doing something that came so naturally to a real father and son that it made her heart ache. She heard Evan ask something, and Rafe's voice reassure him.

She watched Evan's chest puff up with pride, his legs gripping the sides of the gelding with more authority. He *did* look fine. More than fine. He looked positively giddy. How long had it been since she'd seen him look like that? Months. Since before she'd told him they were moving.

And Rafe. He was good with Evan. Spectacular, in fact. Despite the fact that he'd always been certain he'd be a terrible father. That should hearten her, shouldn't it? Make it easier to tell him the truth? But a voice inside warned that paying attention to a child—and knowing that child was yours—were two different things.

Years ago, when they talked of the future, Rafe had told her emphatically that he didn't want children. Carly had no reason to believe that had changed.

But he *was* good with Evan. Maybe if Rafe had the chance to get to know him first, to fall in love with him as she knew he would...

It wasn't yet the right time to tell Rafe he was a father, she told herself. But soon. She'd know when.

She watched for another minute or two, then dragged herself from the window and followed the scent of coffee toward the kitchen. Mingling with that aroma was the smell of freshly baked muffins. Like a beacon of morning light at the end of the hallway, the kitchen boasted tall, naked windows that banked the far wall. They looked out over the San Juans and, more immediately, over the barnyard, where Rafe and Evan were. The kitchen was spare but well equipped, with counters of polished granite and hardwood floors and cabinets. It was a kitchen any woman in her right mind could fall in love with, but Carly wondered how much a man like Rafe really used it.

She was surprised to see Gus pulling a muffin tin from the oven as she hobbled into the room.

"Mornin'," he said cheerily.

"Morning. I mean, afternoon," she replied, feeling her cheeks go pink. "I'm afraid I overslept."

"You're entitled." He poured a steaming mug of wonderful-smelling coffee and handed it to her as she moved to the window. "Coffee? It's good and hot. Rafe said you'd be up soon, so I made a fresh pot."

"Mmmm... Thanks. I'm not very good in the morning until I've pumped some caffeine into my system." She took a deep swig of the rich brew, which tasted as good as it smelled.

"How're you feelin' this mornin'?" he asked.

"Better, thanks." She tipped her head toward the paddock area. "How long have they been at that?"

"Oh, about a half hour or so. Evan's really takin' to that horse. And to Rafe," he added, staring out at them.

She nodded wordlessly, chewing on her lip.

"He ever ridden before?" Gus asked.

"Only the ponies at Griffith Park. And they were attached to metal spokes."

Gus shot her a look. "You ain't worried, are ya?"

She laughed breezily. "Worried? No. Not really. Well, maybe a little."

Gus grinned, his droopy mustache lifting on one side. "Evan couldn't have a better teacher. Rafe's the best. But then, you know that."

Rafe was the best at a lot of things...*including riding,* she mused, completely inappropriately, staring out at him in the paddock. Hauling her wayward thoughts back, she forced herself away from the window and lowered herself onto a ladder-back kitchen chair at the table. It felt ridiculously good to sit.

Gus flipped a hot muffin from the tray onto a plate, then fanned his overheated fingertips. "Muffin?"

Carly realized she was hungry as he set it in front of her. "Thanks, Gus."

He simply smiled and leaned his backside against the granite counter, watching her over the rim of his mug. He wasn't as tall as Rafe, but what he lacked in inches he made up for in pure character. A wreath of wrinkles lined his sun-bronzed face, and his nose looked a bit askew, as if it had seen its share of brawls. And, laconic as he seemed, the glint of mischief in his tobacco-colored eyes hinted that he was wiser than a treeful of owls. In his day, she supposed Gus had been a force to be reckoned with, and perhaps he still was.

"So," she began, searching for conversation, "you're the cook *and* the foreman?"

"Nah. Laurie come by early this morning and whipped up a batch of muffins so we men don't starve to death out here."

She set her cup down, her antennae automatically rising. "Laurie?"

"My daughter."

"You have a daughter?" The photo in Rafe's room flashed through her mind.

"Sure. Grown, with kids of her own now, of course. She and Rafe go way back. That's how I met him, as a matter of fact."

A twinge of illogical jealousy flashed through her. What kind of a woman just drops in on a single man to bake him muffins?

"So…your daughter's…married?" She tried to keep the optimism out of her voice.

"Was. She's a widow."

"Oh." Something more than disappointment flitted through her, but she felt ashamed that it was for all the wrong reasons.

"Goin' on five years now. Her husband Jack and Rafe were on the circuit together. Best friends." Gus took a long sip of coffee, his gaze faraway. "He was a bull rider, like Rafe. A real fine man."

"I'm so sorry, Gus." She was afraid to ask, but she had to know. "How did it happen?"

Gus shook his head. "Plane crash. Reckon it woulda been easier somehow for Laurie if it had been the rodeo that took him. Doin' what he loved and all."

Carly thought of how close Rafe had come to dying for the way of life he'd loved so much. And she thought about Tom, whose death she could never see as anything but a tragic accident. So it was from personal experience that she knew there was no easy way to lose someone you loved. "It must have been very hard for her. And for her boys. But a comfort for her to have Rafe's friendship."

"They don't come no better," he replied simply.

Indeed. How many men, she wondered, would have dropped everything in the middle of the night to rescue a woman who had left him years ago, simply for the sake of a child he didn't even know? Damn few, came the reply.

Still, one question begged an answer. *Why?* With so much behind them. He'd never answered that question for her, and she was reminded once more that she needed to know.

Gus refilled her cup. "You'll get a chance to meet Laurie soon. Said she'd come by with supper some night soon. She's anxious to meet you, too."

"Oh," Carly said, forcing a smile, feeling particularly small and petty. *"How nice of her."*

Just then, Evan charged through the kitchen door like a minitornado.

"Mom! Did you see? Did you see me? I was riding! A horse! A real bronco. Rafe said so!"

She caught him in her arms and sent Gus a suspicious look. *A bronco?* she mouthed.

"Retired," he mumbled into his coffee cup.

"Of course I saw you," she told Evan, giving him a hug. "I was watching you through the window. I was very impressed, buckaroo. You were great!"

Evan planted a wet, unsolicited kiss on her cheek, and her heart gave a sudden squeeze with love for him.

"Rafe says he's gonna teach me to throw a rope, too. Rafe says if I learn fast, sometime maybe I can go with him when he rides out to look at fence lines. Rafe says—''

"Rafe says you should always wash the horse off you before you kiss a lady."

Rafe's deep voice came from the doorway, where he stood leaning one hip against the door jamb, arms crossed negligently across his chest. Carly's pulse gave a little lurch. She still hadn't gotten used to seeing him. He looked, God help her, better than he had nine years ago.

Stronger, leaner, if possible, even more…male.

"She's not a lady," Evan informed him, easing out of her embrace. "She's my mom."

Rafe just smiled that lethal-looking smile of his that had, during his time on the circuit, had females young and old in a collective rodeo dither. Heading for the sink, he gave the faucet a twist, plunged his hands deliberately under the running water, and proceeded to "wash the horse" off them.

Over his shoulder he sent her an undecipherable look.

Carly's gulp was practically audible. Of course, the threat was entirely inferred. He didn't intend to kiss her. He was baiting her. Perhaps this was his way of exacting revenge for past mistakes.

She took a bite of Laurie's muffin, slightly disheartened to find it was delicious.

"So…how are you feeling?" Rafe wiped his hands on a towel.

"Uh, better. Much better, thanks. Listen, I'm sorry I slept so late. I didn't mean for you to have to watch Evan this morning. You must have a million things to do."

"I've been up since five," he said. "Besides, Tampico needed the exercise, didn't he, pard?"

"Uh-huh!" Evan crowed, taking his turn with the bar of soap at the sink.

"Tampico? And that would be…your *bronco?*"

"Retired bronco," Gus reiterated.

"Gentle as a lamb now," Rafe added.

"Really." Carly crossed her arms.

Gus sent a wary look scuttling between the two of them, then set his coffee down on the counter. "*Say,* I see Pedro on his way in. Think I'll go see what he found on that north fence line this morning. C'mon, Evan, I'll introduce you two."

Always game, Evan headed for the door.

"Coward," Rafe said under his breath as Gus breezed by him.

The older man slid his hat on and tipped it to Carly. "Ma'am?"

"Gus."

When they'd gone, Rafe leaned against the counter, made a big show of pouring himself a cup of coffee and took a long, slow drink of it.

She cleared her throat. "Rafe—a *bronco?*"

He grinned. "That's what Evan thinks. Truth is, Tampico was bred for the rodeo, but wussed on every cowboy who ever got on his back. I felt sorry for him, so I saved him from the glue factory. He's my most reliable and gentle gelding."

She relaxed a fraction. "You sure?"

He frowned. "Yeah, I'm sure. You don't actually think I'd put him in danger, do you, Carly?"

"Riding horses isn't without risk." She hardly had to remind him of that.

"Neither is living, but that doesn't mean you should avoid it," he told her. And she knew he meant more than that. "You risk your life walking across the street," he went on, "or getting in your car. You telling me you don't want him to ride?"

She shook her head, hesitantly at first, then with more conviction. "No. Evan loved it. He was positively beaming. It's me. I'm just—"

"Just what?"

"Scared. That's all. In L.A., the closest most kids get to a horse is a four-on-the-floor Ford Bronco—with seat belts and air bags."

Rafe leaned back against the counter, studying her over the rim of his cup. "Our lives are pretty different, aren't they?"

There was no denying that. The chasm that had broadened between them seemed to have grown wider with each passing year. But she had to find some way to bridge it, for Evan's sake. "It's only geography," she said, toying with her cup. "And a few critters. Maybe we're not as different as you think. Not about the basic things, at least. If I seem overprotective...I'm just being a mom, Rafe. He's my child. He's all I've got."

For a long moment, Rafe just stared at her. His expression softened. "I know. You've done a hell of a job, Carly. He's a great kid."

The pleasure his praise brought her was muted, inevitably, by the knowledge that he had missed so much of Evan's childhood already—and by her responsibility for that.

In a perfect world, she would have discovered she was pregnant before she left him. Or, when she called to tell him, that breezy woman with a voice like fine whiskey wouldn't have answered. In a perfect world, she wouldn't have heard the sheets rustle as Rafe took the phone, and he would have wanted to hear what she had to say instead of cutting her off.

In a perfect world, their love for each other nine years ago would have been enough.

But it hadn't been.

"Carly?"

His deep voice dragged her from her thoughts. Guiltily she looked up at him. The words were on the tip of her tongue. *He's yours, Rafe, your son.*

He grinned at her. "How about a helmet?"

She blinked uncomprehendingly. "What?"

"A helmet. I'll get him a helmet to wear when he rides. Will that make you feel better?"

Her mouth opened, but nothing came out. Her mind had gone utterly blank.

He frowned. "You sure you're okay? Your headache back?"

Crossing the short distance between them, he surprised

her by tipping her chin toward the light, whistling at the ever-changing bruise on her cheek. "Hey, that's some shade of green today."

His touch sent a smoldering spark skittering through her like an electric current. He was too close again, and her heart was beating too fast. "I'm a fast healer. We'll be out of your hair before you know it."

He dropped his hand, the moment gone. "You haven't even been here twenty-four hours yet, Carly. You're hardly in my hair."

"Oh," she said with a grin, "give us a minute or two. Having an eight-year-old around is a singularly novel experience. I'm sure you're not used to sharing your house with a whirlwind."

He gestured around the spacious room with his coffee cup. "It's a big, empty house. It could use a little noise. But then, maybe you're anxious to get to that job waiting in Ohio."

Ohio seemed a million miles away just now, and the last thing on her mind. "Right. The job."

"What did they say when you called them?"

"Oh, well…" She picked up her coffee and took a sip, remembering the phone call she'd made from the hospital. "They were very understanding. Generous. They told me to take whatever time I needed."

"That's good," he said, sipping his coffee, too. "Because you're welcome to stay as long as you need to."

Carly wondered how much time she would need. A week? A month? How long did it take to put the past behind you? Would it be as painless as shedding that plaster around her leg? Somehow, she doubted it.

"Hey," she said brightly, "you haven't seen the latest." She hauled herself up on her crutches and demonstrated her new ability, hobbling around the kitchen. "Cruise control."

When she looked up, he was grinning at her. She returned his smile, feeling some of the awkwardness dissipate.

"Congratulations," he said, "Better watch out, though. You'll be causing pileups on the highway before you know it."

The phone on the wall jangled, and Rafe reached for it.

"Yeah? This is Kellard. Oh, right." He shifted the phone to the other hand and moved away from her, lowering his voice. "One o'clock? That's fine. Tell him I'll be there. Thanks, Betty."

He hung up the phone and stared at it for a moment, slugged down the remainder of his coffee, then turned back to her.

"Gotta go get cleaned up. I've got a few things to do in town today. I'll be back by suppertime. How's a pizza sound?"

Disappointment filtered through her. Of course he had things to do. A million things to do. It was selfish of her to want to spend time with him. "Pizza? Fine. Evan loves pizza."

"Sold. I'll pick one up on my way home. Anything to keep Gus out of the kitchen. Coffee is his only talent." He gestured at her cast. "Stay off that leg today, Carly. That's an order."

She sent him a playful salute. "Yessir," she told him, and then he was gone.

Rafe had come here to beg, and though his knees hadn't actually hit the floor, his pride was practically awash with hunter-green carpet fibers.

Damn his pride, he thought, watching Jed Stivers lean back in the tufted leather chair behind the desk and chew on the stogie in his mouth. Rafe would do whatever he had to do to save his spread.

Stivers was thinking about his offer. He could see numbers clicking behind the old man's eyes. Just shy of sixty-five, Jed still had a remarkably full head of silver-gray hair, and the lean edge old cowmen acquired after a lifetime of brutal physical work.

His hard work had paid off handsomely, Rafe thought, glancing around the well-appointed office. Besides running a spread that was the envy of nearly every rancher within a thousand miles, he now employed a couple dozen hands to do the manual labor for him.

He was on the far side of ambition—a concept beyond Rafe's grasp right now. But that very fact that Stivers was finished building his empire, he suspected, was what stood between Rafe and cutting a deal to save his ranch. He shifted in the smaller leather chair across the desk from Jed and ran a finger around the too-tight collar of his white shirt.

Finally, Jed spoke. "You know I like you, Rafe."

Rafe's heart fell a little. He knew that if Jed started out with that, he was sunk.

"Hell, if it was just about friendship—if I needed that adjacent parcel you're offering—well..." He shook his head and sent a cloud of bluish smoke haloing around his head. "But Sunimoto Corp. is bleeding money, and just beggin' for someone to sop it up. They're offering me a fast-cash buyout for that little piece of land, and frankly, I'd be a fool to turn it down."

The "little piece of land" to which Jed referred was more like a thousand acres that lay smack-dab across the northernmost corner of Rafe's land. It also boasted the last dependable source of water for his property following three straight years of soil-sucking drought. Rafe had held the lease on it for the past three years. In four weeks, that lease formally expired. And, along with it, Rafe's dreams of a future.

"...and now that my son James has come back from school," Jed was saying, "and wants a bigger part in the ranch, I'm steppin' back. The truth is, the missus has an itch to travel. She's tired of ranchin' and, after all these years, she deserves it."

Betty Stivers, whose high school homecoming-queen looks had long ago faded, deserved every thing she could get, in Rafe's book. She'd taken the back seat to Jed's career, and paid the price.

"No argument," Rafe said grimly. "But I still have one month to come up with the money, according to my option. All I'm asking is a little more time. You know that without that piece of land, without access to that water, my land is practically worthless. Every other source has dried up, and you know it, Jed."

"What about the banks?"

"Two of them have already turned me down," he admitted. "I'm still waiting on the last two. But I'm working on another angle. Something that's more up my alley."

Jed gnashed the end of his cigar between his teeth and leaned forward, knitting his thick fingers together. "You know I'd rather sell to you, Rafe. Hell, the whole damn countryside is goin' foreign." He gave a good-old-boy shrug, intended to shed any real or imagined responsibility. "James sees dollar signs. Mergers. Business opportunities. I see a way of life disappearing. But that's the way of things, isn't it? Out with the old, in with the new."

He stood slowly and extended his hand to Rafe. "Look, if there's any way I can hold them off, I will. I can promise you one more month. Beyond that..."

Rafe stood, too, and took his hand. "Thanks, Jed. I appreciate whatever you can do."

Outside, the cool air collided with his overheated temper like a slap, but he jerked off his navy sports coat and flung it over his shoulder. Winter was making way for spring. Buds dotted the naked branches of the cottonwoods lining Jed's circular gravel drive. Blue Stellar's jays flitted from tree to tree in a mating ritual as old as time. The world was starting over, just as Rafe's had begun closing in.

Ripping loose the tie at his throat, he gave the top button of his collar a savage twist. He stalked to his car and resisted the temptation to hit something. Anything.

He'd find a way. He had to. He couldn't fail again. Not in front of Carly.

Jamming the key into the ignition of his truck, he cranked the key and got—*nothing.* With a curse, he slapped the steering wheel. *No. Not the truck, too!* He stared hard at the thing for a moment, as if he could will it into submission.

One more time, he cranked the key. This time, the engine hesitated, then coughed to life. "Thank you," he muttered tightly under his breath. With a growl, he headed for town and the half-dozen errands that stood between him and the woman he'd left back at his ranch.

"I hear you've got company out at your place," Chicky Green said as she tallied up Rafe's feed bill. The middle-aged woman with startlingly red hair grinned as she spoke. "*Fe*-male company."

"You heard that, did you?" Rafe said, banking his amusement with a blank expression. Chicky's past life as the bartender of the now defunct Smokey Joe's Suds and Spuds on Main had served her inquiring mind well. She seemed to know all the gossip before even the folks who were being gossiped about knew the scoop. She had a good heart, and he liked her, but he didn't want tongues wagging about Carly when the situation was purely innocent.

She grinned. "You denying it?"

"What, and spoil your fun?"

Chicky winked at him, intrigued. "So who is she? Is she cute? *Married?*"

Rafe sent her a flat look intended to discourage her. It failed miserably.

"I heard you flagged Jim Noble down in the middle of

the night to hop his air-express plane to Nevada. She musta been somebody important.''

He slipped a couple of bills out of his wallet and laid them on the counter. He and Carly had happened long before he'd known Chicky, which was the only reason Chicky hadn't already pegged Carly. "Just an old friend. Nothing more.''

Chicky waggled a red eyebrow and collected his money. "So...she's single, then.''

He decided to throw a wrench in her machinations. "If you don't count her son.''

"A son,'' she murmured. "Hmm... The plot thickens.''

"There is no plot, Chicky. She needed help. I helped her. End of story.''

Chicky drummed her long nails against the counter with a *Sure-it-is* kind of look.

Rafe shook his head, knowing it was hopeless. "Did anyone ever tell you you have an overactive imagination?''

With a look that spoke volumes, she said, "All the time, honey. Listen, if you ask me—''

"I didn't.'' He hefted the sack of grain onto his shoulder.

"If you ask *me*,'' she repeated, punctuating her words with a *cha-ching* of her cash register, "any woman worth hoppin' that bucket of nuts and bolts for in the middle of the night has the potential of bein' somethin' considerably more than just a friend. And you know, honey, I've been tellin' you for years to find you some nice young thing and settle down.''

Rafe grabbed the second sack of grain and grinned. "Hell, Chicky, I've tried, but you keep turning me down.''

Chicky had the grace to blush, as only Rafe Kellard could still make her do. She waved a girlish hand at him and shook her head. "You sweet-talker, you. Some girl's gonna be knee-deep in it when she finally lands you.'' She crossed her arms beneath her ample bosom. "You tell your 'friend' I said hello…and good luck."

Rafe just smiled and headed out to his truck. He was the one who needed luck—to survive the next few weeks with Carly around. He'd spent last night tossing and turning like an out-of-sorts bull thinking about how close he'd come to kissing her.

Kissing her.

Now that would have been a mistake. Make that a calamity. All he needed now was to get involved with Carly again, so that she could walk out on him for a second time. The thought made him mentally groan. Hell, that just might finish him off.

"Hey, Rafe," came a voice from behind him.

Mel Stratton—a bronc rider who'd spent most of his career nipping at Rafe's heels on the circuit—sauntered toward him in a loose-hipped walk, thumbs caught on the front pockets of his jeans.

Mel grinned. "Hey, I hear you're gonna tie the old knot."

"Ah, jeez—" Chicky was even better than he thought!

"What?" Mel said, all wide-eyed innocence. "Ain't it true?"

"No!"

Mel smiled. "I'm just teasin' ya. I did hear about your midnight express to Nevada, though. I reckon everybody has. Ya know, the mill's gotta churn." He rubbed his jaw, abruptly changing the subject. "How's the leg?"

"Fine."

Mel nodded, and Rafe knew he'd already caught the way he was favoring it today.

"Say, I heard another rumor that I liked even less."

"What's that?" Rafe asked, rearranging the sack of grain on top of the others in the bed of his truck.

"That you're thinkin' of ridin' here in town at the PRCA rodeo at the end of the month."

Rafe stopped and turned around. What the hell? Did they have his place bugged, too?

Mel shrugged. "Pedro told Nate Baxter. Baxter told Jeff Pritcher, Pritcher told—"

"Okay, okay. What if I am?"

"Well—" Mel laughed "—I'm here to discourage you, buddy. Frankly, I don't need the competition, if you know what I mean."

"Since when have you been worried about a little competition, Mel?"

"Well, not since you left the circuit, that's for sure. I ain't plannin' to start losin'."

"Then what are you worried about?"

Mel shifted his feet. "Truth is, Rafe, I'm worried about you."

"Aw, hell. I'm touched, really, but don't be—"

Mel grabbed his arm as he started to turn away. "Hey, man, I'm serious."

For the first time, Rafe realized he was.

"I was there, remember?" Mel said.

Rafe remembered. He remembered that ol' Tornado had really been Mel's draw that night five years ago, but Mel had broken his wrist in the first round, and Tornado had been bumped up to Rafe. Nor had he forgotten Mel's expression when he showed up at the hospital to see him the next day. There were still traces of it in his eyes today.

"Take a load off, Mel," he said. "It wasn't your fault."

"I know, I know." Mel hesitated awkwardly and looked around. "Look, if it's the money... I mean... Ah, hell, Rafe, times are hard. I mean, I've had a few good years, and if there's anything you need, anything at all..."

The offer took Rafe by surprise. He felt it creep up his neck and flush into his jaw. If Mel knew he was having financial troubles, how many others did?

He cursed silently. It wasn't Mel's fault. In fact, it didn't even surprise him that he'd offered. He might have done the same if their positions were reversed. *He* was the one sinking. Not Mel. But he hadn't sunk low enough to hit his friends up for money. Nor could he afford any more nasty rumors finding their way back to the last couple of banks he stood a chance with.

"Thanks for the offer, Mel, but I'm fine. I'm just itching to get out of retirement, that's all."

Mel gave a quick nod of silent understanding and backed off. "Right. Hey, maybe I'll see you at the end of the month, then." He forced a grin. "Maybe I'll whip your butt."

Rafe grinned back as Mel walked backward toward his car, pointing a determined finger at Rafe.

"Who knows?" Rafe called after him. "There's a first time for everything."

Or a second.

Chapter 5

It had seemed like a good idea at the time.

With Rafe gone to town, it had seemed like the perfect time for a shampoo. A simple, steamy, hot-water-running-over-the-head-shampoo in the kitchen sink.

What she got was trouble.

Naturally, the first thing she lost was her balance, clutching the kitchen sink in a death grip while she hopped on her good foot until her equilibrium returned. The second was the shampoo, which she knocked off the counter in her blind reach for it as water ran in her eyes.

Feeling for the towel, she blotted her face with it and spotted the shampoo three feet away and rolling. Carly groaned with frustration, already gauging the amount of energy she'd be required to expend to retrieve it.

She grabbed one of her crutches and stabbed at the path of the rolling bottle, managing only to spin it sideways.

Curses!

With her hair dripping in her face, she eased toward the wayward bottle.

"What in hell are you trying to do? Break your other leg?"

Carly jerked a look toward the kitchen doorway to find Rafe glaring at her. In less than the time it would have taken to say, "Foiled again!" he had the shampoo in one hand and her elbow in his other and was guiding her back to the sink over the now wet floor.

"Rafe! I didn't hear you come in."

"Obviously," he said, shaking his head. "Are you crazy, woman?"

"I can do this," she argued. "I just knocked the shampoo off the counter."

"Uh-huh," he muttered, setting the errant bottle down on the counter. "Is this absolutely necessary?"

"Only in the interest of my sanity."

"Your hair looked fine to me."

"That's because you're a man."

He grinned. "I suppose there's some logic in that statement, though exactly what it is escapes me."

She stood there trying to ignore the water dripping steadily onto her T-shirt from her soaking-wet hair. His gaze, however, had no trouble going there. Lingering for a moment on the way her shirt had molded itself against her breasts, those savagely blue eyes swung up to meet hers—decidedly more heated than they'd been a moment ago.

She reached for the bottle. "Okay. Thanks for the shampoo. I can take it from here."

He held the shampoo away. "I think not."

"I beg your pardon?"

"Bend over."

Her eyes widened. "Excuse me?"

"You want a shampoo or not?"

She suspected it was a trick question.

"It's me or nothing," he said, still playing keepaway with the bottle.

She hesitated for more than a moment, then gave a tight shrug. "You."

One dark eyebrow arched significantly. He gestured toward the sink and flipped on the water.

This, a small voice warned her as she did as he bade, *is a very bad idea.*

The first touch—the one near the small of her back—made her jump. The second, firm and sure against her head, guided her toward the water. With unexpected gentleness, he combed his fingers through her already wet hair, easing her fully under the gush of heat. The hot water felt luxurious against her scalp, and his fingers...well, his fingers felt—

"When did you cut it?" he asked, squeezing shampoo into her hair.

It took a moment to compute the question, with her mind a million miles from haircuts. Oh, yes. "Years ago. After Evan was born." His fingers slid against the soapy mass with the skill of a masseur. She suppressed a moan of pure pleasure.

"Funny," he answered, "All these years...I always pictured it long."

The admission shocked her eyes open, and she craned her neck to see him. "Was this before or after you stuck pins in my likeness?"

"Keep your eyes closed, or you'll get soap in 'em."

She obeyed instantly, but held her breath, waiting for his reply.

"Never got that creative," Rafe said, concentrating on the feel of her hair in his hands. "Although I admit that in the beginning there were inevitably devious plots of revenge involved."

"Not exactly what a girl wants to hear from a man whose hands are in such close proximity to her throat."

Rafe chuckled. "It passed." Another lie. The pain never had. It still hadn't.

He flipped the water on again and plunged his hands back into her sudsy hair. His thighs and hips accidentally brushed against the intimately familiar curve of her behind as he bent over her. Good sense warned him to back off, but as usual, he ignored it. Their closeness lost all pretense of accident. With a low, thudding beat, his pulse kept time with the motion of his hands.

Running his fingers up her neck, then down through the silken blond strands, he repeated the action over and over, long after her hair squeaked and gleamed under the overhead lamp. Years ago, he'd done this for her under decidedly different circumstances. There had been a shower involved, and both of them had been naked.

Rafe closed his eyes and tried, without success, to force those thoughts from his mind. Carly was silent under his ministrations, content as a cat being stroked. And for a while, he was content to stroke her.

But when his hands began to ache to stray lower, down her spine and over her breasts, he reluctantly squeezed the excess water from her hair and draped the towel over her head.

When she straightened, her face was flushed. But neither the dusky heat in her eyes nor the confusion in her expression could be chalked up entirely to the hot water. Unsteady, she wobbled against the counter.

Rafe caught her by the upper arms, his hips meeting hers with unplanned inevitability. For a moment, they simply stared at each other, surprised. Her lips parted, and her gaze slid heatedly to his mouth. His best intentions evaporated in that flicker of a moment as his lips found hers and he was reminded of what not even nine years between them had erased.

Elemental as fire, or air, or water, what had collided between them once was still there. He knew it by the way her body swayed into his, losing the rigidity of surprise as his tongue parted her lips. He knew it by the greedy slant of her mouth against his and the way her hands curled into the flesh of his shoulders.

His fingers plunged into the wet hair at the base of her skull. She tasted of mint and honey, and he remembered the rest. No woman's mouth had ever fit his the way hers did. He drew her closer, pulling her flush against him, until her hip was an intimate press against the hardness at the juncture of his thighs.

A whimper of need escaped her as her breasts flattened against his chest and her arms tightened around him. Their tongues mated with the same desperation their bodies felt, swirling against each other, seeking more.

Like a flame fed by air, Rafe's control slipped. He forgot everything but the feel of her mouth on his. Backing her up against the counter, he lifted her against him until her feet nearly left the floor and nothing but their clothing separated their heated flesh.

A few seconds later, her mouth was not enough. He wanted...he *needed*...

His mouth left hers and trailed to the pulse at her throat, where his teeth slid against her skin. He felt the erratic beating of her heart and, from what seemed like a long way off, heard her say his name.

In another moment, he would have taken her right there on the kitchen floor, and sanity be damned. But the sound of his name on her lips—the word tinged with both need and alarm—dragged him up from that place. With his breath a ragged rasp, and his pulse pounding in his ears, he stopped himself with a low, and rather foul, curse.

Carly swallowed hard, shaken to the core by the kiss. But what she saw in Rafe's eyes frightened her most— confusion and, worse than that, accusation. His gaze bored into hers like a hot shaft of iron left too long in the fire. His hands, still locked around her upper arms, tightened.

"Just tell me one thing." His voice was low and ragged. "Why the hell were you carrying my phone number in your purse on some dog-eared newspaper clipping about me? *Why,* Carly?''

Whatever she'd expected him to say, she thought numbly, that wasn't it. She blinked, listening to the harsh sound of her own breathing. Panic welled up inside her. Of course he wanted to know. There was a perfectly logical explanation. But she couldn't give it to him. Not without risking everything. Her head was spinning with what had just happened between them. ''It's complicated.''

''Simplify it.''

She glanced pointedly at his ever-tightening grip on her arms. Instantly he let her go, only then realizing that he was hurting her. Raking both hands through his dark hair, he clasped them together behind his head as he moved away from her.

She opened her mouth, closed it, then began again. ''After your accident, when you were in the hospital...I called to see how you were.''

As if he'd been jolted by an electric shock, he stopped dead and dropped his hands. ''You did?''

She nodded. ''Three times.''

He could only stare at her.

She'd surprised him. Surprised herself. She reached for her crutches and tucked them under her arms. ''You were all over the L.A. news, of course, and they kept showing that clip of the bull and you, over and over...''

He muttered something crass.

''...and I couldn't get past the ICU nurse because she was only releasing the same non-information the hospital was giving to the media, so I finally told them I was your sister.''

Rafe's eyes narrowed. ''That was *you?*''

She nodded.

He swallowed visibly. ''That was Gus you talked to. He told me about your call, but I thought you were some rodeo groupie.'' The anger leached slowly from his expression. ''Why didn't you give him your real name?''

She looked at her hands. ''I—I didn't want to upset you. I just wanted to make sure you were going to be okay.''

''*And* you were married at the time,'' he said meaningfully, watching her.

Her heartbeat slowed to a dull thud. ''That's irrelevant.''

''Not exactly.''

She didn't want to talk about Tom now. She wasn't sure she wanted to talk at all. ''I would have called regardless. But as it happens, Tom did know. He was sitting beside me when the news came on that night. *He* handed me the phone.''

''He was a bigger man than I would have been,'' Rafe said with soul deep conviction.

''Tom was a good man,'' she said, compelled to defend someone who needed no defense. ''He had the uncanny ability to see things as they were, not as they appeared.''

He frowned. ''And how were things?''

If only she had a simple answer for that question. ''Complicated,'' she said at last.

Rafe stared at her for a long moment before pinning his gaze on the darkness outside the kitchen window. ''And my number?''

''You're listed. I must've dialed your number a dozen times in the past few years. But I always hung up before you answered.''

Disbelief crossed his face. ''Why?''

She chewed on her lip, still able to taste his kiss. ''I didn't stop caring about you when I left, Rafe. I just stopped hoping. I'm going to go find a dry T-shirt.''

Rafe's gut tightened as Carly headed toward the bedroom and left him standing there alone. Stopped hoping? For what? he wondered. For him to chase after her? To come crawling to her on his knees to beg forgiveness? For what sin? Being an idiot? Hoping that once, just once, someone would believe in him enough to stick around?

And then he cursed himself for wondering what might have happened if he had swallowed his pride and chased after her.

Flicking on the cold water at the sink, he splashed it on his face. Then, bracing two hands there, he watched the droplets splash against the porcelain. Forget trying to figure it out, he told himself. She'll be gone soon. And with her, the reminder that his best has never been quite good enough.

Evan fumbled with the looped rope, twirling it in an awkward circle that collided with his knees more often than not. This was the third day in a row Rafe and Evan had worked on spinning. Today, they'd been at it for over an hour already, and the sun had begun to set behind the purple ridge of the San Juans.

"Oh, I'll never get it," Evan mumbled, kicking a toe into the dirt.

"Hey, you're not gonna quit on me, are you?" Rafe coiled the rope one more time.

"It'll never work. I just can't make it twirl."

"Not if you think you can't," Rafe said, running his gloved thumb against the rough hemp of the rope. "You know how long it took me to master this?"

Evan shook his head glumly.

"Three weeks."

Eyes widening, Evan stared up at him. "Really?"

"Yup. Day-in, day-out. All I did was work on getting that darned rope to spin in a perfect circle. Know what happened?"

Evan shook his head.

"Same thing as you. I almost lost my nerve. Thought I'd never get it. 'Course, that was before I found my, uh...my lucky dime."

"You have a lucky dime?" Evan said with a doubtful look.

"Luckiest dime I ever found. Yup. Found that dime in the street one day when I was walking in town, and I figured if a penny was lucky, a dime must be ten times as good," Rafe said. "Well, I'll tell ya, soon as I put that dime in my pocket, the strangest thing started to happen."

"What?"

"I started working with that rope again, and darned if it didn't start spinning just right. Just like that."

"Nah," Evan said with a half-convinced grin.

Never, Rafe thought, had the boy reminded him more of Carly than at that moment. He couldn't be sure if it was the way the corner of Evan's mouth lifted in a mischievous, hopeful smile, or the sparkle in his eye. But something tightened in Rafe's chest as he set the rope spinning in lazy circles around the two of them.

"Absolutely," he said. "Pretty soon, I was lassoing everything I passed. Doorknobs, fenceposts—*girls....*"

Evan laughed, but a moment later his expression faded. "But I don't have a lucky dime."

Rafe let the rope spin to a stop and pulled a thoughtful expression. "Right. But hey, it's not critical to have a lucky piece."

"But maybe it would help," Evan said hopefully.

"Hey, maybe you could use mine." Rafe brightened as if he'd only just thought of it.

"Yours? Really?"

Rafe reached into his pocket, praying he had one. His fingers met the warm silver gratefully. He pulled it out and flipped it with his thumb toward Evan, who caught it awkwardly between his arm and his chest, then turned it over in his fingers, examining it for signs of magic. "It looks just like any old dime."

"Ah, that's the thing about lucky charms. Looks can be deceiving."

"But...maybe it's just lucky for you," Evan said at last.

"Maybe. But luck has a way of passing from person to person. Ever notice that?"

He shook his head again.

"Well, trust me. You take this dime, and before you know it, you'll have that rope doin' just what you want." He grinned and added, "The girls'll be running when they see you comin'."

Evan made an appropriate horrified-eight-year-old sound. "I don't *wanna* rope any *girls*."

Just wait, Rafe wanted to say, but he only smiled. "Whattya say? Shall we give it another try?"

The boy tucked the dime in his left pocket, patted it for luck and reached for the rope again. At first the spin was as awkward as the last, bumping against his knees and sailing every which way. Then, gently, Rafe covered Evan's small hand with his own and cocked the boy's elbow higher, guiding the rope in a larger circle until it formed a perfect O.

Evan gasped, eyes wide. "Whoa, awesome!"

Rafe grinned broadly and released his hand. Evan kept the motion going for a full five seconds before the rope collapsed.

"I did it, huh, Rafe? I twirled it!"

Rafe put his hand out. "Gimme five, pard."

Evan slapped his open palm with the authority of a kid who'd just mastered a mountain. "Wait till Mom sees. She won't even believe it!"

"She'll be proud of you, kid," he said, ruffling Evan's blond hair. *I'm proud of you,* came the thought, unbidden.

With a suddenness that nearly stole his breath, Evan collided with Rafe's waist in an enormous hug. Stunned, he absorbed the sensation of the boy's small body molded against him. Rafe's arms hovered just above the boy's back. He was afraid to touch him. To let himself get that close.

A weird sensation tumbled through his chest. He'd never imagined, never suspected, how sweet it would feel—a child's absolute affection. Slowly he dropped his hands to Evan's back and returned the hug, his throat thick with emotion.

"Thanks, Rafe," Evan said against his shirt. "For the dime."

"Hey, you did it, kid. Remember that. Dime or no dime, you've mastered it now. Keep practicing. Someday you'll pass that dime on to somebody who needs it more than you."

Evan nodded wordlessly against his chest, and then he was off and running with his rope, toward the house and his mom.

Carly.

In the three days since he kissed her, they'd exchanged little more than polite conversation. As she'd improved physically with each passing day, he'd pulled back, spending more and more time out on the fence lines, away from her. When they did see each other, the tension between them was so high it practically crackled in the air.

He was the coward. She had wanted to talk—had tried to talk every time he got near. But he hadn't let her. He supposed he was afraid to hear what she had to say: that he shouldn't have kissed her. That they should leave well enough alone. That she was grateful that he'd let her come here to stay, but as far as anything else...

And she'd be right. He'd brought her here to get her memory out of his life, not to drag her back in.

The damnedest thing was, he still wanted her. Right now, last night, the night before. Desire burned like a coal inside him, and he couldn't shake it, no matter how irrational he told himself he was being. He could still feel the way her body had swayed into his, and the way her lips had slid against his, as if she'd forgotten the last nine years. Most telling of all was the way his body responded at the very thought of holding her again.

He told himself there was only one logical explanation for his attraction to Carly—he needed a woman. Any woman. He'd been so busy with the ranch, it had been months since he even thought of sex.

There were a half-dozen he could call right off the top of his head. There was Ellie Monaghan over in Oxford. Or Kathy Lynn Rimmer, over near the Las Platas County line. She'd never turned him away.

Then there was Millie Cahill. He and Millie sort of had an agreement. No strings, no ties. He'd bring a bottle of good wine and a handful of daisies, and she never complained when she woke up in the morning alone.

Or there was always Ruby Winston, the brown-eyed cocktail waitress over at Ludie's in Durango. She was always game, and a terror under the sheets, and—

And she wasn't Carly.

Rafe closed his eyes. A man didn't mess around with a woman like Carly. Kiss Carly Jamison, and irrational thoughts about settling down and raising up a family started bubbling up, no matter how much a man denied them.

Nine years ago, he'd come close to settling down with Carly. Closer than he'd come with any woman, before or since. But he hadn't been much good at it. In fact, he'd stunk.

Buying the ranch was as close as he figured he'd ever come, and his plans had never included a woman as a permanent fixture. As far as fatherhood, his only role model had drunk himself to death by the time Rafe turned twelve. Rafe had survived five years bouncing around the foster-care system before he came to the conclusion that the fairy-tale family he dreamed of as a boy didn't exist and, for someone like him, never would.

But Carly had wanted it all. Kids, a ring, a picket fence;

all of it, and him, too. She'd wanted the perfect package, all tied up with a bow. She deserved that. But he hadn't been the one to give it to her....

Rafe fingered two hands through his hair, took a deep, shaky breath of sage-scented air and stared at the broad swell of land he called his own. Walking to the corral fence, he draped one arm over the rail and dropped his chin against his hand.

In the distance, his cattle grazed, like black smudges of ink against a backdrop of gold. The barn, the house—all of it was his. Four years of sweat and blood had gone into building it. Like a piece of a half-done puzzle, this place had satisfied that long-ago dream of building something he could call home.

Yet it had never kept his bed warm at night or listened to his troubles. It had never made him feel like he could do anything—like that hug from Evan just had.

Rafe was thirty-three years old, and all he had to show for his life was a piece of land, a few head of cattle and a handful of silver-plated trophies that said he had once been the best at what he did.

He wondered what it would have been like if his life had taken another path. What it would be like to know a kid like Evan from birth. To watch him come into the world. To hold him for the first time...teach him to throw a ball, rope a cow...

"A penny fer yer thoughts." Gus's voice came from beside him.

Rafe jumped. He'd been so caught up in his own thoughts, he hadn't even heard the older man coming. Gus wrapped his arm around the rail beside him.

"They aren't worth that much," Rafe said. "Just thinking of things that can never be."

"Lotta that goin' around," Gus muttered meaningfully.

Rafe sensed a lecture coming on and offered a diversion. "Did Pedro bring Red-Eye up from the south pasture?"

Gus's scowl said exactly what he thought of the idea of corralling that loco horse for Rafe's purposes. "Against my better judgment."

"Good. I'll start with him tomorrow in the breaking corral."

"I reckon there's nothing I can say to talk you out of this."

"Nope."

Gus made a sound of annoyance between his teeth and looked away.

Rafe pushed away from the fence. "I think I'll drive into town. Tell Carly I'll be back late."

"Rafe," Gus said, stopping him with a hand on his arm, "I don't know what happened between you two, and it's probably..."

"Definitely—"

"...none of my business," Gus finished, ignoring him. "But she's in there moonin' over somethin', same as you, and tryin' her darnedest to cook you a fancy meal. Now, if I don't miss my guess, that's her way of trying to make up for whatever it is that's set you off like a wounded grizzly the past few days."

Rafe narrowed his eyes. "She's supposed to be resting. She shouldn't be cooking." Accusingly he looked at Gus. "I thought you were cooking."

Gus pinched a space between his thick fingers. "It took her about this long to decide it was in all our best interests to do it herself, I reckon. And it smells pretty dang good, too. So why don't you get your butt in there and tell her you're lookin' forward to tasting it?"

"Stay out of it, Gus."

Gus propped his hands on his skinny hips and shook his head in disgust. "Yer just bound and determined to make things hard, ain't ya? To do it alone."

Rafe turned and started walking. He hated it when Gus got up on his soapbox.

"Well, why the hell did ya bring her here in the first place?"

Rafe whirled on the older man, his mouth curled in an angry scowl. "Because—"

"Because?"

"Because I had to, that's all. Dammit, Gus, I need to put her behind me once and for all."

Gus waited a beat, then followed Rafe as he stomped off toward the truck in the gathering darkness. "Maybe you don't want her behind you. Ever think of that?"

"Maybe that's not an option."

"Tell that to her. She's the one in there cookin' you a meal like her life depends on it."

"Because I put a roof over her and her son's head. Because she's grateful. That's all it is, and all it'll ever be."

"Well, I reckon if ya ignore her long enough, she's bound to get the message loud and clear that she ain't wanted here," Gus said tightly, stopping where he was.

Rafe slowed to a stop in the dusky yard, only feet from escape. Tilting his head back, he stared up at the half-moon rising in the east.

Dammit!

Was that what he'd been doing? Punishing her? For what? Kissing him back?

With a silent curse, he shook his head. Now *that* was irrational.

He hated it when Gus was right. "Okay," he said, turning back to Gus. "So…are you trying to tell me I'm being a jerk?"

Gus raised a hairy eyebrow. "Well, if it walks like a duck, and quacks like a duck…"

Just what he needed. Dime-store philosophy. "Old man, you're a pain in the butt, you know that?"

"That's why you keep me around." His droopy mustache lifted in a grin.

"Yeah, it is," Rafe admitted, punching the old man in the shoulder as he headed back toward the barn.

"Ow," Gus complained, rubbing his shoulder. "And ya got no respect fer yer elders, neither. Where ya goin'?"

"Don't get your panties in a ruffle. I'm stayin' for dinner. But I'm gonna check on Annie one more time," he said, referring to the very pregnant mare in the box stall in the barn. "If that's okay with you?"

Gus grinned. "Okay by me." Watching Rafe go, Gus stuck his hands into his pockets and sauntered toward the pens, whistling.

Chapter 6

Carly sat at the rustic table in the shadow-dappled kitchen, snapping fresh string beans. They gave a satisfying crunch between her fingers. The mindless work suited her mood. Anything more taxing, and she'd have to think. And if she thought, she'd remind herself that Rafe had spent the past three days avoiding her like the plague. And that thought would lead, inevitably, to the next.

The Kiss.

Carly slammed her eyes shut. There she went, thinking again. She tossed half a string bean in the bowl, popped the other in her mouth and sighed. Trying not to think of something was a bit of a catch-22. One had to first think of it in order to *not* think of it. Besides, it did no good. The kiss had happened, and now it lay like a barricade between them.

She told herself that it had been a momentary lapse in control. Hers—*definitely!* His—? Well, the jury was still out on that one. He'd seemed pretty darned in control to her. If anything, it had been a lapse in common sense on his part. They'd acted like a couple of teenagers who'd found themselves in the back seat of a car.

Was it only lust? Or something more?

The truth was, that kiss had laid bare something between them that had lived just under the surface all these years. Despite their best efforts to forget, apparently neither one of them had. Perhaps Rafe regretted bringing them here at all. Clearly, he wanted to avoid entanglements at all costs.

That thought led inevitably to the next: Evan. Would Rafe react the same way when she told him the truth? Would he avoid the entanglement a child brings?

She snapped another green bean and tossed it in the bowl, a little more forcefully than necessary.

Possibly. Probably. How could she know for certain?

Worse, how could she let her son lose yet another father?

Yet...watching them together gave her hope. Rafe had devoted countless hours to teaching Evan to use a rope, when he could easily have buried himself under the ranch work she knew he must have.

And Evan was crazy about him. Was it too much to hope that maybe Rafe's tendencies to run from intimacy were limited only to her?

"Yoo-hoo! Anybody home?"

Carly looked up from the colander full of snap beans, toward the sound of the feminine voice. Evening shadows striped the porch and effectively disguised the features of the woman who stood there.

"Oh!" the woman said as she pulled the door open a crack. Her arms were full of grocery bags. "Hi. You must be Carly."

For a moment, Carly simply stared, thinking Demi Moore must have gotten lost on her way to the studio and somehow stumbled onto Rafe's back porch.

"I'm Laurie," the woman said. "Laurie Anders? Gus's daughter?"

She remembered to close her mouth. *This,* Carly thought with a sinking feeling, *was Laurie?* The photograph upstairs had been an unfortunate understatement.

Belatedly Carly lurched to her feet, knocking over the glass of water by her elbow. She chased the glass as it skidded across the table and caught it inches ahead of disaster. Red-faced, she looked up at Laurie and laughed. "Wait, I think I can do that a *little* more clumsily. I'm sorry. Please, come in."

Water dripped off the edge of the table in a steady stream onto the hardwood floor. Laurie smiled back as she let herself in. She grabbed the hand towel that hung near the door, as if she did it all the time.

"Here, let me get that. Oh, your poor leg! Don't worry, I'm used to this. If it's not me, it's one of my boys. Ask Rafe. I'm the queen of spill-mopping."

Strange, Carly thought, how something so simple as knowing exactly where things were in Rafe's kitchen could seem so intimate.

At that very moment, two boys, one about Evan's age and the other a towhead a couple of years older, came crashing through the door behind her.

"Did not!"

"Did too!"

"Says you!"

"Mom!" complained the youngest.

Laurie sent them a patient look as she wrung out the wet cloth in the sink. "Yes, dearlings?" she said sweetly.

"Jake shoved me."

"Did not," Jake retorted, glaring at his brother.

"Did so. 'Cause I was beatin' him to the paddock. He says just 'cause I promised to clean his room..."

"And *didn't*," Jake pointed out smugly.

"...that he was gonna feed Tampico an' I couldn't do anything."

Laurie's look passed mildly between her two sons. "*You*

promised to clean *his* room? Was there blackmail involved?''

The boys exchanged looks, then went conspicuously silent. Laurie turned to Carly with an amused smile. "Carly, I'd like you to meet my sons, Jake and Jordan. My two lovely sons who only minutes ago swore an oath to be on their *best* behavior tonight." She raised one eyebrow at the suddenly contrite look on the boys' faces.

Jake wiped his hand off on his blue jeans and offered it to Carly. "Nice to meetcha, ma'am."

"Me too. Ma'am," piped in Jordan, trying hard not to stare at the bruise on Carly's cheek. He leaned closer to his mother and whispered, "Hey, Mom, her shiner's better than mine was."

Laurie smiled abashedly at Carly, who was laughing, just as Evan barreled through the door, rope in hand.

"Mom! Mom! Look what Rafe showed me!" He skidded to a halt at the sight of the other boys.

"Oh, Ev— This is my son Evan," she told the boys. "This is Jake and Jordan Anders and their mom, Mrs. Anders."

"Laurie," she corrected with a welcoming smile, extending a formal hand to Evan. "We've heard so much about you. Gus is Jake and Jordan's grandpa."

The boys made tentative introductions, and Jake spied Evan's rope. "Know how to throw it?"

Evan shook his head. "Not yet. Rafe just showed me how to twirl it." He couldn't hide his excitement as he glanced at Carly.

She winked at him and gave him a squeeze.

"Can you?" Evan asked Jake. "Throw it, I mean?"

Jake shrugged casually. "Yeah. I'll show ya if ya want."

"Okay," Evan said.

Jake grinned. "C'mon. Jordan's just learning, too."

The boys headed toward the door without a look back

at the adults. "Wanna hear somethin'?" she heard Jordan ask Evan as they disappeared out the door. A loud, prolonged belching sound drifted in their wake, followed by boyish laughter.

Laurie turned back to Carly and shook her head. "Boys. They're aliens."

The two women laughed together like two old friends. Relief poured through Carly. She found herself liking the woman—despite the resemblance to Demi.

Laurie caught the redolent scent of pot roast cooking.

"It smells wonderful! But you shouldn't be cooking. You're recuperating. You should be eating bonbons by the fire. Watching soap operas and drooling over the diet-soda man in that commercial."

Carly laughed. "The truth is, someone will have to be dabbing the drool from my chin if I have to spend one more day in this house doing nothing, because I'll be a babbling idiot."

"Cabin fever?" Laurie asked in a sympathetic voice.

"Raging," Carly admitted. "I'm not used to staying still for long."

"Rafe know you're pulling your hair out?"

"He's been busy," she said in quick defense of him.

"Humph," Laurie sniffed. "Men are oblivious. How *are* you feeling?" She glanced at the discoloration on Carly's cheek. "Rafe told me you took a pretty nasty hit."

"Better. Grateful," she added. "I don't want to think what would have happened if Rafe hadn't come."

Laurie smiled as she emptied out a grocery sack into the fridge. "Small chance of that. The way I heard it, the phone was still buzzing when he got on that plane. There aren't a lot of women he'd do that for."

Carly suddenly felt quite certain that Laurie could count herself among them. She searched the other woman's face for signs of jealousy, and found none.

Laurie started on the second grocery bag. "Look, I

didn't mean to barge in on you with the thundering horde. I'll just put these things away and—"

"No," Carly insisted. "Stay. Please. You must stay for dinner. There's plenty."

"You sure?"

"Positive. Besides, I could use some company."

Laurie took the colander full of beans and smiled. "Then we'd be glad to. But only on the condition you let me help."

They worked side by side, sharing small talk, tearing lettuce and dancing around the most obvious subject— Carly and Rafe. Laurie talked about her burgeoning catering business, and the mischief her two boys seemed to home in on like a radar beam. They swapped stories, and even touched on the fact that they were both widows—a common bond Carly shared with no other women her age.

"I miss him terribly sometimes," Laurie admitted. "When Jack died, it almost killed me too." The knife she was using on the tomato stilled, and Laurie stared out the window. "Rafe and Jack were best friends. Like brothers. Rafe was there for me, for us, anytime we needed him. He's the best. When he had his accident, I was able to return the favor."

"I'm glad he had you," Carly said, and she meant it.

Laurie dumped the tomatoes in the salad, then regarded her with a tilt of her head. "So...you're the Carly he never got over, aren't you?"

Carly's face flattened with surprise. "Excuse me?"

Gently Laurie said, "Forgive me. I've known Rafe for so long...I guess I'm a little protective. And a little curious. It's just that he talked about you once—in the hospital after his accident. The only time," she added with a smile, "you'll catch Rafe vulnerable enough to admit anything. Actually, he wouldn't have admitted it to me then, except that when he was out of his mind with fever, he called for you."

Shock filtered through her. Her mouth fell open.

"Surprised?"

Beyond words. "You sure he wasn't cursing me?"

Laurie laughed. "Quite sure."

"What did he tell you?" Carly asked evasively. "About us, I mean."

Laurie shrugged. "That it had been serious. That you two were from different worlds, and when things didn't work out, you'd left to pursue a career in law. He said it was for the best, but I saw in his eyes that he'd never really convinced himself of it."

"It happened a long time ago, Laurie. We were both so young."

Laurie nodded with a sigh. "The best and worst time to fall in love. The best because it's usually the first time, and the most…electric. The worst because if it was good, nothing else ever quite measures up."

The truth of her words hit close to home. "Was Jack your first love?"

"High school sweethearts," Laurie admitted with a wistful smile. "He was something. Lived, breathed and ate the rodeo. And he was good. Almost as good as Rafe. You would have thought that might have come between them, but it never did. Rafe pushed him constantly, and Jack loved the competition. They were amazing together."

"They must have met soon after I left," Carly said softly. "I wish I could have known him."

"Me too." Laurie's expression was bright, but her eyes glimmered.

At that moment, the kitchen door opened and the horde descended. The boys played musical chairs at the table, lobbying for best seat, as Gus and Rafe followed them in.

Rafe's eyes lit up when he caught sight of Laurie. "Hey, you," he said kissing her on the cheek with an intimate casualness Carly had trouble imagining. "Didn't expect you guys out here tonight."

"Well, a girl could starve waiting for an invitation," she teased. "So I just decided to barge in and introduce myself to Carly."

Rafe's gaze slid to her with a wary So-you-two-have-met? look.

Laurie waved away his ignorance with a wink at Carly. "Now, we're way past introductions, aren't we, Carly?"

"Oh…yeah," she said. "We're on to favorite designers, classic movies…ya know…the solutions for world peace."

"*World peace,* huh?" Rafe said. "Jeez, Gus, and here we were tinkering with a pathetic little generator, hoping it would keep the electricity running in the barn. Gosh," he said, hitching up his shoulders in his best Bogie imitation, "I guess the problems of two little people don't really amount to a hill of beans…."

"*Casablanca*…" Laurie sighed. "I *love* that movie."

Impressed, Carly laughed. "A hidden talent, Rafe. Bogart impressions!"

"He's got a million of 'em," Gus put in with a grin.

Rafe actually blushed, and glanced at Carly. "Don't believe a word of it."

But somehow she did. This side of him was one she hadn't seen since the early days of their relationship, when laughter came easily and she didn't have to work to coax a smile from him. Laurie seemed to bring it out in him. Carly wasn't sure whether to be glad or jealous of that. She opted for glad, because it was such a relief from the intensity of the past few days.

Dinner was a noisy affair. Above the teasing banter between Rafe, Gus and Laurie, the boys talked a mile a minute, hatching a scheme for a sleepover together.

With all the subtlety of a jackhammer, Laurie suggested to Rafe that he take Carly and Evan on a tour of the ranch by truck tomorrow, before Carly started to redecorate his house out of sheer boredom. The suggestion took him by surprise, but he quickly agreed to it.

Several times during the meal, Carly caught Rafe watching her, but he would just smile and avert his gaze somewhere else when caught. He told bad knock-knock jokes that made the boys groan with laughter. The food all but vanished, and the brownies Laurie had brought crowned a meal that had been a smashing success with all concerned.

Jake and Jordan obviously adored Rafe, who seemed oblivious to his apparent natural talent at enthralling kids. Even Evan, her shy son, discarded caution when Rafe was around. His affection for him was unabashed. Complete.

Carly watched the dynamics with a mixture of trepidation and relief. It was, after all, Rafe who had convinced himself years ago that fathering wasn't in his blood. How wrong he'd been. She wondered if he had any idea what a wonderful one he'd make. Then again, playing favorite uncle had the added benefit of no responsibility. Therein lay the rub.

After dinner, Rafe regaled the rapt boys with a tale or two about his bull-riding days with Jake and Jordan's father. Laurie listened quietly, smiling at the bittersweet memories and watching her sons listen to stories about their father. Carly's heart ached for them all, but she found that Laurie wasn't one to dwell on the sadness. She had a story of her own to tell about her late husband and a miniature donkey with a passion for denim that had everyone laughing, including Carly. Gus embellished it by adding a part none of them had ever heard, until they were all holding their aching sides at the hilarious picture he conjured up.

Finally, Laurie gave Gus a peck on his stubbled cheek and started to clear the table. The boys, miraculously, pitched in.

Evan fit in so well in the whole picture, it seemed as if he'd always belonged. Carly could almost imagine them a family, her and Rafe and Evan. Almost. But it was a dream that had no chance of coming true. They would never be a family, and Evan would only have a father if Rafe accepted him—and then only part-time.

She knew time was growing short. And the longer she put off the telling, the worse it would all be. She had to tell Rafe. Soon.

"Can we feed Tampico, Rafe?" Jordan asked, clearing dishes off the table for his mom.

"And we haven't seen Annie yet," Jake said. "When is she gonna have her foal?"

"Any minute," Rafe said, getting to his feet. "All right. Who wants grain and who wants hay?"

"Me!" all three boys said in unison.

Rafe grinned. "We'll sort it out." As the boys stampeded for the barn, followed by Gus, Rafe reached for his hat and turned back to Carly.

As his gaze met hers, she glimpsed the same smoldering heat that she'd seen there before. And something else. Resolution. About what, she had no way of knowing, because before he could say anything, the phone rang.

Laurie was closest and picked it up. She held it out for Rafe. "It's for you. Rance Taylor."

Rafe's expression went blank, and he took the receiver. "Yeah? This is Kellard." He switched the phone to his other ear, glanced at Carly and Laurie, then turned his back on them. She and Laurie exchanged looks.

"Uh-huh," he murmured. A long pause. "I understand. No, it's business. Right. No. Thanks. Don't bother." His voice went flat as he said goodbye and hung up the phone. A full five seconds passed before he turned around, slid his hat on and headed for the door.

Laurie broke the oppressive silence. "Everything okay?"

"Great," he replied, trying for sincerity. "I'm gonna go and, uh, see about Tampico, or he'll be getting triple rations of grain, if I know those boys." He stopped and turned back to Carly. "Thanks for dinner, Carly. It was great."

After he left, Carly stared at the door and sighed.

"He's great, the dinner was great, everything is...great. So...why do I get the feeling it's not?" She glanced up at Laurie. "Who's Rance Taylor?"

A frown furled Laurie's brow. "A banker in town."

"A banker?" The wheels began spinning in her brain. "Does Rafe need money?"

"I don't know."

Carly glanced at the door. "I've seen him sitting up late with his books several times late at night. He's been pre-occupied, worried about something, but he hasn't talked to me about it. Whatever that phone call was, it didn't sound good. Do you think he's in trouble, Laurie?"

"He's a very private man, Carly, especially about his problems. He doesn't talk about his problems with me. Have you tried asking him?"

She shook her head. "Even if I did, he probably wouldn't tell me." She stood and walked to the window, staring out at the dim light over the barn. "To say things didn't work out between us is only half the story, Laurie. I left him. I walked out. He went off to a rodeo one day, and when he got back, I wasn't there. Did he tell you that?"

"Not exactly, but I gathered as much," Laurie said. "You must have had your reasons."

Carly turned to stare at Laurie.

"Surprised I'd say that?" Laurie asked.

"Yes," Carly answered.

"I've been married, remember? And I know Rafe," she explained. "And yes, I love him—as a friend. A good friend. But that doesn't make me blind to the little things he does to keep people at arm's length. The dance takes two. If it had been all your fault, I suspect you wouldn't be here now.''

"Why *am* I here?" she wanted to know.

"You don't know?" Laurie said, pouring more coffee into her cup.

"I know he didn't have to bring us here. He could have hung up the phone that night and pretended not to know me."

"You and I both know he wouldn't have." Laurie got up and came to stand beside Carly at the window.

"Then it was simply obligation?"

"Right," Laurie said wryly. "That was obligation you saw in his eyes every time he looked at you tonight."

Hope cropped up from the dark edges of Carly's mind. Irrational hope. And it struck her that she'd always harbored it somewhere deep inside—the hope that maybe he didn't hate her completely. Maybe in some little corner, he still felt something for her, too. There was, of course, another possibility—Evan. Could he suspect her son was his? Was that what really had brought him to her? If it was, she hadn't seen so much as a flicker of that in his eyes since that first day. Carly swallowed hard. All the worse, she knew, when she did tell him the truth.

Together, she and Laurie looked out at the yard, where, beneath the halo of light from the barn, they could see Rafe leaning against the barn door, staring out at the darkness. Behind him, the three boys darted in and out of the light like moths drawn to a candle's flame.

"When I pictured him over the years," Carly said softly, "it was like that. Alone."

"And stubborn as a mule?" Laurie observed.

A smile lifted her mouth. "That, too. One minute you think there's a chink in those walls he's built around himself, and the next he's slathering more mortar up there."

"Those walls aren't as impenetrable as he'd have you think," Laurie said gently, tucking a long, dark strand of hair behind her ear. "Talk to him, Carly. He needs you. He just doesn't know it yet."

Chapter 7

The truck rumbled over a cattle gate with a bone-jarring rattle. Rafe glanced in the rearview mirror at Evan, who sat in the jump seat beside Mack, transforming the grinding of the grates into sound effects of his own imaginary world of starfighters and automatic weapons.

If anyone was to see them driving along, they might be mistaken for a family, he mused with a grin. Mom, Dad, the kid and the dog. For a moment, he allowed himself to slip into that picture, as if it were one of those carnival attractions where you stick your face in a cutout hole and assume someone else's life for a photo. Like a Hollywood set, it was all front and no back.

He glanced at Carly as she took in the snow-dusted mountains and the sprawling valley that comprised his ranch. Everywhere she looked, spring was taking hold. Green sprouted through the crust of winter brown like a foal's spring coat, and here and there splashes of early wildflowers dappled the palette with reds and yellows. Punctuating the landscape like so many black dots, his cattle wandered lazily under the warm May sun, a few curious enough to look up from grazing to stare as they drove by.

Carly sighed, shaking her head. "If I said it was beautiful, that would somehow seem…inadequate. It's…spectacular. It takes my breath away."

Rafe smiled, feeling like the kid who's just won a licorice stick from the teacher. "I thought you'd like it."

"Oh, I don't just like it," she said, leaning out the window, her elbows on the sill and her silvery hair catching the wind. She lifted her face to the sun, closed her eyes and let it pour over her. "It *smells* so good. I still haven't gotten used to it. After living in L.A. it smells like heaven."

"After living in L.A.," Rafe said dryly, "any place would smell like heaven."

"Hey, no bashing my ex-hometown," she said, pulling her head back inside with mock outrage. "Yes, there are third-stage smog alerts, runaway crime and total gridlock on the freeway at any given hour, but—" she shrugged "—the weather's good. And earthquakes only happen on a bothersome scale every twenty years or so."

"Oh, there's a plus," he said with a grin. "So what's Ohio got that L.A. doesn't?"

"A scaled-down version of all of the above, I'm sure," she admitted with a smile. "And hey, they say you don't really *need* three hundred and twenty-six days of sunshine to ward off psychosis. And then, of course, there's the added attraction of a law partnership."

"A partnership?" This was news.

"Junior partnership, actually, but a step in the right direction. To wit—away from the public defender's office."

Rafe kept his eyes on the road. "I thought you liked your work."

"I like the law," she said. "I just didn't like rubbing shoulders with the lowest common denominator of society on a daily basis anymore. Or watching them walk because I was doing my job well.''

''So what's waiting in Cincinnati?''

He watched her search out some imaginary thread on her jeans and pay it particular attention. ''Room to grow, for me and for Evan. I'll be able to pick and choose my cases. Maynard, Barnes and Griffith built their reputation on sticky-wicket cases no one else would touch. They've won some huge cases, which allow them to do pro bono work for clients other firms would reject out of hand as being unprofitable.''

''That's where you come in?''

She smiled. ''That's been my specialty for years. But this time, I set my hours, and choose my cases.''

''And Evan? What does he get out of it?''

''Me,'' she said, glancing back at her son. ''Oh, and definitely a dog.''

Rafe glanced in the rearview mirror again. Evan was tussling with an exuberant Mack in the back seat. They were wild about each other, after only a few days. Mack would miss Evan when the boy left. So, Rafe realized with startling clarity, would he.

A sinking feeling settled in the pit of his stomach. Leaving was a topic they'd managed to avoid these past few days. Not that he wanted them to stay, he told himself quickly. Both he and Carly understood that this whole thing was temporary. Carly had her life and he had his. That was the way he wanted it, and the way it had to be.

''What's that?'' Evan shouted, pointing to a strange-looking rock formation poised in the middle of a pasture.

''That's Bread Loaf Rock,'' Rafe said, glad for the distraction. Indeed, the massive boulder looked just like a loaf of bread, with a slice off the end lying beside it.

''It's kind of a landmark. A hundred and fifty years ago, the Ute Indians made their winter camp here every year.''

''There's Indians here?'' Evan asked, wide-eyed.

Rafe nodded. "Not like the old days anymore. But yeah, they still live around here. They thought the rock was good medicine."

"Medicine?" Evan repeated.

"Luck. Fortune," Rafe explained.

"Like the dime?" Evan whispered in his ear.

"Sort of, yeah," Rafe whispered back.

"Okay," Carly said, pulling her head in the window. "No secrets in the peanut gallery."

Evan winked at Rafe, who winked right back. "Did you buy your ranch from the Indians, Rafe?"

Rafe shook his head. "The Indians believed that no man could own a piece of land. He could only use it for a while. It was all part of the Great Spirit."

"So you're just borrowin' it?" Evan asked, leaning his elbows on the seat behind Rafe's shoulders.

The truth to that was closer than either Evan or Carly knew. "You might say that."

Carly was staring at him, and when he turned to look at her, she made no attempt to hide it. A smile played on her lips, and some unasked question had deepened her blue eyes to a smoky gray.

He momentarily forgot the road, and had to swerve back on it when he felt the wheels leave the gravel.

Mack barked and Evan laughed with eight-year-old glee at the unexpected thrill. "Do that again!"

But his mother had braced one cautious hand against the dashboard, and Rafe took that as a no.

"Hey, there's a creek just up the road here. Feel like stretching your legs a bit?"

"Yeah!" Evan shouted, ruffling Mack's ears.

Carly eyed her cast with a glint of humor. "I don't know about stretching, but I'll do my best to hobble."

They stopped near the headwaters of a spring-fed creek that could have graced any postcard. Rushing clear water tumbled over sparkly granite rocks that tangled in the roots of three towering ponderosa pines, forming pools and waterfalls as it went. Evan's eyes went round at the possibilities, and he and Mack were off and running before Rafe's feet hit the ground.

"Hey, don't get too close to the water!" Carly shouted after him.

"Don't worry, I'm only gonna look for rocks. C'mon, Macky!"

"It's not moving fast enough to hurt him," Rafe said, and Carly relaxed a fraction, stretching the stiffness from her back and legs.

"I forget that exploring creeks and climbing trees are the things little boys are supposed to do," she said, watching her son tackle his first boulder with zest. "Back home, in the city, you watch them like a hawk, every move, every step. You're always afraid of a car, or a crowd, or a stranger."

Shoulder to shoulder, they watched Evan pick up a rock, examine it under the brilliant sun, then stuff it in his pocket. "Here, he's just a boy, exploring the edges of his world. He loves this place, Rafe."

The breeze carried Carly's scent to him. Distracted by it, he nodded. "It's what I've always dreamed of."

Carly pulled her gaze from her son, surprised. "Always? Even back when we were together? Did you dream of it then?"

"Since I was a kid."

"You never told me."

"Didn't I?" he asked, knowing he hadn't. He shrugged. "I was just a cowboy then, riding for pocket change. I never quite believed it myself. I only dreamed of it."

"And I was just a student, dreaming of becoming an attorney."

Touché. "And here we are."

A companionable silence stretched between them, and then she chuckled. "Do you remember the day we met?"

He rubbed his jaw, feigning deep thought. "Hmm-mm."

She laughed and slugged him in the arm.

"Ow!" he said, suppressing a grin.

"Rat. Of course you remember."

"Okay," he said, throwing his hands up in surrender. "Maybe I do have some dim recollection."

"I was broken down, with steam billowing out of the propped-up hood of my Nissan on the side of the road—a road not too unlike this one. And you, knight in shining armor that you were, stopped to help a damsel in distress."

A smile softened one corner of his mouth. "You were all in a flutter about being late for a class at the college, as I recall."

"I never did make it to that class, or any others that day, come to think of it. We ended up spending the whole day together. Talking, drinking coffee and eating bear claws while we waited for the shop to find a water pump for my car."

His mind sifted through the memory. He remembered hoping the shop would never find that part. That they could stretch out that afternoon forever.

He said, "I remember you looked like you'd just stepped out of some preppie catalogue, and there I was in my crummiest worn-out jeans and a pair of knocked out boots that had walked through half a dozen cow pies that day."

"I didn't notice."

"I know," he said, letting his gaze drift over her features. She'd always been as oblivious to his shortcomings as he was aware of them.

"I do remember that I liked the way those old jeans fit you, though." Looking up at him through a sweep of lashes, she grinned. "You kissed me that day. Remember that?"

And the next day, and the next and the next. His gaze

landed heatedly on her mouth, his body tightening with the memory. "Mmm. I was young. Impulsive. Guess I haven't changed much."

"Impulsive can be good."

He wondered if she was talking about nine years ago, or the other night in the kitchen. Or now. Breaking the golden top off a stem of long grass, he toyed with it between his fingers. His heart thudded against the wall of his chest. "We had our moments, didn't we?"

"Mmmm-mm. Great moments. I wish—" She stopped short of blurting out whatever she'd been about to say.

"What?" he wanted to know.

She shook her head on a deep sigh. "I was going to say, I wish things could have been different. But I guess things worked out the way they were supposed to. I mean, look at you. Look at this. You have this ranch—"

"And you got married and had Evan," he added.

Carly's lips parted, and she looked down quickly at the ground. "Yes."

He should have been mine, came the thought unbidden, but Rafe quickly quashed it. It did no good to think about things that couldn't be. "I guess we both got what we wanted. He's a great kid, Carly."

Her eyes darted to him with inexplicable urgency. "Oh, he *is,* Rafe. He's a great kid. The best."

He wondered briefly about the hard sell, knowing it was unnecessary. "Tom must have been proud of him."

A frown formed between her eyebrows. She found something on the ground to look at again and nodded wordlessly. The dried grass rattled in the wind with a sibilant sound.

Dammit! he thought. He'd made her cry.

"Hey, I'm sorry," he said, touching her arm. "I didn't mean to upset you by talking about Tom."

That one small touch was a mistake. Both of them knew it. She pulled her arm away with a quick denial. "You didn't. *Really*," she said, flicking a knuckle across her cheek.

And pigs can fly.

"Hey, Mom!" Evan called from the rock he was balancing on, waving something minuscule in his hand. "Look what I found!"

"Be right there!" She waved back, looking relieved. "We'd better go see."

"Carly?"

She turned back. "What?"

He thought better of it. Obviously, she still had deep feelings for Tom. Why else would she have reacted so strongly to the mention of his name? The realization dulled something inside him. Something that made no sense, even to him. What did it matter if her heart still belonged to another man? It had never really belonged to him.

"Nothin'," he said with a disarming smile. "Let's go see what he wants."

They kept a cautious space between them as they made their way to where Evan was scurrying around the creek edge, loading his pockets with rocks like a squirrel in autumn. Carly filled the conversational void by firing questions at Rafe about the names of the mountains and the creek and the trees anchoring it. Rafe answered them all, watching the pleasure in her eyes as she took in the land. She had a mind for details and she stored it all away—like Evan with his rocks—for some future use.

Rafe, too, stored it all away, the memory of this morning—this time with Carly and Evan. Too soon, they'd be gone, and when she left this time, she'd take another chunk of him with her. And somehow, this time, he knew he'd never get it back again.

He didn't want to think about how close he was to losing it all, about her leaving, about anything. He wanted—just for now—to stand beside her and imagine what could have been.

* * *

The next day started out badly, and went downhill from there.

By 9:00 a.m., three Japanese in suits and construction helmets and a miniature imported pickup truck had tracked him down in the south pasture and begun some rapid-fire conversation Rafe couldn't begin to understand. Their translator, whose command of English was tenuous at best, had considerable difficulty explaining their reason for interrupting Rafe in the middle of pulling a heifer from a mud bog. By the time the translator had pulled the survey scope out of his truck to illustrate their purpose—namely, surveying the land they were about to buy out from under him—Gus had to physically restrain Rafe from delivering the full-body tackles he had in mind.

The astonished businessmen scurried into their truck like rats to a woodpile and disappeared down the road behind a cloud of dust. It was a good bet they'd have a fascinating story to tell their grandchildren about the crazy American cowboy who had come at them like a banshee after their innocent request.

By eleven, the sight of circling vultures had led Rafe to two dead calves and the all-too-distinguishable prints of a mountain lion surrounding them. They were the fourth and fifth in as many weeks. A grim pattern. Cats didn't normally work this far down, and definitely not in daylight. This time, however, steam was still drifting from one of the partially eaten calves. Rafe cursed his luck.

The print showed that the cat favored a paw from which it had a missing toe. There was a good chance it was wounded.

It had struck like a phantom and disappeared the same way. He'd followed the tracks into the rocky outcrops at the base of the nearby mountains, then, abruptly, lost them. He decided to leave the dead calf as bait, and would assign Pedro night watch over it tonight. He held out little hope that Pedro would catch sight of the renegade cat. It had a full belly, and might not strike again for days.

By four, with his patience stretched thinner than bale wire, he realized that he'd only begun to see how bad this day could get.

Rafe cinched the hold rope tighter around his gloved hand and pounded his knuckles shut against it. His heart knocked against the wall of his chest like an out-of-control jackhammer. Cold sweat dampened his gloves and slid down between his shoulder blades. Beneath him, the stallion stirred restively, shifting his massive frame against the rails of the enclosure like a coiled half-ton spring. Every muscle, every warning, twitched in the beast's hide.

In the distance, lightning streaked across the darkening afternoon sky like an empty threat. The thin, windswept clouds held no rain. The breeze carried the tang of summer, and the promise of heat.

"I'm ready," he told Gus, sliding his feet toward the horse's shoulders.

When Rafe looked up, Gus was simply scowling at him, not moving anywhere closer to unlatching the gate.

"I said, I'm ready," he repeated.

"Well, I ain't," Gus retorted, drawing the back of his hand across his dry mouth.

"Open the gate, Gus," Rafe said deliberately.

"This is a stupid idea, Rafe."

"You got a better one?"

Gus's scowl deepened. "Gimme a minute."

"I'm running out of those."

"You can't trust this devil, Rafe," Gus said, nodding at Red-Eye. "He'd as soon pound your brains out as look at ya."

Indeed, the stallion rolled a killing look back at Rafe in retribution for daring to sit on his back. A green bronc, Red-Eye had been purchased along with a half-dozen other horses seven months ago from a spread west of here that was going under. Better men than Rafe had tried gentling him by more conventional methods, but to no avail. He showed real potential as a rodeo bronc, but woefully little as a cow pony. Which was exactly why Rafe had chosen him today.

"My fingers are going numb, Gus. Open the damned gate."

Still Gus didn't move.

"Pedro?"

The ranch hand who'd been watching the exchange from atop the nearest rail straightened instantly, shooting a nervous look at Gus. "*Sí*, boss?"

"Open the gate, or you're fired."

Pedro flushed and moved toward the rope holding the gate. "*Sí*, boss."

"He won't fire you, and you know it," Gus told Pedro.

"Wanna risk it?" Rafe asked Pedro, who shook his head with a grim smile.

"Aw, hell. Don't say I didn't warn ya," Gus grumbled.

"Clock it," Rafe commanded, and Gus reluctantly pulled out his stop watch.

Pedro nodded to Gus as he yanked the jury-rigged rope, which slipped off the post, and swung open the gate with a bang.

Rafe left his stomach behind as Red-Eye exploded into the enclosure with the force of a pipe bomb, took three long strides, then sunfished upward in a torturous twist.

For what seemed like minutes—while Rafe's body hung suspended somewhere between horseflesh and outer space—he struggled to stay upright, perpendicular to the animal's back. As with the kid who'd learned to balance on two wheels, it was a knack that returned to him, despite how long it had been.

Then, with body-numbing force, he slammed downward again, colliding with flesh and bone so hard it made his teeth clack together and his neck snap. Distantly he heard the whoops of his ranch hands and the grunting fury of Red-Eye. He felt the protest of every muscle in his body, reminding him that he wasn't twenty-six anymore. Then everything slowed down, as if a video-camera button had been pushed. The world slid past him—up, down, sideways, in a blur of browns and greens and cerulean blue, in a violent collision of wills—his versus Red-Eye's.

Hang on, he chanted over and over. *Hang on. Hang on.*

And then the earth was flying up to meet him like a fist. Rafe threw his hands out to break the fall and rolled. He took the brunt of it on his back. The impact stole his breath and sent him careening like a top toward the corral fence.

From the corner of his vision, he saw Pedro leaping in front of Red-Eye, waving his arms like a madman before the horse could swing back around toward Rafe. His stalled lungs heaved as he instinctively reached for a fence rail to haul himself out of harm's way. Awkwardly he pitched himself between two rails and landed on the other side, just as Pedro flung himself out of the corral beside him and the stallion's hooves came down deafeningly in the dirt behind them both.

"Ay, Díos!" Pedro managed in a strangled whisper as Red-Eye whirled away. The ranch hand panted in panicked, chugging breaths.

Rafe simply closed his eyes and focused on breathing, sprawled in the dirt like a staked out hostage. His ribs burned, and his leg— Hell, his knee felt dislocated. But he knew it wasn't.

"How long?" he gasped.

"Six point eight," Gus snarled back.

He suppressed a groan. "Felt longer." Like an hour.

Dimly he heard Pedro say, "Oh-oh," and he cracked open one eye. A dozen feet away, standing in open-mouthed, outraged horror, was a hundred and fifteen pounds of trouble.

"Ohmygod—"

"Carly," Rafe croaked, "what are you doing here?"

"What am *I* doing here?"

"Ah, jeez—" Rafe edged up on his elbows, ignoring the pain in his side. He was covered with dirt and—he dabbed at the damp trickle on his cheek—bleeding. "It looks worse than it is. Carly—"

She spun around on those crutches faster than nobody's business and hauled that pretty little behind of hers in the opposite direction.

"Where are you going?" he shouted after her. "Hey!"

Anger was carrying her almost effortlessly toward the house, despite the ten pounds of plaster on her leg. Rafe muttered a curse and winced as he struggled to his feet.

Gus folded his arms over his chest with an I-told-you-so attitude. "Well, if you want my advice—"

"Old man," he snapped, his patience gone, "when I want your advice, I'll damned well ask for it. That goes for riding *and* women! Understood?"

Gus grinned and sauntered off toward the barn.

Rafe swore again and reached into the corral for his trampled hat. He hissed in a breath at the pain in his bad leg and the achy heat in his side.

Nobody'd said it wasn't gonna hurt.

He should have been prepared for Carly's reaction—but he wasn't. What the devil was she so mad about? That was just what he needed—one more adversary. Each step he took fueled his own anger. Here he was sneaking around his own place, hiding from her, as if he were doing something wrong. Whose place was it, anyway? And what right did she have getting angry over him riding again? None. That was what. Not a blasted one.

He limped toward the house, passing Evan hooking lassos around the gatepost. Mack, lying next to Evan, whined and thumped his black tail at Rafe, raising a cloud of dust.

"Hey, Rafe, look what I can do!"

"Great, kid. Not now."

Evan's face fell. "But—"

Ahead, the door to the house slammed behind Carly. "Later," he said, too sharply, then pulled himself back to soften the blow. "Hey, why don't you go see Gus? He could use a hand with feeding."

"Okay." He heard Evan's downtrodden mumble behind him, but decided to deal with that later.

He took the porch stairs two at a time. At the top, he stopped, pressing two hands against his rib cage, waiting for the ache to subside before yanking open the screen door and heading for Carly's room.

He didn't get that far.

She was in the living room. It was the chinking sound of crystal against crystal that gave her away. She looked up as she lifted a glass of bourbon to her lips. With an undecipherable look at him, she knocked it back, sending it down her throat in one burning gulp. She gasped and choked, coughing with all the aplomb of a teetotaler.

"What are you doing, Carly? You're not a drinker."

"Oh, really!" she squeaked, sending him daggers while she wiped the back of one hand across her mouth. "And you're not a rodeo rider anymore."

"I don't recall being drummed out of the association," he snapped, heading for the bourbon himself.

"Well, there oughta be a rule against suicidal cowboys competing. That's what you're going to do, isn't it? Go back to riding? Why else would you let that loco horse throw you around the corral?"

"What if I am?" He slugged down a drink, savoring the burn as it made its way down.

"Correct me if I'm wrong," she said evenly, her eyes whiskey-darkened and angry. "But do you or do you not have only one remaining kidney after your little dance with that Brahma bull four years ago?"

He was too surprised that she knew that to deny it. "So?"

Her jaw dropped and she slammed the crystal tumbler down on the desk. "So! *So?* No one in his right mind would risk the other one on some foolish..."

"Call it what you want."

"...idiotic adrenaline rush!"

"You done?"

His jaw went rigid with the same stubborn pride Carly remembered. She wanted to shake him, stamp her feet, beg. But she wouldn't. It had never gotten her anywhere before, and she was sure it wouldn't now. So she braced herself and asked, "Why? Why now?"

"What difference does it make?"

"What dif—?" The evasiveness in his voice only now dawned on her. "Did you really think it wouldn't matter to me? You obviously didn't expect me to see you—working out—all the way on the other side of the barn. What's going on, Rafe?"

"Nothing's going on," he hedged, touching the cut on his face and glancing at the red stain on his fingers. "I miss it. That's all."

Her chest tightened with apprehension. "You miss bruised ribs and concussions? Getting trampled on by an animal ten times your size?"

"I rode for seven years with hardly a scratch."

"If you don't count near-death experiences."

"You're making a big deal out of nothing," he said, enunciating every word. Beneath the veneer of civility, she sensed a simmering explosion waiting to happen.

Welcoming it, she said quietly, "You and I both know that's not true."

He'd been avoiding her eyes. Now he pierced her with a single look. "Drop it, Carly."

Outside, thunder rumbled warningly, like the distant sound of war.

"Not until you tell me why you're willing to risk all of this—" She swept her hand around the high-windowed room and toward the acres that stretched below the San Juans. "Everything you've worked and sweated for, this house, this ranch—"

"This ranch—" On an oath, he turned and, with one vicious swipe, raked a stack of papers off his desk. "This ranch won't be worth the deed it's written on if I *don't* ride."

Carly stared at the papers still fluttering to the floor, then back up at Rafe.

"Is that what you wanted to hear?" He sent an errant few papers airborne beside the others, then braced his flattened palms on the desktop and stared at the mahogany grain. "Satisfied now?"

She ignored the papers and moved beside him. "Tell me."

"Tell you what?" he said, not looking up. "That I'm gonna crash and burn because I was fool enough to count on good weather? Because I never expected a friend to sell me out? Because," he said, lowering his head between his splayed arms, "I wanted it too much?"

She reached a hand up to touch his back, but stopped herself, afraid of the contact. "I don't understand."

The sigh he heaved came from somewhere deep inside him. Reluctantly he told her about the lease with Jed Stivers, about the water—the creek they'd sat beside only yesterday morning, about Sunimoto Corporation and their rush to eat up Colorado grazeland. He told her about the three expensive, failed attempts he'd made at drilling for water, and he told her about the banks.

Carly listened with a lump in her throat as he talked, knowing what it had cost him to admit any of this to her. Yesterday, he'd shown her his ranch, and she'd seen first-hand what the place meant to him. The feeling still vibrated inside her, as well. But to risk his life for it? His future? She couldn't let this happen.

"So, I'll ride," he finished, running both hands through

his hair. "And I'll win. Because I have to." He walked to the window and stared out.

She found it hard to breathe. She knew what was coming, but felt helpless to stop it. Like the proverbial elephant in the living room, it crowded her thinking and hurt her ears with its noise.

"Please, Rafe, reconsider. Let me look at the contracts," she suggested, a little desperately. "I do that for a living. Maybe I can find—"

"There's nothing. I've looked at every angle. I'm out of time, Carly."

"Then, let me help you. I can—"

His eyes had gone glacial. Cold. If she'd tried to humiliate him more than he already had been, she couldn't have chosen a better path. Two spots of color appeared in his cheeks. "You want to help me? Don't stand in my way. This is my problem, not yours, Carly. I'll manage. I won't lose it."

"There's more at stake here than just your ranch, Rafe."

He shook his head. "Without this place, I'll have nothing. I'll *be*...nothing."

Carly's heart hammered in her ears. She felt faint. Gripping the table behind her, she took a deep breath and dived off that cliff whose edge she'd been teetering on for nine long years.

"That's where you're wrong, Rafe," she said slowly. "You'll always be Evan's father."

Chapter 8

A deafening silence thundered through the room. Outside, the real thing rumbled across the sky, as lightning illuminated the room and flickered across Rafe's face like an old-time movie. His thought processes had slowed instantly to the speed of cold molasses. "Wh-what did you say?"

She was a deer caught in headlights, looking like she wanted to run, to hide, yet hopelessly frozen to the spot.

"What did you say?" he repeated, louder this time.

She swallowed heavily. "He's yours, Rafe. He's your son. Not Tom's."

Rafe's fists curled into tight balls at his sides, whitening his knuckles. Somewhere, deep inside him, since that first phone call from Nevada, he'd been unconsciously anticipating those words. But when they came, he couldn't take them in. Or believe them.

"You're *lying*." His voice sounded hollow, strangled.

She shook her head, her backside colliding with the desk

behind her. "All you have to do is look at him, Rafe. He's yours."

Look at him? he thought, in a cold sweat. He'd been looking at him for the past week. Talking to him. Touching him. And all along, he'd been a part of him? Flesh and bone of him?

Pictures flashed in his mind: the shape of Evan's face, his jawline, even his ears. Familiar. How could he not have seen it? Was it because he hadn't wanted to see it? Rafe bowed his head and squeezed his eyes shut. No, she'd told him Evan was Tom's. Hadn't she? He'd seen the picture—Evan and Tom fishing. Father and son. So much alike. And he'd believed—

"He's eight, Rafe. And four months. He's yours. You're his father."

Had all the air been sucked out of the room? His chest refused to expand. Rafe blinked, calculating a twelve month calendar and counting backward through the years.

Dear God.

Anger, hot and explosive burned through him. "All this time—" he gritted out, staring at her in disbelief. "And you didn't...you couldn't have—"

She covered her mouth with her hand. "I'm...I'm sorry."

"Sorry? You're *sorry?* Dammit, Carly, when the hell were you planning to tell me? As you were walking out the door for the second time?"

She shook her head miserably. "Rafe...please—"

"Damn you."

She flinched as if he'd struck her. He wanted to, God help him! All these years!

A son. He had a son?

Carly steepled her hands over the bridge of her nose muffling a cry. "I'm sorry, Rafe. I...oh, God...I tried to tell you. I wanted to tell you."

His legs felt mired in concrete. His pulse wanted to

pound, but it felt thick and slow. "You *wanted* to tell me? Nine years?" he said through clenched teeth. "Nine goddamn years, and you couldn't find a single opportunity?"

"I did try. I called you a month after we—" She closed her eyes. "A woman answered the phone."

His mind reeled. "A *woman!* Are you saying you didn't tell me because a woman answered my phone? Christ, Carly, it could have been a cleaning lady, for all I know."

"But it wasn't. We both know that she was in your bed."

Numbly Rafe's mind thumbed backward nine years, to a time he'd worked hard to forget.

Yes, he remembered. He'd forgotten that other woman's name, after all these years, but he hadn't forgotten the shock of Carly's call or the fact that she'd waited a full month to call him. "You never said anything about being pregnant."

"I—I never got that far."

"Damn," he muttered, remembering in some back room of his mind that he might have, possibly, cut her off. "And that was it? You spent your twenty cents and you figured your responsibility was done?"

She edged around the desk. "Rafe, you're angry right now—"

He heard her squeak of fear as he shoved a ladder-back chair out of his way and sent it crashing to the floor. His mouth had a cruel slant to it. "You don't think I have a right to be?"

She looked around desperately for an escape route as he moved toward her.

"I just find out that I've got a son and I've missed the first eight years of his life because you found it *inconvenient* to tell me about it?"

"Not inconvenient. It was a choice. I made it and I had to live with it." Her eyes burned red, and she fought back tears, but they leaked out the corners of her eyes. "And if

I had told you? Trapped you into a marriage you didn't want with a child you didn't want? Would it have made you stop running? From us and what we could have had?''

"You left *me*, dammit! I came home and you were gone. Lock, stock and barrel."

Her mouth quivered with emotion. "You walked out of our relationship long before I did, Rafe. You just hung around to watch from a safe distance as it crumbled. I told you I wanted children. You didn't. You made that perfectly clear. You didn't want any of it, Rafe. Not marriage, not a family—"

"And who the hell gave you the right to decide that I shouldn't know I *had* one?"

"A child isn't something you can take or leave, Rafe, or some...some abstract idea that might or might not be interesting to you. I did what I thought was best for Evan. But don't you think for a minute that I haven't asked myself every day of his life if I'd done the right thing!"

Rafe's eyes did a slow, contemptuous rake down the length of her. As if he'd stripped her naked, she crossed her arms over her chest and hugged herself. He leaned close, his voice almost a whisper.

"Tell me, Carly, did Tom even know you had a bun in the oven when you got him to marry you? Or did he die thinking Evan was his?"

Her stinging slap knocked his head sideways. With the speed of a striking snake, Rafe grabbed her wrist and jerked her toward him. Her flesh gave beneath his fingers. Her breath came fast and hard, and her breasts brushed against his rigid forearm with each rise and fall. But the steel had returned to her eyes, the kind he'd expect to see in a courtroom. Gone was the fear, and any trace of uncertainty. In their place was perfect, hollow control.

His mouth lifted in what anyone else might have mistaken for a smile. "Well, at least you were honest with one of us," he said, releasing her arm without gentleness.

"Where are you going?" he heard her ask as he tore his hat and black duster from the rack beside the door.

"Out," he said, jerking the door open and fitting the Stetson on his head. "Oh, and, darlin'? Don't wait up."

The door rattled in its frame, knocking two picture frames beside it askew.

Carly stood listening to the fading sound of Rafe's truck as it disappeared down the road, spitting gravel. Somehow, she remained standing, breathing. She felt like a scooped-out pumpkin whose guttering candle flickered inside. For years she'd anticipated this moment, knowing it would come. Her rehearsed lines were nowhere to be found, and her pride was a smudge on the floor.

Slowly, she slid down beside the desk, bracing her back against it and stretching her plaster-encased leg out in front of her. She dropped her face into her hands.

An awful, overwhelming fatigue sucked at her. Or maybe it was regret. Too late, a voice said. No going back.

It was over, and he hated her. No surprise. He had every right. In his place, she supposed she would hate him, too.

It didn't matter, she told herself, pressing the heels of her hands to her eyes. All that really mattered was Evan, and what all this would do to him.

Evan.

"Oh, God," she moaned to the air as her palms grew wet. Evan was in the middle of this, where he'd always been. Only now everything was changed. Never again would it be just the two of them. Whatever Rafe decided to do about this, his specter would be there between them. She only prayed that he could put aside his hatred of her for the sake of his son.

But as evening shadows closed in on her and the sky rumbled with thunder, Carly feared she'd made a terrible, irreversible mistake. One that they would all spend a lifetime paying for.

* * *

Durango, the tourist mecca of western Colorado, pre-
ferred to deny the existence of places like the Blue Lagoon
Saloon in its travel brochures. Its location on the fringes
of Durango city limits made that convenient. A locals'
hangout, the bar had passed its prime years ago, and
looked most at home with a handful of chopped Harleys
parked out front. It wasn't the sort of place Rafe regularly
frequented, but he'd come here because he craved ano-
nymity and a place in which to lose himself.

Inside, faded flocked wallpaper, curled at the corners,
covered the parts of the walls that beer-advertising mirrors
didn't. A handful of worn tables and chairs sat in some
semblance of order in the center of the room, while a juke-
box and four Naugahyde-clad booths—one of which Rafe
had occupied for the better part of the evening—lined the
far side of one wall.

The red-headed cocktail waitress, whose name, she'd
informed him, was Susie, slid a neat shot of whiskey toward the center of his growing stack of empty shooters.
He'd formed a hexagon with the empties, and now he considered how the new addition might expand the design.

"You sure you want another one, honey?" she asked,
leaning with both forearms against his table, so that the
tomato-red wraparound top she wore gapped intentionally
at her ample cleavage. Rafe didn't even pretend not to
look.

Her cocoa-colored eyes went soft with concern for him.
"You look like you've had enough."

He wasn't gonna touch that one.

Instead, he appeared to think hard about her advice for
a moment. Then, with a shrug, he said, "Nope, not yet."
With a disarming smile for Susie, he knocked back the
shot in one gulp. He made a face as it burned down his
throat. He waited for this last shot to take its effect,
but—nothing. He felt appallingly, annoyingly sober.

Susie shook her head in sympathy. "Oh, honey, who-ever she is, I hope she knows what she's throwin' away."

He didn't want to talk about *her*. He didn't want to talk at all. Holding up his empty glass, he said, "One more time, Susie."

"Look, sweetie," she said slowly, patting his hand as if he were dim-witted. "We close in twenty minutes. Why don't you just set here a while, drink some nice, hot coffee, and let me call you a cab?" The bartender floated into Rafe's line of vision, carrying, coincidentally, a steaming cup. Susie set it down in front of him. "You oughtn'ta be drivin' in your condition."

The coffee's strong scent wafted to him like a slap of cold air. Well, hell, he thought. He'd been eighty-sixed! Couldn't they see he was nowhere near drunk enough yet?

"Go on, now," Susie urged in a motherly voice. "Take a sip. You'll thank me in the mornin'."

"Yeah, sure," he said, hoping she'd go away. "Fine." He took a sip of the dark brew to pacify her. She smiled with a little nod, having done her good deed for the night, and drifted off to another table with her cork-topped tray.

For a long time, Rafe stared into the dark coffee, not really seeing it. Instead, Carly's voice echoed in his head

He's yours, Rafe. Your son. Not Tom's.

His hand tightened around the warm mug and he cursed her again. How could she? he asked himself for the hundredth time. How could she have kept it from him all these years? Who the hell was she to decide for him? She'd been afraid of rejection, she'd said. A muscle jumped in his clamped jaw. She'd never given him the chance to prove her wrong. It went to the heart of the very thing that had killed their relationship in the first place.

Trust.

She didn't trust him. He sure as hell couldn't trust her. And there they were, at opposite ends of the same story, with Evan in the middle.

He thought of the blond-haired boy who'd looked at him
with Carly's eyes. His son. His blood. It struck him then
that Evan was his *only* blood relation. Not, of course,
counting his faithless mother, who'd ditched him and his
father when Rafe was just about Evan's age and had never
been heard from since. For all he knew, she was dead, too.

He'd learned young not to count on others, and he supposed that was why he'd chosen rodeoing as a career. No
one to count on or blame but himself. No one to be responsible for. No one to answer to. He was happy being
alone. It suited him.

Another lie, in a long string of lies he'd told himself
over the years. He'd *gotten used* to being alone. That was
the real truth. Then, just when he had all his cards stacked
tenuously atop one another, Carly had shown up and
punched a hole in his paper house.

You walked out of this relationship long before I did,
her voice echoed. *You just hung around to watch from a
safe distance while it crumbled.*

Had he? Hell, that ship had sunk beneath them, but
she'd been the one to bail. And even if there was any truth
to the words, right now, he didn't give a damn. He didn't
want logic muddying up his personal sense of betrayal.

Rafe plunged his fingers through his hair, pressing
against the back of his skull, where violence simmered like
a throb.

"Well, if it ain't Rafe Kellard," a voice beside him said,
in a tone that made Rafe look up with slow malice. Sometimes, he mused, life was good.

The bloated cowboy standing beside his table grinned
goadingly at Rafe with tobacco-stained teeth set in a face
only a mother could truly appreciate. He opened up his
considerable stance to encompass the handful of captive
onlookers scattered across the bar. "Rafe Kellard," he announced, "the ex-world champion bull rider! What's the
matter, Kellard? Drinkin' over your loss o' nerve?"

Swamp-Tooth hooted at his compatriot nearby, who laughed with drunken appreciation.

Rafe twirled his cup between his fingers, a smile of pure malice creeping to his mouth. Go on, he thought. I dare ya.

"Hell," Swamp-Tooth went on, oblivious to his own personal safety. "I seen women take bigger hits than you and come back. But not you. Why is that, Kellard? That bull knock the nerve right outa you? Too yellow to get back up again?"

Rafe felt the rush of his blood as he got slowly to his feet, his gaze pinned on Swamp-Tooth and the appealingly broad plane of his jaw. The whiskey pumped through him like warm courage. "Hey, don't hold back, pal. Say what you really think."

"I lost a lot o' money on you that night," Swamp-Tooth growled, backing up a step.

"'Zat right?" Rafe said evenly, though the room was doing a slow spin.

"That's...that's right. Practically ruined me, you bastard."

Rafe made a tsking sound between his teeth. "Now that's a real shame. What'd you say your name was?"

His eyes narrowed. "I didn't."

"Good," Rafe said with a chilling smile, "'cause I prefer to keep this sort of thing between strangers." His fist caught the other man's jaw hard, knocking his head backward with a satisfying *crack*. Swamp-Tooth stumbled backward and crashed into an empty table, splintering it beneath him. Then, like a steer too dumb to get out of the rain, Swamp-Tooth shook his head and charged back at Rafe, bear-hugging him around the waist and sending them both crashing into the booth where Rafe had been sitting. Glasses clanked and scattered beneath them, and he heard Susie shout something to the bartender. Rafe dodged his opponent's fist, which slammed into the tabletop with a sickening thud.

"Owwww!" Swamp-Tooth roared, his breath fetid with tobacco and alcohol, and took Rafe with him as he rolled to the floor.

Everything seemed to lose order then, as Swamp-Tooth's friend jumped into the fray, followed by a half-dozen others who simply hungered for a brawl. Glass shattered, wood fractured, and general mayhem ensued. Rafe tossed Swamp-Tooth in the direction of the bar, where he collided with a stack of glassware.

The bartender ducked a thrown beer bottle, which smashed into the neat glass shelves of liquor behind him. The crash was deafening, but Rafe was too busy fending off blows from Swamp-Tooth's compatriot to worry much about it.

A surprise punch to the gut temporarily blinded him, but not for so long that he didn't see the wooden chair coming down in his direction. He dodged it easily, then sent his attacker sprawling into a thicket of brawlers, scattering them like ninepins.

Swaying woozily, with adrenaline and alcohol still rushing through him, Rafe looked around for more comers, with his fists up around his chin. He could taste the blood on his teeth. For a moment, he thought, all was right with the world. He felt invincible. Vindicated.

But the moment was fleeting.

In the next few seconds, he heard the sound of sirens and he realized—with an oath—that the day's bad luck had only begun to rear its ugly head.

The blaring ring of the phone made Carly shoot bolt upright in Rafe's bed, as if she'd taken a shot from a cattle prod.

"*What?*" she said to the dark room, still lost in some dream.

The phone rang a second time. Loudly.

Blinking, she looked at the glowing digital readout on the bedstand clock. Two-thirty-seven a.m. She'd been asleep for exactly forty-five minutes. Who in the world would be calling at this time of night? A dozen awful possibilities flitted through her mind, each worse than the last, and all of them concerning Rafe.

Her heart thumped in her ears, and she fumbled for the receiver in the dark. "Hello?"

A long silence answered her.

"Hello?" she repeated, more urgently.

Finally a voice said, "Is Gus there?"

Carly squeezed her eyes shut with relief. Thank God. At least he wasn't dead in some ditch somewhere. "Rafe?"

"I wanna talk to Gus," he said, as if he didn't know it was her answering his bedside phone.

Irritation made her purse her lips. "He's not here. He went to Laurie's for the night." She heard a mumbled curse on the other end of the line and the squeak of his grip on the handset. Another long silence.

"*I* won't do?" Carly asked at last.

"No," came the gruff reply.

Carly wasn't in the mood for games. "Fine. Goodbye." She started to hang up the phone.

"*Wait!*" he shouted, loud enough for her to put the receiver back to her ear.

"Carly? Don't hang up."

Her eyes rolled up to the ceiling. "I thought you didn't want to talk to me."

"I don't," he said with resignation, "but I only get one phone call."

She frowned. "I beg your pardon?"

"I said," he reiterated through gritted teeth, "I only get one phone call."

"Ahhh…" She paused significantly. "Outa dimes?"

"No. Dammit, Carly, this isn't funny."

No, it wasn't. "Let me guess. Drunk and disorderly?"

He growled some reply.

"Excuse me?"

"I said yes!"

She winced and held the receiver away from her ear. She could hear the alcohol in his voice, and she could hardly miss the anger. "Don't tell me you got in a fight."

"Sort of," he admitted. "Okay, I got in a brawl. I need Gus to come bail me out."

"Rafe, it's two-thirty in the morning. You want me to wake Gus and make him trudge down to lockup to bail you out now?"

Silence again as he contemplated that, obviously none too clearly.

She rubbed a hand across her eyes. "Why don't you just sleep it off down there?" she suggested. "I'll call Gus in the morning and he'll come and get you. All right?"

Silence.

"All right?" she asked again.

"Fine."

"Rafe?"

A long beat. "What?"

"Are you okay?"

He hesitated, as if he were considering some flip answer. But he surprised her. "I've had better days."

Her heart twisted. "Me too," she said quietly.

"Yeah," he said quietly back. "Look, I gotta go."

"Okay."

The connection clicked off from his end, followed by the too-loud buzz of the dial tone. Carly stared at the phone for a moment before hanging up and sprawling back down on the bed.

She stared at the ceiling for a long time, her insides vibrating as if she'd just stuck her finger in a light socket.

A brawl? She tried to picture Rafe taking his anger with

her out on some unsuspecting soul foolish enough to get in his way. That he was capable of such violence didn't surprise her—she'd seen it in his eyes last night. But the uncharacteristic vulnerability in his voice just now had caught her off guard.

She rolled her cheek against the smooth, cold sheets, gathered a pillow to her stomach and hugged it tight. Hope was a dangerous thing, but it crept into her heart without regard to safety. Tomorrow, she thought, they'd talk. Then they would see.

Tonight she wouldn't sleep a wink.

Rafe lay with his hands propped behind his head, staring at a dust mote swirling through the shaft of morning light that spilled through the high, barred window of the wretched-smelling communal cell. Snores and snorts of his sleeping fellow inmates echoed through the sterile gray barracks. He longed to join them, but sleep had come only fitfully, punctuated by disturbing dreams that had him running from some demon chasing him.

The symbolism wasn't lost on him.

He was sober now. Except for the dull throb behind his eyes, he was clearheaded enough to think rationally about the things Carly had said yesterday. The part about him running from their relationship, about stepping back, only to watch it crumble...

Reluctantly he admitted to himself that she might be partly right. He'd spent hours this morning poring over the end of their relationship—honestly—perhaps for the first time since she'd left.

He'd spent years blaming her for leaving him. But the truth was, he'd always known she would go. What was that saying about self-fulfilling prophecies? Maybe the sabotage had come from his own fears. From that first day they met on the road outside of town, he'd known Carly was destined for better things than life with a cowboy like

him. He had never fit in with her intellectual friends from
school. Like them, she'd been aimed for the big city, and
he'd known in his gut that she'd be good at lawyering.

As much as he wanted her, he'd known that loving
Carly was just another word for holding her back. One
day, sometime in the future, no matter what she claimed,
she'd hate him for standing in her way. She'd get bored
and restless, like his own mother had, and she'd go.

So…maybe he *had* stepped back.

Maybe he'd let her think he'd left her before she could
leave him. But in his heart, he hadn't. Somewhere, some
little piece of him hoped that maybe he was wrong. That
maybe she loved him enough to see past the door he'd left
open for her.

The last night they were together—before he left her for
yet another road trip—she'd asked him if he loved her.
He'd made love to her with slow, tender passion so that
she'd know how he felt, even though he couldn't bring
himself to say it. Because to say it would have been like
blackmail.

He remembered she'd cried afterward. At the time, he
hadn't understood why. But after she left, he'd believed it
was because she'd made her choice right then.

Had they made Evan that night? he wondered now.

Evan, who looked at him so trustingly with Carly's eyes,
and smiled with that tilting grin that now reminded Rafe
of his own.

He wondered why he hadn't seen it before. He'd looked
at Evan that first morning in the hospital with the possibility ripe in his mind. So why hadn't he seen it? Or even
pursued it with Carly? Could it be that he'd been scared
to know? To find out? Was it easier to deny the possibility
than to face the truth?

Rafe punched his vinyl-covered pillow and cursed.

He wanted to hate her. He'd worked on that emotion all
night. He'd nurtured it with whiskey, and fed the betrayal

he felt with justifications. In the light of the day, however, none of it seemed to hold water.

And now they'd come full circle. Together, but separate. A family, but not.

"Hey, Rafe, you got company," the deputy said, breaking into Rafe's thoughts.

He pushed up on his elbows and winced at the sudden pain in his head. His old friend Deputy Dan Tarvy hitched a thumb toward the doorway with a wink and a grin. Finally, Rafe thought. At least Gus would find him something for this headache.

"Thanks, Dan," he said, throwing his legs over the side of the cot while cradling his head in his hands.

"Someday," Dan whispered, leaning close to the bars as he unlocked them, "you'll have to tell me your secret, buddy. One thing you always had was taste."

Rafe was about to ask what the hell he was talking about when a pair of crutches moved into his line of vision.

"*C-Carly,*" he stammered.

She bit her lower lip, taking in the cuts and bruises on his face. "Impressive."

He got to his feet, bracing one hand against the cell wall until the room stopped revolving. He clamped a hand against his splitting skull. "Ohhh—"

"Headache?" She arched a sardonic eyebrow.

He pinched the bridge of his nose between his thumb and his first finger. A fellow inmate snorted in a close imitation of a hog at a feeding trough.

"What are *you* doing here?" he muttered.

"Oh, I was in the neighborhood. Just thought I'd drop by. Get a firsthand look at the local jail." She glanced at the motley assortment of men sharing his cell. None of them looked any better than he did. "Friends of yours?"

He glared at her in reply.

She raised her eyebrows. "Hmmm… Except for the tattoos, they all bear a striking resemblance to you."

"Very funny," he said, gathering his battered Stetson from the stripped bunk he'd occupied. Bending over nearly did him in. "I thought Gus was coming."

She smiled tightly and headed down the hallway. "He picked me up at the ranch this morning and dropped me off. He thought maybe this was more up my alley."

"Your Honor, my client has proven himself an exemplary member of this community for over ten years. Mr. Kellard has no blemishes on his record. He's a hardworking cattle rancher upon whom several employees depend for their livelihoods. What happened last night was certainly unprecedented and he's expressed sincere regret about the whole incident." Carly saw Rafe glance sideways at her. "Therefore, I ask the court to consider this, along with the Blue Lagoon Saloon's agreement to drop all charges subsequent to restitution by my client."

The sixty-something black-robed woman behind the bench shifted her half glasses down her nose and glanced at Rafe. Carly joined her. Despite, or perhaps because of, the numerous cuts on his face and the dark bruise under his left eye, he stood there, eyes hooded and distant, like some dark archangel fresh from battle with a foe. The crisp white shirt Carly had brought for him stood in stark contrast to his freshly shaved sun-bronzed face, and his dark blue jeans hugged his hips low and tight.

A shiver of desire went through her as she took in the sight of him. Irrational, she told herself, for he could obviously not want her less than he did now.

Judge Abigail Weldon seemed neither immune to nor swayed by Rafe's looks, but Carly caught her tearing her gaze from him just the same.

Tapping her pencil thoughtfully against her desk blotter, the judge cleared her throat. "I'm inclined to agree," she said. "This was a first offense. And according to this police report, Mr. Kellard didn't brawl in that saloon alone."

"Yes, Your Honor, that's true. Another man did, in fact, start the fight. But in the interest of expediency, my client has informed me that he's willing to accept full responsibility for the disturbance."

"Am I to understand that the plaintiffs have already received restitution in the amount of—" she looked down at the file in front of her "—twelve hundred and sixty-five dollars?"

Beside her, Rafe made a strangled sound.

"Yes, Your Honor," Carly said evenly. "That's already been taken care of."

"It's *what?*" Rafe's clamp-jawed hiss felt hot against her ear.

"Not...now," she mouthed, nudging him in the ribs and smiling at the judge.

"Very well," the judge said, writing something on the file before looking up and folding her hands in front of her. "Mr. Kellard? I am going to drop the drunk and disorderly charges against you, as well as willful destruction of private property considering all parties have agreed. Whatever your reasons were for taking apart the Blue Lagoon Saloon, I assume there won't be a repeat performance any time in the near future?"

"No, Your Honor," Rafe said sincerely.

"Splendid," Weldon said with a judicial smile. "Miss Jamison? A pleasure."

"Thank you, Your Honor," Carly said, gathering up her papers and her briefcase. "I would return the compliment."

"Hang on to her, Mr. Kellard," Weldon told him, in a startling departure from usual judicial procedure. "Reciprocity can be a valuable thing."

Rafe smiled tightly and took Carly's briefcase from her as the judge told the bailiff to call up the next victim.

"What the hell does reciprocity mean?" he muttered to her as they moved out of the courtroom.

"Give and take. Quid pro quo," she said, balancing on her crutches as he opened the double doors for her. "The California state bar and the Colorado bar have a reciprocity agreement which allowed me to argue in front of the judge today. That's all she meant."

Rafe looked back at the judge as Carly went through the door. Somehow he suspected she'd meant a hell of a lot more than that.

They were almost home—with more than thirty minutes of nearly silent white-knuckle driving behind them—before he broached the subject of the Blue Lagoon payoff.

"Where'd you get the money, Carly?"

Carly kept her gaze pinned to the road, where the high desert grassland rushed by in a blur of greens and purples and fragrant smells. "Consider it a loan, if you wish."

"I wish you hadn't done it in the first place."

"You'd rather spend another night with the tattooed trio?"

Against his will, a smile played at the corners of his mouth. "I'll pay you back."

It was as much of a thank-you as she was likely to get. But she hadn't done it for thanks. She'd done it for him. "There's no hurry. Besides, I owe it to you, after your coming all the way to Nevada to get me and—"

"I've got the twelve hundred in my account, Carly. I said I'll pay you back. And you can bill me for your fee."

She winced. "There is no fee, Rafe," she said carefully. "Not for you. Not ever."

He pulled into the ranch drive, slowed to a stop and shifted the car into park. With his hands braced on the steering wheel, he stared at the house. "Where's Evan?"

Carly's heart raced and plunged like a balky racehorse. "Gus took him to Laurie's with him this morning. He's going to spend the night with the boys. Gus is staying another night, too. He thought it might be easier for Evan.''

Disappointment flitted across Rafe's expression. ''Does he know?''

Sunshine beat down on her through the open window. She wanted to open the door, run, hide—anything but talk about the inevitable.

''Does he know about you, you mean?'' she asked. ''No. I thought it was something we should tell him together. But he's known for a long time that Tom wasn't his natural father. Tom knew, too, by the way,'' she said deliberately. ''Right from the start.''

Rafe's chest lifted, and he tilted his head back against the seat's headrest. ''Did he know about me?''

''Yes. He knew everything.''

Rafe turned to her with a frown. ''What everything? That I didn't want children? That I was a jer—?''

''He knew that I was still in love with you.''

Rafe's lips fell open. ''What?''

Idiot, she berated herself. Stupid, stupid, stupid… Dizziness assailed her. Why was it so hot? The musky scent that belonged to Rafe triggered its automatic response in her. Palpitations, dampness on her palms and in other places… She opened the truck door and wrestled her crutches outside.

''Wait a minute,'' he said, grabbing her by the upper arm.

''Please, Rafe—''

''Dammit, Carly, what do you think I'm made of, stone? You can't just drop a little bomb like that and walk off—''

''It doesn't matter anymore'' she lied. ''It's ancient history.''

''Is it?'' he demanded.

A chill ran through her as his question vibrated between them. ''Isn't it?''

He let go of her arm and simply stared at her, as if she'd

asked a question that was outside the realm of his possibilities.

Then, the tension in his features dissolved and an absurd laugh worked its way up from his chest. "I don't know. Hell, I don't know anything anymore. Three weeks ago, I seemed to have a handle on my life. I knew who I was and what I was. Where I was going. Now, I'm about to be out of a job, and probably a home. And suddenly I'm—I'm somebody's father. *Me.* And you want answers? Better get in line."

"I don't want anything, Rafe, except for your son to know you. That's all."

With his two hands gripping the steering wheel, the smile slipped off his face and he stared out at his ranch. "I want that, too."

Relief, quick and sharp, stabbed through her. She'd waited so long to hear those words. Last night she'd been so afraid. She'd underestimated him again. Had she done that all along? All those years ago?

"Look, I've got a lot of work to catch up on," he said, unable to look her in the eye. "We'll talk about this later."

"Sure." She started out of the truck and braced the metal crutches under her arms, cursing her need for them. But she hadn't taken a step before his voice stopped her.

"Hey, Carly—"

She turned back to him with a questioning look.

He swallowed thickly, staring straight ahead. "What you told Tom—about us...was it a lie?"

It was a moment before she could reply. She shook her head. "No."

Chapter 9

"You sure he's okay there? I hate to impose on you like this, Laurie," Carly said, fidgeting with the phone cord until its coils had wrapped around her whole hand.

"Impose?" Laurie laughed. "You have no idea the favor you've done me. For the past two hours, the three of them have been in the tree house, deeply entrenched in some sort of secret club constitution.

"I sent some snacks and drinks up on their dumbwaiter about an hour ago, which promptly vanished," she added. "So I guess they're okay. Meanwhile, I've managed to bake ten dozen crepes and seven dozen popovers for the party I'm catering tomorrow night. If anyone should be doing the thanking around here, it's me."

Carly smiled, too, relieved that at least Evan seemed to have found a place for himself here. "Evan took leaving L.A. and his friends there pretty hard. I'm so happy he's become friends with Jake and Jordan."

"The feeling's mutual." She paused. "Uh, speaking of friends, how's Rafe?"

Carly looked out the kitchen window. Fifty feet away, she could see Rafe wrestling a portable generator for some small part that didn't want to budge. He'd doffed his shirt, and the sun beat down on his muscled torso, emphasizing everything that was right with the male physique. Carly chewed on her lip. "He's fine. Cranky, but all in one piece." Yes, definitely all in one piece.

She could almost hear Laurie shake her head. "Funny, it's not like Rafe to go off the deep end like that."

"I know. It was my fault, Laurie," she admitted. "We had a...disagreement. Actually, it wasn't even anything as simple as a disagreement." If only it was.

"Carly, I wasn't prying. You don't have to tell me anything."

The quiet understanding in her voice was almost too much for Carly. She couldn't handle sympathy when she felt so guilty. She wondered how Laurie would react once she knew the truth. She wanted to tell her. She craved the counsel of another woman, a friend, but not before she'd straightened things out with Rafe. And Evan. "Thanks," she told her. "Just promise me one thing, okay?"

"Sure. Anything." Laurie sounded puzzled.

"If Rafe comes to you, and he probably will, because he needs someone, even though he doesn't want to admit it...if he comes to you, take care of him for me?"

A long silence stretched between them. "You know I will. But, Carly, we're just—"

"Friends, I know," she said quickly. "Just take care of him. Promise?"

"You still love him, don't you?"

Laurie had an uncanny ability to unvarnish the truth and ask questions that went straight to the heart of things. "Yes," she answered, surprising even herself.

"Whatever it is that's going on with you two," Laurie said, breaking into her thoughts, "don't give up on him yet. He's just a man, like any other man. He needs. He hurts. He retreats. But eventually he tries again. He's a tough nut, Carly, but underneath it all there's this soft center that craves what you have to offer. And despite the way he's acting, I think he's crazy about you.''

Carly glanced out the window again in time to see Rafe kick the recalcitrant generator and stomp off. She smiled sadly and shook her head. "I wouldn't bet on that."

Laurie sighed. "You were right when you said he needed someone. He does. I've been telling him that for years. Trouble is, somebody claimed his heart a long time ago. I just didn't know until we met that it was you."

Carly's eyes burned as she shifted the phone to her other ear. Outside, Rafe was nowhere to be seen. "I wish you were right, Laurie. I wish to God you were."

Rafe had given up on the hundred and one chores left on his list well after the eleven o'clock news ended. He'd ridden out with Pedro to find another dead calf, with signs of the cat everywhere, but no cat in sight. Pedro had come up empty last night, too. Rafe was too tired to pull another all-nighter, but tomorrow night he would stake out the pasture himself.

Exhaustion pulled at Rafe as he stumbled through the front door. Carly had left several strategic lights on for him, which he methodically switched off as he made his way toward his bedroom.

He'd missed lunch, and dinner had appeared anonymously on a covered plate in the barn office sometime after seven. Carly was nowhere to be seen. He'd told himself that was just as well, because he had neither the desire nor the energy for another confrontation.

But as he sat alone under the naked lightbulb, eating the meal she'd cooked for him, he'd found himself missing her company and contemplating what life would be like when she and Evan left. Predictable again.

And quiet. And dull. And lonely.

And what about his son?

His son! A fresh wave of disbelief rolled over him. He was a father with a son. Rafe swallowed hard. It was something he saw every day, but he had never envisioned himself in the role. He and his son, together at a ball game, or a park playing catch. Helping the boy with his homework, or lying on their backs together in the sun, chewing on alfalfa and shooting the breeze.

And despite never having considered it before, he wanted all of it now. He'd been cheated out of the first eight years of his son's life. He wasn't about to miss the rest.

The next obvious thought froze those daydreams in mid-fantasy. Evan still didn't know. How would he react, and how would they tell him? "Hey, son, you don't really know me well, but I'm your dad," or "I know this will be a little hard to understand. It was for me, too...."

Rafe squeezed his eyes shut. Somehow or other, he'd find a way. They'd work it out.

Then Evan would be in Ohio and he'd be here.

Hell, there were summer vacations. Holidays. Carly would just have to let Evan come.

But would he want to? And what would Rafe have to offer if he lost this place? He tried to envision bringing Evan to some small apartment in town, then forced the image ruthlessly from his mind.

He wouldn't, *couldn't* lose this place now. He supposed Carly had thought she could sway him against risking the rodeo again, now that he knew about his son. In fact, it had only made him more determined to do whatever it took to keep the ranch. It was the only legacy he had for Evan.

And what about Carly?

A strangled feeling crawled up his throat.

Sharing Evan, they'd have to see each other from now on. How the hell would he manage that? And when she found some other guy to marry, could he watch that man hold her, knowing they shared a bed at night? A shudder drove through him.

Walking down the dimly lit hallway to his room, he passed Carly's door. She was asleep—had he actually expected her to wait up?—her door firmly shut, her lights decidedly out. But he paused there, imagining her sprawled languidly beneath the thick blankets on her bed.

Tom knew I was still in love with you. With you. With you…

Why, Carly? he wanted to shout. Why, if you were still in love with me, did you stay with Tom? Did he love you like I did? And what sort of a man would share your heart with someone else?

Anger was the automatic response to that question, but his body's reaction was something else altogether. It had him picturing her naked and willing beneath him. Wanting him as much as he wanted her at this very moment.

He looked down to find his hand poised above her doorknob.

He swore, backed up, and careened down the hallway as if the hounds of hell were after him.

The sound woke her. An unfamiliar, awful sound. She had no idea where it had come from. She sat up in bed, cocked her head and listened.

There. Again. A panting, thrashing, muffled cry.

Rafe.

Carly threw the bedclothes off and lurched out of bed. Grabbing only one of her crutches, she hobbled in the dark toward his room, groping her way along the pitch-black hallway until she came to his door. Inside, the sound escalated.

"Rafe?" she said, fumbling for the light switch. Damn! Where was it?

"Son of a—" came his guttural cry again. "Ahhhhh—Gaaawwd!"

Moonlight spilled onto his bed, and Carly saw him frac-
tionally as he thrashed through it, arms and legs flailing at
some invisible enemy, his sheets tangled around him like
a shroud.

"Rafe!" She crossed the distance to the bed in a heartbeat, discarding the crutch to lean over him. "It's all right.
It's a dream. A *dream*. Wake up!"

She made the mistake of getting in the way of his arm,
and he caught her hard across the cheek.

"Uhhh—" she cried as she fell back across the bed in
the dark, holding her face. His hands found her, and he
crushed her shoulders in his grip.

He cried out something unintelligible, wrestling her off
him until she was pinned to the mattress by his superior
weight. Even in the dark, she could see that his eyes were
wide-open, and his expression was fierce.

Real fear shot through her as she felt her air being cut
off. "Rafe!" She was choking, clawing at his arms with
her nails. *"Rafe—!"*

Disoriented, unfocused, Rafe *saw* her for the first time.
In the dark he blinked, his chest heaving.

"C-Carly?"

Her fingers dug in more deeply, in the only reply she
could manage.

On a foul oath, he pushed his weight up and off her in
an instant, still tangled in the sheet and straddling her hips.

Carly pressed her head back and sucked in air.

He grabbed her by the shoulders in fear. "Christ, Carly!
Did I hurt you?"

She shook her head with a cough, still getting her breath.
"I'm—I'm okay." She touched a hand to the forming
bruise on her cheek.

He had to lean over her to flip on the green ginger-jar
lamp beside the bed. He pulled her hand away with a hor-
rified expression. "Did *I* do that?"

"I got in your way. It's—"

"I'm...oh, God, I'm sorry." He swallowed hard, obviously distressed. His chest heaved, the washboard hardness of his abdomen sharply defined in the moonlight. Her gaze fell to the dusting of dark hair that veed toward the brutal scars that wound around his ribs. It was the first time she'd seen them, and she was hardly prepared. Suddenly she knew what he'd been dreaming about.

He rolled off her, onto his back. The sheet came with him, barely covering the fact that he was naked underneath. He ran both hands down his sweat-slick face.

Carly turned onto her side. "It was my fault. I walked right into your arm. You were asleep." Silence stretched between them punctuated by his harsh breathing. "Hey, you okay now?"

He was not. Not by a mile. "I didn't mean for you to..." His voice drifted off, and he looked away, unable to face her.

She touched his arm, thinking to comfort him. His skin felt warm and damp, and her fingers curled around the solid muscle there. "Don't turn away, Rafe."

It took him a moment to respond. "It was just a stupid dream."

"It's over." But she knew it wasn't. Not for him.

"Every time, I think the outcome will change. I'll avoid the hooves, or roll away in time to miss that goddamn horn. But—" he shuddered "—it's always the same." He sent her a warning look. "Don't say it."

"I wasn't going to," she answered, thinking that there was no better reason not to compete again than this. Her thumb stroked the curve of his biceps, and without contemplating the wisdom of it, she pressed her lips against his warm, bare shoulder. He tasted salty, and the heady scent that belonged to him was dangerously male.

If she'd been thinking, she would have gotten out of his bed, away from the heated perfection of him. She would have run, knowing that one touch might betray her, send her headlong into what she'd been working so hard to deny since she came here.

But she didn't go. And when she looked up, she found him watching her—his eyes smoky with confusion and desire.

Rafe lifted her palm to his lips and pressed an aching kiss there. What might have passed for chaste under any other circumstances was nothing of the sort here. It was a flagrant warning that rocketed through her like a stab of heat. Rafe's eyes searched hers as he rolled toward her. Uncertainty warred with smoldering need.

She should run. Flee. Do the sensible thing.

His fingers slid through her hair to cup the back of her head.

Now, common sense told her. *Go now.*

The sheet slipped away from his naked hip as his knee moved to cover her thighs. Carly heard a whimper and knew it was hers as he pulled her close, his mouth a heartbeat from hers.

"Tell me to stop," he whispered. "Tell me this is crazy."

"It is," she said, curling her hand around the nape of his neck.

"Yeah," he whispered back, then claimed her mouth possessively in a hard, hungry kiss that left no doubt about his intentions. Slick and hot, his kiss slanted across her mouth, first one way, then the other, without a final destination. His tongue mated with hers with the same urgency that had them clinging to one another like drowning sailors amid the ruined bedclothes. As if there were no one else in the world to hang on to and the ocean were closing in.

The surf seemed to pound in her ears as his mouth shifted to her throat, leaving a moist trail from behind her ear to the swell of her breast. Her thin T-shirt proved no obstacle to his quest as his hands gathered it upward until he found what he was searching for.

On a gratified sigh, he cupped both her breasts in his large hands, plumping the weight of them and brushing the rigid tips with his thumbs. Each touch seared her, made her skin quiver with wanting. Oh, she'd forgotten. It had been so long. So very long...

It was lust, but more. She knew that. It was this man, whose hands knew her so well, whose mouth made her want things no other man could make her want. She threaded her fingers through his thick, dark hair.

She still loved him.

She'd tried to deny it for so long, but no more. He belonged to her and she to him. They belonged in this bed together. His loving now was raw with hunger, as was hers for him.

"I love you," she breathed, almost inaudibly. If he heard over the rustling of the sheets, she didn't know, and she hadn't the nerve to say it again. He made no reply, but instead teased her breast with openmouthed kisses, then took one nipple into his mouth and sucked hard.

Carly arched toward him on an inhalation, an explosion of sensation shattering her will to think. Pressure built deep inside her. It circled like a bird toward the center, spiraling with each rhythmic flick of Rafe's tongue.

His left hand trailed down her ribs, over the jut of her hip, to slide down her thigh and back up along the inside. Carly felt his violent shudder of arousal as he found the spot he sought.

He groaned impatiently at the silky barrier of her panties, and she heard the fabric tear as it disappeared down her hips. The sound excited her, and she twined her good leg around his, drawing him up hard against her. The velvet steel of his arousal pressed against the apex of her legs. She needed... Oh, she wanted...

"Rafe—" she breathed. "Oh, Rafe, please—" She buried her fingers in his hair.

A rough sound like a growl came from deep in Rafe's throat as he fought to control the inevitable. She was writhing under him, driving him crazy. Her skin felt like silk, all hot and smooth and damp with his loving. And she tasted sweet, like honey. He nuzzled her breast and the soft underside of it as he explored the depths of her slickness with his fingers.

In a rush of physical memory, it all came back to him—each curve, each hollow.... He knew her body as well as his own, but it had been so long. He couldn't get enough of her.

His gut knotted. He had to be inside her, to sheathe his aching flesh in her heat. He had wanted to make it good for her, but the way she ran her hands up his thighs pushed him beyond his limit. They'd fought this for too long now, but it had been a useless battle. There was no fighting it anymore.

Calling up every ounce of restraint he could manage, he pulled himself away from Carly and reached for the wallet on his bedside stand and the small foil package he always kept inside. It was one thing to be impulsive, another to be arrogant enough to think that what had happened before couldn't happen again.

When he turned back to her, he knew his moment of caution could have cost them the fire that had nearly burned out of control. But he saw that it hadn't. Carly watched him, her eyes still smoldering as she slid her hands up his ribs and spread her fingers across his chest. A small, grateful smile tugged at her lips. Then she kissed him with an openmouthed urgency that reignited the blaze all over again. He abandoned all the rational arguments against what they were doing. He was beyond everything but the urge to be one with Carly.

She slid her hands over his chest, skimming over the

awful scars that marred his side. For a moment, he grew still, bracing himself for her reaction.

She raised up and tenderly pressed her lips against the worst one. Rafe swallowed hard.

"Incredible, isn't it?" she murmured, smoothing a thumb across the jagged white scar.

"What?"

"The body's capacity for healing." Her gaze lifted to his, and for a moment he wondered if she was really talking about visible scars at all.

"It's ugly," he said, lowering himself into the cradle of her hips, hoping to distract her from what he'd rather forget.

"No," she whispered, nuzzling his shoulder. "It's your strength. Your resilience. It's who you are."

"Who I am," he repeated, dropping his mouth against her neck. "This is who I am, Carly." His tongue swirled against her heated skin, and he heard her moan softly. "Scars and all. Can you handle that?"

Her hand slid down between them. "Try me."

Her first touch made him suck in a breath between gritted teeth. A tremor went through him, and after a moment he clamped a hand over hers to make her stop. His entire body was throbbing.

With a restraint that belied the fierceness he felt, he said, "It's been a while for me, and I'm dangerously close to losing it here."

Her lips parted as she watched him, and with only a slight shift and a deep groan of intense pleasure, he buried himself inside her. A small quake moved through her. It almost undid him. For five thundering heartbeats, he held himself still.

"Wait," he told her in a breathy plea, holding her hips still between his hands. "Ah, Carly, what you do to me—"

"Rafe...don't stop..."

He started to move. Slowly at first, matching her movements. Then faster. He breathed her name against her throat with each deep, hot thrust and felt the tiny muscles at the core of her give and take as the tension in her built.

She urged him on with whispered entreaties, delivered heatedly against his sweaty flesh. The friction of her softness against his rough chest was nearly unbearable. Her hips undulated beneath his in an ancient rhythm that called him relentlessly deeper.

Her soft cries drove him mad with need, and he held on to control by the barest thread. His breathing grew harsh as they moved together, hands clutching feverish flesh. In a haze, he felt her climb to the top of that wall and stand teetering on the brink of it. With the finesse of a painter, he stroked her over the edge.

Something shattered in Carly, a pleasure so exquisitely painful that she cried out at the force of it. Her body arched into his, and his arms curled underneath her and held on tight. Over and over her body convulsed with Rafe skillfully holding her there on the knife's point.

Then, his rhythm increased again, faster and harder than before. The guttural sound of his breathing joined the creaking of the bed. A moment later, he crushed her against the mattress as he spilled himself into her with a strangled groan.

Collapsing, his weight half on, half off her, he lay sprawled with his cheek on her shoulder and his right arm pulling her close.

Carly closed her eyes and, for a long time, held him, loving the press of his weight against her. For years she'd tried to convince herself that good sex was all they'd shared together and that was what she missed. Now she knew that wasn't true. What they'd shared was more than sex. It was more than two people groping in the dark toward some kind of self-gratification. The bond they shared went deeper than lust.

He was the other half of her. The missing piece. And

she wondered how she'd gotten along all these years without it. And how she'd go on without him again when it was time for her to go.

Rafe brushed a thumb along the side of her face, and it came back damp. He raised up on one elbow. "Hey, are you crying?"

"No. Yes." She squeezed her eyes shut. "I'm sorry."

"Did I hurt you?"

She shook her head, her fingers threading through his hair in tempo to her heartbeat. "No. No. It was just—" *I've missed you*, she thought. Covering his hand with hers, she held it there against her cheek. She never wanted to let go. "Are you sorry this happened?"

"I'm sorry about your cheek. This...?" He shook his head. "This was probably a mistake, but it was also—" his thumb brushed her chin "—inevitable."

Tears leaked out of the corners of her eyes. She couldn't stop them. Rafe leaned close and kissed the moisture, then covered her mouth with his. His kiss tasted salty, and she wrapped her arms around his neck, drawing him closer. Unlike his earlier kisses, this one was heartbreakingly tender and said all the things he couldn't.

Finally, he lifted his head and brushed the hair out of her eyes. "We're both adults, Carly. We knew what we were doing when we started it."

"I'm not sorry," she said fiercely, her fingers curling through his hair. "I've never been sorry about loving you."

"Shhh..." Her words made him ache. He hadn't known until tonight how much he yearned for this. This feeling—as if he'd been dead and was alive again. She'd done it. For a moment, he allowed himself to imagine what it would be like to lie here beside her every night, holding her in his arms.

"I know you thought I left you for Tom or some other man."

It was the last thing he'd expected her to say. Silent, he
held her, unsure how to answer that.

"I didn't. I didn't meet Tom until after I left. He was
ten years older than me. He was ready to settle down, and
he fell in love with me, even though he knew I was pregnant with another man's child." She breathed deeply, as
if resurrecting these memories of Tom came from some
painful place inside her. "He was good and kind, and
when he asked me to marry him, I said yes."

"For Evan's sake?"

"Partly," she said truthfully. "I wanted Evan to have a
father. But to say that I wasn't still reeling from our
breakup would be untrue. I was. I was also young and
scared and alone. Tom was safe. An anchor."

And he wasn't Evan's real father. Rafe clamped down
on the stirrings of anger that still swirled around the
thought. Only an idiot would feel jealous of a dead man
at a time like this, but Tom had shared a part of Carly that
Rafe had never gotten to share. He'd been a father to the
boy Rafe had sired, and slept with the woman Rafe had
only known in his dreams for the past nine years. The
anger was irrational. Low.

But there was another side to his anger.

Nine years ago, Rafe thought, he had been another man.
He'd lived on the sharp edge of a razor, riding broncs and
bulls and spitting at danger for fun. What kind of a father
would he have made? It took only a moment to come up
with the answer: lousy.

His accident had been a revelation. A reincarnation, in
a way. It had stripped him of the need for danger and given
him this place. But he wondered, with his future still in
turmoil, whether he'd really changed all that much? He
still had no idea how to parent a kid. Laurie's boys were
the closest he'd come to kids in years, and while he enjoyed the time he spent with them, he wasn't responsible

for them. That responsibility, he suspected, was a whole different story.

One thing he did know, however. He'd let Carly down nine years ago. He'd let the ball drop, and Tom had simply been there to pick it up.

Her skin felt warm beneath his hand. "Did you love him?"

"Yes. Very much."

Somehow, it relieved him to hear her say it.

"But it was never—" she began.

"What?"

Her eyes slid shut. "I can't explain it. We shared a life, Evan, even a future for a while. But…"

Rafe brushed the hair from her eyes, waiting.

"He didn't—" She stopped, staring at the ceiling in the dark. "He didn't make me feel—"

His thumb skimmed the air-cooled tip of her nipple. "This?"

A shudder tore through her, and her eyes slid shut. "Yes."

A fierce possessiveness poured through him as his hand slid down her belly and found the dampness between her legs. "Or this?"

She inhaled sharply. "Yes."

He felt himself grow hard against her, knowing he would take her again and again until they were spent. And he wouldn't think about tomorrow. Or about how loving Carly had never been enough to hold her. Dipping a finger into her, he felt her whole body convulse. Then, he kissed her deeply, not wanting any more talk.

As he shifted his weight onto her cooling body, Carly sank into the bed, surrendering to the onslaught of his mouth. Words failed her, as they always seemed to do around Rafe. But as his mouth slid downward, his tongue swirling against her damp, heated skin, she forgot to think, and allowed him to drag her back to heaven with him.

*   *   *

Morning light filtered into the room. Dust motes danced in the shafts, like schools of fish moving in the same direction. The red numbers on the digital clock on the bedside stand read 7:45. Rafe's head rested on her shoulder. Light played off his lashes and the dark stubble on his jaw. His skin felt warm and smooth, and she adored the weight of him sprawled against her.

Her body craved sleep, but she couldn't close her eyes. She'd inventoried his every muscular curve and hollow and stored it away in her memory. Last night might have to last her for a lifetime.

She looked down to find him watching her.

His eyes were half-open and a lazy grin tugged at his mouth. "I half thought I'd wake up and find out I dreamed it."

"No such luck, Buster," she said lightly.

"You got that backwards, Legs. I've got you right where I want you."

She sighed, edging down until her chin rested on top of his head and his arms curled fully around her. "This wasn't supposed to happen, was it?"

"Uh…no. But you know what they say about best-laid plans—" He grinned at the pun. "Sorry."

She grinned back. "Did I tell you how amazing last night was?"

He rolled over on top of her. "Remind me." He dropped kisses on her ear, her throat, her collarbone, while her fingers traced the smooth muscles of his back.

"We should—" she was distracted by his tongue drawing slow circles toward her breast "—talk about this, don't you…think?"

His mouth found her nipple. "About this?"

"No," she answered breathlessly. "About…*this*. Us."

He lifted his head. "Us?"

Carly's lips parted just as the phone rang, making them both jump.

"Damn," Rafe muttered. "Don't get it."

"It could be Laurie. She said she was going to drop Evan off this morning."

Rafe reached for the phone. "Hello?" His gaze slid up to Carly, and he rolled off her. "Sure, just a minute," he said, handing her the phone. "It's for you."

She sat up with a frown, pulling the sheet with her, and put the phone to her ear. "Hello? Oh, Mr. Maynard." Carly ran an automatic hand through her tousled hair and held up one finger. "Uh…yes. Oh, gee, I appreciate that. Really. I— Yes, the leg's better. Uh-huh. My head, too. The dizziness is almost gone." She glanced up at Rafe and rolled her eyes. "When? Um, I'm not exactly sure yet. No." She chewed on her lip. "I understand. Of course. I get my walking cast on next week. I'll call you then? Yes. Well, actually, I…"

Rafe went cold and stopped listening. Her walking cast. That phrase struck him as ironic as hell. She'd be walking right out of his life with the damned thing. He got out of the bed, pulled on his jeans and shifted around on the floor beneath the discarded pile of clothes for his shirt. Behind him, he heard her quietly hang up the phone.

"Hey," she said.

"Hey," he replied, not looking at her.

"That was the—"

"Law firm."

"Yes. Where are you going?"

Back to reality. He looked at his watch as he clapped it around his wrist. "It's late. I've got a million things to do."

"Rafe?"

He turned back to her after a deep breath. "Yeah?"

She threw her legs over the side of the bed, taking the

sheet with her. "Don't go yet." There was a plea in her voice.

He leaned over and kissed her cheek, careful not to touch her anywhere else. Gently, he said, "I'm not going anywhere, Carly. I live here, remember?"

Stung, she lowered her eyes.

Rafe cursed under his breath as he shoved the tails of his shirt into his jeans. Of course she was the one leaving. What the hell had he expected? It was understood, right? Hell, yes. Even if he wanted her to stay—which, dammit, he didn't—what did he have to offer? Unless he could win that rodeo competition, he was back to square one. But that wasn't her fault.

He rubbed a fist along his stubbled chin. "That was out of line. Sorry."

That earned him an undecipherable look. "No, you're right. I am the one who's leaving."

"We're both adults," he said rationally. "We can deal with this like adults."

The certainty was fading from her eyes. "Right. And...*how* exactly do we *do* that?"

He sat on the edge of a chair and pulled on one worn boot. "We chalk what happened last night up to bad judgment."

"Well," she said on a breath of humorless laughter, "there certainly was that. On the other hand—"

"Throw in a couple months of loneliness," he added pulling on his other boot, "some healthy lust, and there you go. We just put it behind us. Forget about it."

"Forget about it?" Carly blinked at him.

"No harm, no foul. We both enjoyed it, right? You're not gonna walk away from here with a baby this time. We were careful." Shrugging on a fleece jacket, he stared intently at the zipper as he fumbled the mechanism.

Careful with everything but our hearts, Carly thought.

"I think it's best," he said, not looking at her, "if it doesn't happen again. Agreed?"

Her heartbeat echoed in her ears. Damn him. She'd gotten used to her aloneness. Complacent about her nunlike existence. She'd assumed she could go on indefinitely that way. Then he'd walked back into her life and sabotaged all that. He'd given her a taste of hope, then snatched it away.

Well, it *was* best. Absolutely. Her life was full—meaningful, even. She had a job and a future waiting for her in Cincinnati. And after all, she reasoned, what had really changed? It was the same old song. Rafe Kellard, the king of noncommitment, was giving her the brush-off once again.

She hugged the sheet around her. She was past being hurt by him. She wouldn't let him into her heart. She had to keep her priorities straight—what was important was Evan.

"Agreed," she told him. "We'll scratch sex right off our 'to-do' list." She reached for the T-shirt he'd discarded on the floor by the bed and pulled it on. "Let's see, that only leaves…telling Evan you're his father and, hmmm…working out those pesky details."

"Carly—"

"Other than that—breakfast. Are you hungry? I'm suddenly starving." A blatant lie. "I think I'll go change, then make some coffee and eggs, if you still like them. Sunny-side up, right?"

Rafe narrowed a look at her. "Carly, don't do this."

"Do what? Accept the obvious? That I'm sitting here in this bed all by myself because you're too scared to think we might have something here?" She stood, reaching for her crutches and waving off the dizziness that had nothing to do with head injuries and everything to do with injuries of the heart.

Rafe grabbed the crutches and held them from her. "You know as well as I this would never work."

"And why is that, Rafe? Because you might lose this place? Because I'm an attorney? Because the moon is full?"

A muscle jumped in his jaw as he stared at her.

She went on. "You know, what happened between us last night wasn't about any of those things. But the sad thing is, you think it was. Well, that's never what I've been about, Rafe. And it never will be. But you can go on choosing to believe that," she said, grabbing her crutches out of his hand, "if it makes it easier for you."

She breezed past him on her damned crutches, wishing like hell she was graceful and erect, and cursing the sadist who'd invented plaster casts.

Chapter 10

A bluesy Rickie Lee Jones ballad about ghosts echoed through the kitchen when Rafe returned from feeding the stock. He'd spent the past twenty minutes trying to think of what to say. Naturally, he'd failed. He couldn't think of a thing that could set things right between them. Carly was angry and he was a heel. And despite her denials, their lives were too complicated to be as simple as she claimed.

So they sat across the wooden table from one another, pretending to be hungry. Neither was, but they both stabbed at the overcooked eggs and half-burned sausages on their plates and moved them around to make it look as if they'd eaten. Rafe nursed his coffee, hiding behind the rim of the mug to watch Carly avoiding his glance. The damned awkwardness was louder than the music.

The smell of something burning suddenly stung his nose. Leaping up, he snatched two blackened pieces of toast from the toaster and waved off the smoke.

Carly slapped a palm against her forehead. ''Ugh! The charcoal! I knew I forgot something.''

Rafe tossed them in the garbage. "I can make more."

"Please don't. Enough carcinogens for one meal," she said, fork-wrestling a blackened sausage.

He cleared his throat. "We need to talk about Evan."

"Ah, yes. Item number two."

Ignoring the barb, Rafe slid into his chair and took a swig from his coffee mug. "We need to tell him the truth."

Her fork settled back against her plate. "I know."

"So?" he asked. "What have you told him already? About me, I mean."

"Only that his real father and I were together once and that we'd made him out of love."

Rafe didn't take his eyes off her. "Does he think I didn't want him?"

"No," she answered. "I never told him that. Tom was his father for most of his life, and that was what he knew. I told him the truth last year, and he seemed to accept it. He's never asked me that question. He's only eight, Rafe."

"He's never wondered why I'm not in the picture?"

"Maybe," she allowed, "but if he has, he hasn't voiced it."

They sat facing one another, still as stone. Rickie Lee's voice filled the silence stretching between them. The morning sun poured over Carly like honey, gilding her fair skin and shining on her hair. Rafe cursed himself for noticing, but was helpless to stem the pang of longing evoked by seeing her at his kitchen table.

He stood, shoving his hands in his pockets.

"Rafe," she said gently. "I know you're worried—"

"Worried? Hell, that's the understatement of the century. I mean, what do I know about kids? I've never had any. I don't know the first thing about fathering one. What if I screw up like my old man?"

"You're not your father, Rafe. You won't ever be. Evan's crazy about you."

"How do you know?" he shot back. "I brushed him off the other day when I was chasing you back into the house. He wanted to show me something, and I—"

"Children are very forgiving. If you're expecting perfection of yourself—"

"Dammit, Carly, don't give me psychobabble."

"There's no need to yell."

"I'm not yelling!" he heard himself shout. He pulled back, dragging a hand down his face. "But, dammit, Carly, you're his mother. You've always been his mother. Of course he'll forgive you. Right now I'm just an interesting diversion with an impressive buckle on his belt. How the hell do you know how he's gonna react when he learns I'm his father?"

A noise from the doorway drew both their glances. Rafe's heart fell when he saw Evan standing in the doorway, a stricken expression on his face.

"Evan!" they both gasped at once.

The painted wooden box in his hands crashed to the floor and splintered as he turned and ran out of the house like his tail was on fire.

"Oh, no," Carly breathed, her fingers against her mouth. "Evan, wait!"

Rafe muttered something crass. "How much of that did he hear?"

Carly reached for her crutches. "I've got to go to him."

Rafe put his hand out to stop her. "Wait. Let me talk to him. It's between us right now, anyway."

"No, I have to—" Tears brimmed in her eyes as she struggled to her feet. "Oh, God, Rafe..."

He laid a hand on her arm. "You want me to be a father to that boy? Let me go. I'll talk to him. We'll try to sort this out. Okay?"

She nodded silently, and Rafe took off after Evan.

Laurie, Gus and the boys were halfway up the steps when Rafe burst through the front door. Her smile froze at the expression on Rafe's face. "Hi, Rafe. What's going on?"

"Did you see Evan?" he demanded, his gaze scanning the empty yard. Sweat had popped out on his forehead, and he was breathing as if he'd run a long way.

With her arms full of a sleeping bag and overnight things, she laughed. "Of course I saw Evan. He just hopped out of my car and ran in ahead of us. He wanted to show you the box he made for..." She glanced at the front door where Carly had just appeared behind the screen and the gears began clicking. "Uh, Gus?"

Gus was already way ahead of her. "Boys, why don't we go see that bull Rafe's got penned up over in the corral? I think Pedro would even let you feed him, if you ask real nice."

Jordan tugged at Rafe's sleeve and whispered, "I saw Evan and Macky run to the barn."

"Jor-dan! Why didn't you say something?" Laurie stared at her youngest son.

Jordan shrugged. "Nobody asked me."

Rafe took off down the steps at a lope toward the barn as Gus herded the boys in the direction of the bull pen. Laurie turned to Carly, who stood watching Rafe go.

"Are you all right?" Laurie asked.

Carly shook her head, holding her fingers against her mouth.

"If you want me to go, I'll—"

"No." Carly pushed open the screen door. "Please come in. I think I could use some company right now."

Rafe found Evan in the farthest corner of the loft, behind a stack of hay bales. In the dim light, he made out the small figure with arms crossed over his bent knees, head down atop them.

He sat down in the soft, fragrant hay beside him. Evan abruptly turned ninety degrees away.

"Hey, pard. I know you're upset."

Silence.

"Ev? Look, just give me a chance to talk here, okay? This is hard for both of us."

"My dad's dead," Evan said into his arms.

Rafe's throat closed around a knot. "Yeah, I know. Your dad, he was a special guy. And I know you loved him."

Evan's back grew rigid.

"And see, I'd never want to take that away from you. I'd never want to interfere with that. That's special, you and your dad. He loved you very much." Evan sniffed. "Look, Ev, I don't know how much you heard in there—"

"You were fighting."

"No, we weren't fighting. And definitely not about you. We were just trying to decide the best way to tell you."

"You lied," the boy said accusingly, tears streaming down his small cheeks.

"How'd I lie, Evan?"

"You s-said you were just a friend of my Mommy's—"

"That's true. A long time ago, we were good friends. Actually, more than friends. We, uh…we loved each other."

Evan tipped his damp face sideways and glared at Rafe.

"But," he continued, "for some reason, things didn't work out and we broke up. When your mom found out she was gonna have you, well, she decided that Tom would be the best daddy for you. And so he was."

"He *was* my dad."

Rafe knew what he meant. In every sense of the word that Evan understood, Tom had fathered him—he'd tucked him in, read him bedtime stories and taken him fishing. Tom was the one who'd been there, not Rafe.

"You're right. He was. But now I am, Ev. I'm your dad now and you're my son."

"You s-said we were just partners."

Rafe reached out and touched Evan's small back with his large hand. The boy seemed small and suddenly fragile. "Well, we're that, too. It's just that now we're even more."

Angry, Evan rested his forehead on his arms again. "If you were my real dad, you would've come to see me, but you never did."

And there it was. Boldly put. Rafe rolled his eyes beseechingly at the roof overhead, then ran a hand over his stubbled jaw.

"I know this is gonna be hard for you to understand, Evan, but if I'd known about you, I would have come to you in a heartbeat. But I didn't know until yesterday that you were really my son."

Evan took that in, and his eyes narrowed. Rafe could see the wheels turning. Damn, the kid was quick.

"That's not your mom's fault, so don't blame her. She did what she thought was best for you, and you gotta admit, Tom was a pretty good choice. But if I'd known, Evan, nothing could have kept me from you," he said fiercely. "I want you to believe that. And nothing ever will again. You're stuck with me, kid."

From the bottom of the loft came the sound of Macky's whine, and from above them the flutter of swallows wings as the birds built nests of mud in the rafters.

"You—you want to be my dad?" Evan asked.

"Do I want—?" Rafe felt his voice go, choked off by the longing in Evan's question. "You bet I do, Ev. I want it more than you can know."

Something broke inside the boy, and he lurched toward Rafe, wrapping his arms around Rafe's broad shoulders. Rafe grabbed and held him tight, the joy of holding his son unbearably sweet. The bite of that emotion stung his eyes.

After a moment, Evan pulled back, apparently realizing the eight-year-old uncoolness of his embrace. He shifted his jacket straight and fisted away the moisture on his cheeks. "Are you and Mom gonna get married?"

Rafe's mouth opened and closed as he searched for an answer. Married, to Carly? The idea tugged at him, but he rejected it just as quickly. For the same reasons they'd broken up years ago, he couldn't drag her into his life now.

"Uh...well, you know, that's a tricky thing."

Evan blinked, knowing a no when he heard it. "But you said—"

"I know, I know. I said I'm gonna be your dad, and I am. But your mom and me, we've got different lives. She's got a job in the city, and I'm here."

"You could move."

"No, Ev. But you can visit me here."

"But don't you love my mom anymore?"

Rafe looked at his hands. Hell, the kid could ask questions. Love her? Hell, he wanted her, Rafe told himself, thinking of last night. He missed her when she wasn't around, and he felt singularly alive when she was. But love her? He couldn't...wouldn't...allow himself to love her. He couldn't afford to.

"What's important," Rafe said carefully, "is that we both love you and want what's best for you. It's gonna take some working out, but we can do it. Whattaya say?"

One small shoulder lifted in a shrug of assent. It wasn't the enthusiasm he was hoping for, but Rafe decided it would do. It was going to take work on all their parts to make this work. "I think your mom would like to talk to you, too, only she can't make it up this ladder with that leg of hers." He got to his feet brushing hay off his jeans. "She's real worried about you." Rafe extended his hand to the boy. "C'mon, son."

"Sticky," Laurie summed up succinctly, after Carly sketched out the ironic twists and turns that had led her and Rafe to this moment.

"Like glue," Carly agreed, feeling as if she'd been swimming in the stuff.

With a sympathetic nod, Laurie added, "One good thing about glue...when it dries, it doesn't stick to your feet."

"I'll try to remember that, if I can ever extricate myself from it."

Laurie sighed, smoothing her palm across the wooden table. "I'm not sure what I would have done in your situation, and frankly, it's unfair to even speculate. There's nothing more fragile and inexplicable than a relationship. And no one looking at it from the outside can ever really comprehend it.

"Jack and I," she mused, "we were easy. We loved each other from the moment we laid eyes on each other. If you asked anyone we knew if there were problems, they would have laughed. But, the truth is, there were. Nothing I could explain or would even want to. We were lucky enough never to have to face the kinds of problems you and Rafe have. But," she said on a shaky breath, "I'd take them in a second to have him back."

Carly's throat tightened, and she covered Laurie's hand with her own. The thought of losing Rafe, even if they never resolved their differences, was almost too much to bear. And Laurie's unbiased support meant more to her than she could have said.

Laurie tossed her silky dark hair with a flick of her head, refusing to be maudlin. "Anyway, you've told him now, and you can only move forward from here. It'll take him some time. But personally, I think if he didn't care, he never would have ended up in that bar the other night, nor would he have landed himself in jail over it. And you know what?" she said, getting up to pour more hot water into their teapot. "He's gonna make a hell of a daddy. My kids adore him."

"I know," Carly said, dabbing at her nose with her

overused tissue. "So does Evan. Or at least he did, until—"

"Don't worry. He'll come around. He's still little, he can adapt. It's you and Rafe I'm worried about."

Carly sipped the remnants of her tea dejectedly. Me too, she thought, but she said, "Don't worry. We'll be fine."

"And roosters quack."

Carly gave a teary laugh. "Only if they marry ducks."

"Well, Rafe isn't married to anyone, honey, and the only prospect I see is you."

Laurie poured them both a second cup of tea, and they sat sipping in silence. Finally, she asked, "What is it *you* want, Carly?"

"I don't know," she answered on a sigh. "It seems foolish to hope for something that can never be. It's not enough that we share a child. That can't be what holds us together. Rafe's always had trouble accepting love, and mine, he just plain doesn't want."

"What about *you?*"

"Me?" She looked at Laurie, then toyed with her cup. "You know, it's funny—if you'd asked me that question a few weeks ago, you would have gotten another answer. I knew where I was going, what I'd be doing. My life was laid out in a nice linear path. That's what I thought, anyway. However—a good knock on the head made everything a little bit clearer."

"Funny," Laurie commented, "how near-death experiences tend to do that."

"Exactly. You know what I realized?"

Laurie smiled and shook her head.

"That all the years I thought I was chasing something, I was really running away. From Rafe and what we could have been. But Evan—he's that part of us, that love, that never truly died. But Rafe's pushing away again, just like he did before. He's convinced that if he allows himself to love me, he'd be standing in my way, or something idiotic like that. That's so far from the truth…but I can't seem to make him see it. I love him, Laurie, so much it hurts. And there's nothing I can do to change that.''

"Then don't."

Carly swallowed back the lump forming in her throat. "But if he won't—"

"You're a lawyer. Convince him."

Carly blinked. "You make it sound so simple."

"Not simple," Laurie said, covering Carly's hand with hers. "But what have you got to lose? Think of it this way—if this were a case, how would you go about proving him wrong?"

For a long moment, Carly stared into the sunshine pouring through the kitchen window, thinking. "I'd…convince him that the underpinnings of this case were set in quicksand," she said slowly. "That the logic was faulty and the evidence slanted."

"Aha." Laurie grinned like a creamery cat.

Carly's eyes widened. An idea began to take shape in her mind. Of course. The answer had been there right in front of her all along. It seemed so simple, really, but it would require a two-pronged approach—the second of which was decidedly riskier than the first. It held the potential to destroy everything, and she wouldn't use it unless she had to. But Laurie was right. What did she have to lose? She had only one answer to that.

Rafe.

"Thanks, Laurie," she said, the beginnings of a smile curving her lips. "Do you know you'd make a great attorney?"

"No," Laurie quipped, "but if you hum a few bars…"

That night, Carly leaned over her son's bed and pressed a kiss on his forehead. Tugging the covers up under his arms, she smoothed them straight with unnecessary fuss and sat down beside him. He looked different tonight, as if the day's happenings had chiseled new wisdom into his features. And the bed seemed somehow smaller than it had the night before. Or had Evan grown?

Macky had assumed his position on the rug beside Evan's bed, having temporarily abandoned Rafe for his younger clone. Carly scratched Macky's belly with her toe.

"Mom?"

"Mmm-hmm?"

"If Rafe is really my dad, what am I s'posed to call him?"

She brushed the last wrinkle from the sheets and smiled down at him. "Well, that's sorta between you two. What do you want to call him?"

A frown creased his small brow. "If I called him Dad, that would be like Daddy wasn't *really* my dad."

"I see."

"And if I call him Rafe, then it's like he isn't my dad."

"I see your dilemma." Carly stared at her son in wonder at the unexpected depth of his reasoning. They'd talked earlier, when Rafe and Evan came back from the barn. They'd spent tears and anger, and she'd answered a hundred questions. But this one wasn't about the past, it was about the future. And for the first time, she felt the stirrings of hope.

"Why don't you wait awhile and see what feels right to you?" she suggested. "I'm sure that would be okay with Rafe."

He nodded thoughtfully. "Mom?"

"What, sweetie?"

"How come you don't love Rafe anymore?"

She swallowed hard. "That's a complicated question, Evan."

"Is it 'cause you loved Daddy?" he asked intently.

"Yes. I did love Daddy. But there's room in my heart for lots of different kinds of love. I love you and I loved Daddy. I'm absolutely nuts about Macky...."

Evan giggled, and Macky thumped his tail against the floor, knowing he was being discussed. She gave him another rub with her toe.

"But what about Rafe?" Evan persisted. "Do you still love him?"

She nodded. "Yes. Yes, I do, honey."

"Then how come you can't be married together? Rafe says it's 'cause you have different lives. But they're not so different, are they?"

"Not so different." She pressed another kiss on his downy forehead. "But when you grow up, things get more complicated. Sometimes mommies and daddies just can't live together."

"Why not? 'Cause they don't love each other enough? Like you and me?"

She nipped his nose between her fingers and grinned. "You and me, we're a team, right? We stick together no matter what."

"No matter what," Evan repeated, as if it were a litany between them.

"And I'll love you till the sun turns blue," she said.

"And the moon turns green," he finished, and they both giggled as she tickled him into distraction.

In the darkened hallway, Rafe stood stock-still, listening to the exchange between Carly and their son. Leaning his head back against the wall, he searched the dark hallway for guidance.

Complicated? Hell, things were getting downright mind-boggling. How easy it would be to wrap his arms around them both and beg them to stay. To be his family. He longed for that.

And coming from a man who sat on the brink of disaster, it shamed him to want to drag the two people he cared most about in the world down with him.

Like his father before him.

The old man had hauled him down into the whirlpool of alcoholism after Rafe's mother walked out. Rafe could still remember the humiliation of moving from place to place when the rent got too steep, and the awful embarrassment of letting his friends know that Chet Kellard was a blood relation.

He'd grown up with a keen understanding of a man's responsibility. It had been his dream for most of his life to find that stability and lock it down. Yet it continued to elude him.

In another week, he'd say goodbye to Carly and Evan, then do his damnedest to save this leaky vessel. One way or another, he vowed, he'd make his son proud of him.

Even if it killed him.

The next evening, Rafe decided they should all get out of the house. J.J.'s Pizza Emporium was doing a booming business as a grateful Carly and a thrilled Evan went through the door Rafe held open for them. They were met by the tinny sound of "A Bicycle Built for Two" coming from a player piano.

J.J.'s was decorated like a turn-of-the-century ice cream parlor complete with "gas" lamps, filigreed ironwork and costumed waiters. As a concession to the twentieth century, however, several old-fashioned pinball machines stood in one corner, surrounded by a line of children.

Evan couldn't stop staring.

"Pretty impressive," Carly murmured as they made their way to their table. The incredible fragrance coming from the huge ovens made her mouth water.

"Wait till you taste it," he told her.

"Can I have a quarter, Mom?" Evan begged.

Rafe pulled several out of his pocket and handed them to Evan. "It's my treat tonight."

"Thanks," Evan said shyly, and ran off to join the handful of kids surrounding a machine.

"Hey," Rafe called after Evan. "What do you want on your pizza?"

"Just cheese," Carly told him.

"Oh," Rafe said, pulling Carly's chair out for her.

"It's all he ever wants on it," she added, seeing Rafe's discomfort. She shoved her crutches down beside her. "It's some kind of a secret pact all children make together to force parents to order a second pizza with everything." She grinned.

"I still have a lot to learn."

"That's half the fun," she replied.

"Well, Rafe Kellard!" A pretty dark-haired twenty-something waitress in a Gay Nineties pinafore practically skidded to a stop at their table. "Where have you been, darlin'? I've missed you!"

"Michelle?" Rafe said, flushing, as her gaze slid to Carly and back again.

"Oh, 'scuse me," Michelle said in an embarrassed twang. "I was just so happy to see you, I didn't notice you had company."

"Michelle, I'd like you to meet Carly Jamison. Carly? Michelle Quatro."

Carly smiled, wondering if the strategic pinning of the younger woman's pinafore was done simply to emphasize the size of her perky breasts. "Hello."

"Hello," Michelle answered.

"Michelle was the rodeo queen last summer in Durango's pro rodeo," Rafe clarified.

"Really?" Carly said, impressed. She bet those perky breasts had something to do with that. "Congratulations."

Michelle waved her hand. "The judges were either pizza eaters or skiers. I teach downhill up at Purgatory in the winter season," she explained.

Carly nodded. "Ah."

"So, Rafe," Michelle went on, "how's that ranch of yours? Keepin' you busy, huh?"

"Sure is, Michelle. Awful busy."

Evan bounded up to the table. "I need two more quarters, Mom. Can I? Pleeease? I almost got a free game!"

Carly watched Michelle take Evan into the picture as Rafe pulled out two more quarters. "Here you go, son," he said. Evan managed a "Thanks" before he was gone again.

"Cute kid. Yours?" Michelle asked Carly.

She hesitated, unsure of how Rafe wanted to handle this.

"Ours," he said proudly, meeting Carly's eyes. She smiled back at him.

"Oh," Michelle said. It sounded like a little hiccup. "I suppose you folks would like to order now."

Rafe winked at her. "That'd be great."

The pizza was the best Carly had ever had, thick and gooey and cheesy. Evan's nonstop dialogue ranged from his pinball coup to Rafe's promise to take him along with Gus for the branding tomorrow. Rafe and Evan had been working steadily on Evan's riding, and the chance for a firsthand look at cattle branding had Evan practically jumping out of his boots. Carly wished she could go along and watch, but knew it was a male-bonding thing between them, and better left to the men.

As the evening progressed, the tension that had been with them for the past few days seemed to melt away. This was the most relaxed she'd seen Rafe in days. He told awful jokes, and Evan did his best to outdo him. They all laughed and laughed.

Once or twice, as Evan was amusing them with the story of exactly how he and Macky had come back covered head to toe in mud this afternoon, she'd caught Rafe watching her. When their eyes met for the second time, he didn't look away. Instead, he held her gaze with his for a long, bittersweet moment that left them both shaken.

Just as Evan took a breath, Rafe spotted an older woman with fire-engine-red hair coming toward their table. Her

smile was as bright as her hair. "Well, it's about time you
gave your friend here time off for good behavior from that
ranch of yours, Rafe. Hi," she said to Carly, offering her
hand. "I'm Chicky Green. I run the feed store, and me
and Rafe go way back. It's a pleasure to meet you."

Carly couldn't help but smile. "Hi, I'm Carly Jamison.
And the pleasure's mine."

Chicky tsked at the cast on Carly's leg. "I heard about
that accident you had in Nevada. Why, Rafe went tearing
out of here like nobody's business in the middle of the
night on Jim Noble's cargo pl—"

"Hey, Chicky." Rafe bussed her on the cheek, cutting
her off. "In for pizza tonight?"

Chicky touched her cheek and grinned. "Yes, and it was
quite tasty, thank you. Now, Jamison...Jamison... That
name sounds awfully familiar. You from around here?"

"Years ago. I was a student at Fort Lewis College."

As if the pieces had just fallen into place, Chicky exclaimed, "*Jamison!* Carly Jamison? You're a lawyer,
aren't you? I remember now. You became a big-time pub-
lic-defender lawyer in Los Angeles, didn't you? There was
a write-up in our local newspaper about you a few years
back, after that case you won for that movie star's son.
What was his name?"

"Garrison," she said, glancing at Rafe and wondering
if he'd read that story, too. She found him watching her
with a wary sense of pride. "Tim Garrison."

It was one of the cases she was most proud of. For
reasons of his own, Tim had refused his mother's expensive personal attorney in favor of Carly's experience and
personal conviction about his innocence. She'd sweated
blood over that case, and in the end she'd cleared his name
and uncovered evidence to convict another man. For once,
she thought, justice had prevailed.

"That's right," Chicky said. "Letta Garrison's son. And

they caught the real killer only a month or so later, didn't they?''

"Yes," Carly said, the memory of that victory still fresh in her memory. "Yes, they did. A full confession."

"Right," Chicky said, pleased that she'd gotten it straight. "There was a 'local student makes good' kind of personal-interest story in the paper about it."

Carly vaguely remembered the phone call she'd gotten in the middle of a harried week from an overeager reporter from Durango. It had taken her by surprise, but she'd never imagined anything had really come of the brief conversation they had.

"You know how those newspaper reporters exaggerate things," she told Chicky. "I just did my job."

Chicky wasn't buying. "Sure you did." She turned to Rafe teasingly. "And your taste is certainly improving."

"Oh," he said watching Carly, "it hasn't changed that much over the years."

Heat shot through Carly at his look.

"So," Chicky went on, "tell me you're stayin'. We could use a good lawyer in this town. One who didn't slither out from under some rock."

"Actually…" Carly began.

"Carly's got a job waiting for her in Cincinnati," Rafe put in. "A partnership."

Chicky didn't try to hide her disappointment, and she and Rafe exchanged some uninterpretable look. "Well, that's a shame. A pure shame. I—I should say congratulations. I was just hopin' you might've found somethin' here to keep you." Her gaze slid back to Rafe.

Oh, she'd found something, Carly thought, toying with the straw in her soda. "I love this place," she said, staring at her drink. "I always have."

"Well, that's—" Chicky began.

Rafe touched Evan's shoulder and said, "Evan, this is

Ms. Green, an old friend of mine. Chicky, I'd like you to meet Evan. My son.''

Chicky didn't appear to be the sort of woman who was easy to surprise, but shock flickered across her expression. ''Well, dust my jingle bobs.'' She held out her hand formally to Evan. ''It's a real pleasure to meet you, Evan. A *real* pleasure.''

Evan shook her hand gravely. ''You've got pretty hair.'' He grinned at her blush. His smile had never reminded Carly more of Rafe's than it did now. Not even Chicky could miss it.

''I can see you've inherited your daddy's wicked charm. You know, he can charm those freckles right off your nose—'' she slid a meaningful look to Rafe ''—*if* he puts his mind to it.''

''Now, Chicky,'' Rafe drawled mildly, ''you know I reserve all my charm for you.''

''That's your first mistake, Rafe Kellard,'' she said, jabbing him in the chest with her finger. ''Carly, don't be a stranger. Rafe's friends are special to me. If you ever need anything, you just holler, you hear?''

''Thanks, Chicky.'' When Carly took the other woman's hand, she couldn't miss the covert squeeze of emphasis. ''I will.''

''Evan. You come see me, you hear? I keep a candy jar full of licorice just for boys like you.''

Evan's face lit up and Chicky turned to Rafe. ''And you—I'll talk to *you* later.''

Properly chastened, Rafe watched Chicky's regal exit with resignation. First Gus, now Chicky. As if he didn't have enough to worry about, without battling the town's matchmakers. Chicky practically ran the whole damn town, knew everybody and everything about them. It was killing her that she didn't know what was going on with him and Carly.

But more than that, he knew that Chicky really cared about him and that she held out a faint hope that someday he'd find someone to settle down with. Well, she'd be waiting until the cows came home for that, he thought, because Carly Jamison was already as good as gone.

Chapter 11

Smoke from the branding fire curled lazily against the indigo sky and mingled with the sharp tang of singed hair and the baleful lowing of cattle. From the edge of the fire, Rafe looked out over the operation with a bittersweet sense of pride, wondering if this was the last time he'd be branding. They'd been at it all morning, and they were nearly done with the first batch of spring calves.

In the distance, he saw Gus, riding Rafe's cutting horse, Bogus, and Evan—aboard Tampico—cutting calves from the herd. Macky was hard at their heels, doing his part as the cow dog he thought he was.

Evan, whom Rafe had outfitted in miniature leather chaps and a serious hat, looked the part, but had yet to successfully drop his loop over a calf. He seemed content, however, to help Gus as one of the men. They'd gone over the rules a dozen times this morning before riding out: no wandering off, no getting near the irons and no arguing about the rules. Carly had stayed behind, giving her best impression of calm.

Rafe's thoughts had drifted to her this morning more often than he wanted to admit. He'd recalled the way she looked last night at J.J.'s, her silvery-blond hair ruffled by the evening breeze, every bit the lady he knew she was. They'd looked like a family, and for a few moments, he'd indulged himself in what-if fantasies. What if she wanted to stay? What if his ranch was solid? What if nine years hadn't come between them?

But none of that mattered. Reality was what mattered. His truth was right here on this ranch—struggling to make ends meet and holding all the fragile strands together. It was what he was—who he was. But his truth and Carly's were worlds apart. If he was going to fail, he couldn't do it in front of Carly. He knew that much about himself. She meant too much to him for him to let that happen.

Rafe had hired three extra hands for the day of branding. All of them worked together like an efficient machine— roping calves, doping wounds, castrating bulls and marking them with the Rocking K brand.

Pedro's savvy around branding irons was legendary, and he rarely botched a branding. With the steady hand of an artist, he burned the hide just enough to peel, but not sear—leaving a clear, readable brand.

Ben Yeager, one of the men Rafe had hired, expertly cropped the ears of each calf to match its mother's crop. And the other two, Sam Thurston and Cal Baker, stretched the calf out by its legs. After Rafe had vaccinated the calf and doped it for screwworms, Cal removed his knee from the neck of the poor, put-upon creature and unheeled it. It bolted upright, bawling for its mama.

Rafe looked up to find Gus and Evan riding toward him, a cloud of dust swirling in their wake. Gus handed over the calf to Ben.

"Drop-split the right, and over-slope-split the left," he called, specifying the earmarks.

Ben repeated it, then threw the calf to the ground, and he and Cal stretched it out for Pedro.

"Doesn't it hurt 'em?" Evan asked Rafe as he pulled up beside him.

"A little," he said honestly, "but it also protects them. They'd be easy prey for rustlers and disease if we didn't do this."

Even after a morning of it, the city boy in Evan still flinched as he watched Pedro do his job. He was working hard to be one of the men. But Rafe knew the adjustment had only just begun. Still, it pleased him immensely that Evan wanted to fit in.

Gus dismounted nearby as Rafe filled a syringe with vaccine. The older man groaned as his feet hit the dirt. "Lordy, these bones are gettin' too old for this type of work."

"That'll be the day." Rafe sent liquid squirting out of the tip of the needle. "Couldn't have anything to do with it being close to noon, or that food basket Laurie sent over for the crew, could it?"

Gus's eyebrows went up innocently. "Basket?"

Evan laughed. "*You* know, the one you were sniffing earlier in the back of Rafe's truck."

Gus reddened with a grin. "Oh, you mean *that* basket! Well, come to think of it, my stomach is nearly ticklin' my backbone. Whattaya say we break for some grub? I'll even do the fixin'."

Cal released the calf Rafe had just injected. He straightened. "I say, since that's the last calf in this group, let's eat."

They did so standing around the tail of Rafe's pickup, feasting on gourmet sandwiches Laurie had concocted of turkey, roasted peppers and some kind of unbelievably good sauce. As always when Laurie packed a basket, she'd included a pie—this time cherry. Rafe knew she was experimenting with new recipes for her catering business and this basket was, in a way, test marketing. Nobody complained about their guinea-pig status, least of all, Gus.

Half an hour later, they were mounted and ready to herd up a new bunch of calves into the makeshift pen. Gus stayed behind to clean up, while Rafe took Bogus and followed the others toward the scattered herd.

The land here swelled and dipped in ancient furrows born of the fisting San Juans millions of years ago. Arroyos, cut from long-ago streams, angled sharply across the landscape, then vanished under a canopy of fragrant chaparral and sage, whose shade the cattle sought out.

It was only at times like this, that Rafe begrudged them that small comfort, because it made rounding up calves twice as difficult. But his men were experienced, and the whole procedure made Macky feel wildly self-important.

They'd been working for nearly a half hour when Rafe dropped his rope around a cow's horns, enticing her from a thicket of chaparral. Her calf, like the others, followed unsuspectingly. Lost in thought, Rafe made his way to the summit of the arroyo.

Once there, he spotted Ben a few dozen feet away, hauling his own find toward the branding corral. In the distance, he could see Cal and Pedro heading for the rapidly filling pen.

It took a moment to notice what was missing from this picture.

Evan.

It struck him like a sickening jolt of cold that the boy was nowhere in sight and that Rafe had seen him last right before he headed down into the arroyo. He'd been thinking about Carly and the ranch and everything else but what he was supposed to be thinking about.

Panic edged through him as he searched the horizon.

Nothing.

"Evan!" he shouted, cupping his hands around his mouth.

Nothing.

He dropped his rope and kicked Bogus toward the pen at a lope. He pulled up sharply near the truck.

"Where's Evan?" he shouted at Gus.

Gus's hand stopped halfway to the syringe bottle he was reaching for. "I thought he was with you." The same awful dread crept into Gus's expression. There were a hundred places for a boy to get lost out here. A hundred places to fall.

"Dammit!" Rafe swore. "He was right there. I lost track of him somehow." *How could he have lost him?*

Cal edged his horse toward them. "I thought I saw him go that way," he said, pointing west. "I thought he was followin' you, Rafe."

The direction he was pointing was fifty yards beyond the arroyo Rafe had descended into.

"Ben, Cal, Pedro!" he shouted. "Drop what you're doing and spread out. He can't be far. I saw him not fifteen minutes ago. But he doesn't know this country."

Pedro mounted up, yanked his rifle from the boot of his saddle and checked the load. Rafe watched him, feeling his chest go tight.

Pedro slid a dark look over at him. "*El gato*. The cat—he is still out here somewhere, *jefe*."

The weight of the situation descended on Rafe full force. The cat. Of course. The goddamn cat who'd been slaughtering his livestock like they were sitting ducks at a carnival.

He tore his own rifle from his boot and spurred Bogus back in the direction from which he'd come. What were the odds of that cat coming down here now, in daylight?

The answer sent a chill down his spine. The last two calves he found had still been warm by three in the afternoon.

The thought of telling Carly he'd lost her son flashed through his mind with sickening dread. What had he been thinking, losing track of Evan that way? What the hell kind of father misplaced his son in the middle of a field?

He pulled up short, listening. He heard nothing but the gentle breeze pushing the air to the east, and the sound of the nearby cows chewing their cuds.

He cupped his hands around his mouth and shouted Evan's name.

Evan had gone farther than he intended. It was the sound of the calf bawling that had drawn him here, in this thicket of chaparral and some thorny bush that kept plucking at his new leather chaps. In fact, he'd thought Rafe was right behind him, but when he turned around, he couldn't see him anywhere. Besides, he was so close to the cow, he didn't think Rafe would mind, once he saw how he'd rescued it from the tangle it was caught in.

After all, Evan reasoned, he hadn't been able to rope a single cow all morning. He was afraid Rafe might be sorry he'd brought him if he didn't do something to help the roundup.

He ran a hand down the hide of the bawling calf. "It's okay," he told it, plucking gingerly at the nasty prickered branch that had wound around its legs and back. "I'll get you out of here. Rafe'll be so proud of me, maybe he won't even brand you. Maybe," he said, ripping the branch aside with the toe of his boot, "he'll let me take you home and put you in the barn. I could call you—"

Evan frowned at the prickly tug on his back. The branch he'd just released from the calf had caught him across the flannel of his shirt and held tight. He twisted, trying to untangle himself, but only managed to make it worse. Another bit at the back of his jeans.

"Ow!" Evan bit out in frustration. But the more he struggled, the worse it got. Humiliation stung his eyes. He was stuck, just like the stupid cow! He'd *never* be a cowboy at this rate.

Calf and boy stared at one another in unique empathy.

The sound of a breaking branch drew Evan's gaze behind him. He couldn't see anything, but bushes. "Rafe?" he called, half hoping it wasn't, so that he couldn't see what a mess he'd made of things.

No one answered, but Tampico shied and took off running past him, down the gulch.

"Hey!" he called after him. "Where're you going, you stupid horse? You can't just leave me here!"

The sound came again.

"Gus?"

A low rumbling sound, like an L.A. car with a bad engine, came from just beyond the brush. Evan's mouth went dry.

"P-Pedro?" The word was barely a whisper.

The huge cat appeared like a ghost through the curtain of green twenty-five feet away. Evan's mouth fell open, and his eyes went round. He tried to scream, but no sound came out. He tugged at his trapped shirt, trying to rip it from the thorns without taking his eyes off the cat, but it was hopelessly tangled. His fingers fumbled stiffly for the buttons on the front of his shirt.

Pop went the first. Then the second. He ripped off the third and fourth as the cat started toward him. "N-nice kitty," he whispered hoarsely as he yanked his hands out of the sleeves. "Go away. G-go away!"

The cat snarled loudly and started for Evan at the same moment he screamed and bolted for the exit to the canyon. Pumping his legs as hard as he could, he waited for the feel of the sharp claws digging into his back.

What he heard was a gunshot, so close it made his ears ache, and the heavy thud of something falling behind him.

Breathing hard, Evan kept running blindly through the thicket. Branches slapped at him, and tore at his bare skin, but he didn't stop until he heard Rafe's voice close behind him.

"Evan!" On foot, Rafe plunged through the underbrush toward him, throwing his rifle aside to kneel down and grab him hard in his arms. Evan pressed his face against Rafe's shirt and clung tight. He felt like a baby, crying the way he was.

"Oh, God, Evan—oh, my God" was all Rafe could say. Evan could feel him shaking and smell the sharp tang of his sweat.

"I'm s-sorry," he cried into Rafe's shirt. "I w-was trying t-to help that c-calf, and—"

Rafe grabbed his shoulders and pushed him back to look at him. His face was angry and red. "Do you realize you almost got yourself killed?" he practically shouted.

Evan stared at him in horror.

"If I hadn't found you...if I hadn't gotten here in time—"

"I'm s-sorry, R-Rafe."

"I *told* you not to wander off, didn't I? Didn't I tell you to always keep me in sight? That was the rule, Evan. What were you thinking, going off like that on your own?"

"I—"

Pedro crashed through the bushes behind Rafe, holding his rifle out straight. He stopped dead at the sight of Evan and Rafe. Gus came next. When he saw Evan, he braced his hands on his knees and bent over, breathing hard.

Evan felt sick to his stomach. Rafe was still looking at him, waiting for an answer. But he couldn't talk. Instead, he squirmed away from Rafe's angry hands and ran past Gus.

"Evan!" Rafe called, but he was gone.

"I'll get him," Gus said.

Rafe covered his face with his hand. "Take him home, Gus. Take him back to the ranch in the truck."

"Sure. He's gonna be fine, Rafe." He looked down at the dead cat. "Thank God you got here in time."

Rafe couldn't answer. He kept thinking about two hundred pounds of claw, muscle and fur chasing Evan down like he was a rabbit. He squeezed his eyes shut. Sweet Jesus. What if—?

Ten feet back, the calf—still entangled in the wire— bawled miserably. Rafe started automatically toward it, but Pedro stopped him with a hand on his shoulder.

"*Jefe.* I'll do it. And then I will look for Tampico, *sí?* He's run off somewhere."

Rafe nodded and got to his feet. His knees were shaking, and his legs felt like gelatin.

Pedro didn't leave. "It was God's will that you found him," he said, in an attempt at comfort. "It was not his day to die, no?"

Rafe didn't feel comforted as he bent down and picked up his rifle. Leaving Pedro behind him, he forced his legs to move in the direction of the camp. He was to blame for this. Not God. Not Evan. The boy had been his responsibility, and he'd failed him. What had he been thinking about? Carly...the ranch...his own bloody future?

And had he thought the boy wasn't scared enough, that he had to yell at him? He remembered the look of betrayal on Evan's face. Why hadn't he just held him? Why hadn't he been able to say that if he lost him it would have killed him, too?

His own father's drunken voice rang in his ears: What's the matter with you, boy? You're just like your mama. Never be no good to nobody. You're too damned selfish!

Well, what the hell? he thought grimly. His old man had been right about something after all.

He caught Bogus's reins and shoved his rifle back in its boot. Mounting up, he pointed the horse toward the house and kicked it into a full, lathering gallop.

Carly was waiting on the porch when Rafe and Bogus returned. For the past half mile, she'd watched him slow the animal to a walk to cool it down. By the time he reached the yard, she could see it was going to be bad. For once, she was grateful to have the crutches for support. Her legs were still shaking.

Rafe dismounted and tied the horse to the hitching rail near the house. He started up the steps, stopping when he'd reached her eye level, his face grim. "Carly, I'm…I'm so sorry."

"Rafe—"

His voice was haunted. "I don't know how the hell it happened. One minute he was right there, and the next—"

"I know." Her voice quivered with emotion she had yet to get under control.

"Is he okay?"

"He's inside resting. He'll be okay."

Rafe squeezed his eyes shut. "I'd give anything if I could take that moment back. You trusted me with him, and what did I do? I—"

"You saved his life," she finished.

His eyes, clouded by self-recrimination, lifted to hers. "I almost got him killed."

"You told him to stay with you. Over and over. I heard you."

Rafe turned on his heel and sent a fist crashing into the porch upright. "He's eight, Carly. It was my job to watch him. I was going after a cow and, hell, I don't know…I forgot about him. I was thinking about a million other things—the ranch, the loan…you."

"Rafe, don't do this to yourself," she said, touching his shoulder. He flinched and moved away, unwilling to allow her to comfort him.

"It was my fault, Carly, not his. Mine. I told you I'd screw up—I warned you I'd make a lousy father."

"Do you think you're the first father to lose track of his son? Do you think Evan's the first boy to disobey a direct order? Or that I haven't messed up now and then as a mother? Rafe, I could say the same about the car accident.

I put his life in jeopardy driving through that storm. He could have been killed. We both could have. If only I'd confirmed those reservations, or if I'd pulled into the far lane..."

She rubbed a hand across her forehead. "What I'm trying to say is that life is unpredictable. You saved him. If you hadn't been there to shoot that cat— God, I don't even want to think—"

"That's just it, Carly. I knew that cat was out there. He's been harassing my cattle for weeks, now. I *never* should have taken Evan out on that range and risked his life. I just— It never occurred to me that..." He broke off, turning away from her.

Fresh tears stung her eyes. She knew only too well what he was feeling. Gus's retelling of the incident had left her shaken to the core. She could have blamed Rafe, but she chose not to, because she knew he'd die before he'd intentionally let anything happen to Evan. And seeing him this way only confirmed that.

"They say what doesn't destroy us, makes us stronger," she told him. "Evan learned a valuable lesson out there today. Thank God you were there to see that he survived it."

Rafe shook his head, unconsolable. "And I yelled at him. Jeez, there he was, shaking like a leaf, and what do I do? You should've seen the look on his face."

She grabbed his arm and forced him to look at her. "Gus told me everything, Rafe. In your shoes, I would have reacted the same way. He was wrong to wander off like that. It almost cost him his life. He's never faced such a consequence before. It shook him up. Badly. And yes," she admitted, "I'm sorry it happened. And I know you are, too. I wish we could protect Evan from all the bad things that happen in the world. But short of keeping him in a plastic bubble for life, that's just not possible. Rafe, *look* at me."

Reluctantly he did.

"Thank you." She wrapped her arms around his neck and held him tight. "Thank you for being there and saving his life."

He buried his face in her hair, and inhaled deeply. "Don't," he murmured. "Don't thank me."

She nodded against his ear. "It's over." But she knew it wasn't. Rafe's confidence as a father was too fresh, too raw, to absorb this sort of a blow. Nothing she could say would repair it. It would take Evan to heal it.

"Why don't you go inside? He's waiting for you."

Rafe nodded and pulled away from Carly, knowing that if he didn't, he'd do something he regretted—like kiss her, or drag her to his room and bury himself inside her until the gnawing fear disappeared.

Instead, he left her standing alone on the porch, knowing that there were more important needs to be met than his own.

Inside, Carly had built a fire in the river-rock fireplace. The scent of piñon eased him as he moved toward the small boy curled up on the couch watching a cartoon.

He'd been crying. His face was red and his nose looked like Rudolph's. Through a sweep of lashes, he looked up at Rafe, wary as a wolf cub in a bear's den. Strange, Rafe thought, but it was like looking at a mirror image of himself.

"I'm sorry, Rafe," he said in a small voice, tears of shame reforming in his eyes.

"Me too."

"I didn't mean to go off like that. I was only tryin' to help that calf."

The cushions gave as Rafe sat down beside Evan. "I know. I didn't mean to yell at you like I did. I was just real…scared."

"*You* were?"

Rafe let out a breath of laughter, and he bent his head

down toward Evan. "Yeah, see the gray hairs you just gave me?"

Evan's mouth quivered at the corners. "I don't see any gray hairs."

"Just wait. You will." Regarding his son with a shake of his head, Rafe explained, "It's my job to protect you Evan, 'cause I'm your dad. When I yelled at you, it was only because I was so relieved that you were okay. If anything had happened to you, Ev...I—"

Evan blinked at the moisture in his eyes. "Then you—you still want to be my dad?"

A knot fisted in Rafe's throat. "Are you kidding? C'mere, son," he said, and welcomed his boy into his embrace.

The next few days slid by too quickly for Carly. The branding took another day, and with the big cat gone, Rafe allowed Evan a second chance at the job. He shone brightly, following every rule to the letter. He even managed to rope a cow. When the two of them came back from the long day's work, Evan couldn't stop talking until Carly had heard more than she ever wanted to know about the process of branding, marking and castrating cattle.

But it was the look on Rafe's face that really touched her. Pride, love—that indefinable emotion a parent feels when he looks at his child. The fire he and Evan had walked through had forged a bond between them that might otherwise have taken years to build. Whatever obstacles lay before them, Carly knew that somehow they'd surmount them—together.

Rafe made no attempt to hide the fact that he was still practicing on Red-Eye. Neither of them mentioned the nasty bruise that appeared on his cheek, or the way his limp grew more pronounced as the days passed. The topic was off-limits to Carly.

* * *

She thought that the sound of wind buffeting the windows of her room and whistling into the cracks of the house had awakened her. But as she sat up straight in bed, a dark figure loomed over her.

A scream hovered in her throat, but Rafe's urgent whisper quickly cut off the sound. "Shhhh, Carly, it's me."

She blinked in the darkness and, from the smell, dimly wondered if a horse had wandered into her room with him. She reached for the lamp switch and nearly gasped when she saw him. He was naked from the waist up, his face and torso were smudged with dirt and blood, his tousled hair was littered with straw. Good Lord! "Rafe, wha—?"

"I need your help. The mare's foaling. She's having trouble."

Carly rubbed her eyes. "Shouldn't you call the vet?"

"Phone lines are down somewhere with this wind. Pedro and Gus are gone for the night. Will you help me?"

"Yes," she replied without hesitation.

"Get dressed. I'll meet you in the barn."

Carly found him there a few minutes later, leaning over the prostrate mare. She wasn't moving, but Carly could see contractions rippling her belly, and the odd, faraway look of hopelessness in her huge brown eyes.

Setting aside her crutches, Carly knelt down near her head, stroking her gently. Her breathing was labored and wheezing. "How long has she been like this?"

"I checked her at ten and she was on her feet," he said. "Something told me to come out here again at one, and she was on her side."

Carly glanced at her watch. It was 3:45 a.m. "Is that long for a horse?"

"When the foal is turned wrong, it is," he answered plunging his arm into a bucket filled with a strong-smelling antiseptic. Outside, the wind battered the side of the barn, making it moan.

"I've been trying to turn it for the last two hours with

no luck. I need an extra hand, or I'm gonna lose both of them.''

"Tell me what to do."

Rafe stretched out behind the mare. "It's a back presentation, but the foal's head's pulled around. It'll break the mother's pelvis if I can't get the head rotated back into position." He slipped the noose of a small rope around the fingers of his left hand and gently eased it into the mare's birth canal. "I've got to—" he gasped with exertion "—loop it around the foal's jaw...and..." A contraction tugged at the mare's belly, and Rafe winced as his arm took the full force of it. Every muscle in his body was straining.

"I've gotta pull the head around. When I get it...you take the end of this rope and—"

Rafe gasped, mouth open in concentration as he searched for the small jaw of the foal. Carly watched helplessly, wishing there was something more she could do.

"Dammit," he muttered. "I can't...get... C'mon, mama, let me have her—"

Carly lowered herself to the straw behind him and took her position, in case he managed to get the rope where he wanted it. It seemed like hours before he did, though only a few more minutes passed.

"Okay—" he gasped. "Now...tug gently...gentle pressure on that rope as I...pull the head around."

She pulled back firmly and felt the rope give.

"Keep going...keep going— *Stop!*" Rafe struggled some more to slip the rope around behind the foal's ears before he removed his arm and joined Carly on the rope. Breathing like a spent marathoner, Rafe watched the foal's muzzle, eyes and ears appear. The rest of the foal came easily, sliding onto the blood-spotted straw like a slick package.

It was a perfect little filly, all legs and blazes and stubby tail covered with the membrane of birth. But it took only moments for Rafe to realize that it lay still and glassy-eyed, staring sightlessly at the barn wall. The wind outside howled, and Carly's heart stuttered to a stop. It couldn't be dead. Not after all this!

"Rafe! She's not breathing!"

He cleared the mucous from the foal's nose and mouth and blew into its nostrils hard. Two quick pumps on her chest, and the foal jerked to life on an inhalation. The foal's long, spindly legs moved in the hay, and she blinked up at Rafe. Then, because the mare made no movement toward her baby, he dragged her up toward its mother's muzzle.

The spent mare actually lifted her head at the scent of the baby and sniffed it with curiosity. Then, with long, instinctive strokes from her tongue, she massaged the newborn foal as nature intended.

Rafe sat back on his heels, still breathing hard. The smile of victory he sent Carly betrayed none of his exhaustion.

Carly threw her head back and laughed in exhilaration. Rafe joined her, falling over in the straw and sprawling across it. Carly fell beside him and rolled toward him, still buzzing and enthralled by what they'd just done together.

She leaned on her elbows in the straw beside him. "You were great."

"Damn, I *was* good, wasn't I?" He chuckled with feigned machismo.

"Incredible," she agreed. "How did you know how to do that?"

Rafe sighed. "Been around horses my whole life. I've watched a few of these. I got lucky. I almost couldn't hook that jaw."

"But you did." Her voice was awe-filled. "You're amazing."

He slid a look at her and grinned. "I couldn't have done it without you. Thanks for not getting squeamish on me."

"Squeamish? Humph." She chuckled. "I've never been accused of that. And I might remind you that I've been through this myself," she reminded him. "So I did have some empathy for the poor mare."

Rafe's gaze drifted over her face lazily, as if, one by one, he were memorizing each feature. "I hope," he murmured, "you had an easier time of it than she did."

But of course, he wouldn't know that, Carly thought. He'd missed the birth of his son. She swallowed hard, knowing that was another thing she could never give back to him. She forced a playful grin. "Compared to this one? Evan was a walk in the park. Well, maybe not a walk. A jog."

He grinned.

"Or a full-out sprint." She sighed. "Anyway, my doctor said I was 'built for babies.'"

His eyes, as deep a blue as the sky, probed into hers. "Why didn't you have more?"

She looked down at the straw. "It just...never happened."

"You didn't try?" he asked, still watching her closely.

"We didn't *not* try," she hedged, feeling uncomfortable with the whole topic. "It's just that I never...conceived."

Rafe's mouth lifted in a tight smile, and he lurched to his feet. "God, I'm a mess." He headed for the bucket filled with soap and water and cleaned the muck of the ordeal off him. When he'd finished toweling himself off, he reached a hand down to Carly and dragged her to her feet.

Momentum carried her into his naked torso, and she stopped herself with her palms against his chest. For a moment, neither of them moved. Carly's heart thudded in her ears so loudly, she wondered if he could hear it. Beneath her palm, she could feel his heart pounding, too. His gaze drifted from her eyes down to her mouth and back again.

She returned the favor. "Hey, you clean up real good, Kellard."

"Yeah?" His amused gaze locked with hers.

"Yeah," she said, making no effort to disengage her hips from his. She waggled one eyebrow. "Say, did I ever tell you about my veterinarian fantasy?"

"Oh-oh," he said.

"Mmmm... See, there's a barn involved. And hay. Lots of hay."

Rafe eyes darkened as she ran a finger down his bare torso. "Aha. And in this fantasy, who are *you*?"

"Another veterinarian, of course." She laughed and raised up on her toes and kissed him fully on the mouth, threading her fingers behind his neck and pulling him toward her.

Balance lost, they shrieked with laughter as they fell atop one another on a soft pile of clean straw there in the birthing stall. They rolled over, locked in a mirthful, lustful kiss that turned from playful to hungry in a heartbeat. Rafe's tongue demanded reply as the kiss deepened and shifted in intent. Carly answered willingly, melting into him like heated candle dip, aching for this. How she'd missed the feel of his mouth on hers—his hands against her skin.

He ripped aside her opened pea coat and his hand found her breast. Carly's head fell back, and she arched into his touch. Through the fabric of her blouse, his thumb raked over her aroused nipple. His mouth left hers and trailed down her throat.

Then, he stopped.

Breathing hard, Rafe lifted his head. Carly did the same, a question in her eyes.

"This," he said, pulling the edges of her coat together, "is not a good idea, Carly."

Her whole body was on fire. "Why not?"

He swallowed thickly. "I think you know why."

"What are you afraid of?"

He shook his head, silent.

"Me? Are you afraid of me? The future? What?"

He slid his hands down her arms, breaking her hold on him. "It's not fear. It's common sense. I—I can't do this now." He sat up, and she followed.

"This? You mean *us?*" A shaking came from somewhere deep inside her, from that place of hopelessness she wouldn't allow to steer her life. "Do you have a timetable for it, Rafe? Because if you do, I'd really be interested in knowing what it is. I mean, I almost died a couple of weeks ago in an accident that definitely wasn't on *my* schedule, and you never know when something like that might come up again suddenly."

He looked away and closed his eyes, obviously shaken by her words.

"Look at me, Rafe, and tell me that what just happened between us—what happened the other night—was just about sex. Go on," she dared him.

"In three days, you're leaving—"

"What if I wasn't?"

Rafe's mouth fell open, but no sound came out.

"What if I stayed here instead?"

The wind howled outside, rattling the barn. "What are you talking about? You've got a job waiting. A partnership…"

"Answer my question."

"It's not a fair question. It's not even an accurate one."

"What do you mean?" she asked, confused.

"I mean, in a week, a month, maybe even a year, you'll be climbing the walls out of boredom. You'll grow to resent me for keeping you from what you love—"

"Dammit, Rafe, you're—"

"And when I lose this place, which I'm about to do, then what? You and Evan and I will move into a little apartment in town somewhere?"

"Do you think that matters to me?"

"It matters to me!" he shouted, shoving to his feet and stalking angrily to the stall door. He stopped and hung his head, his fist curling against the wood. "It matters to me."

She regarded him quietly. "You think you know me, but you don't. What gives you the right to decide for me what I want or need? It was you who decided I was better off without you nine years ago. You who decided that I could never integrate my life with yours and be happy. So you stepped aside, didn't you?"

"And I was right," he said.

Shock filtered through her. He'd actually admitted it. "You were wrong then, and you're wrong now," she said, her voice shaking. "I love you, Rafe."

Rafe froze at her words.

"Did you hear me?" she pressed. "There, I said it. No more taboos, or unspoken subjects. I *love* you. I've loved you for half of my life, it seems. And I know you better than anyone. Do you think I can't see what you're doing here?"

"I'm trying to be honest with you," he said tightly, reaching for the shirt he'd left hanging over the stall.

She shook her head. "That kiss just now—*that* was honest. Can you look me in the eye, Rafe, and tell me it meant nothing to you? That I mean nothing to you?"

He turned sharply and met her gaze. "Do you think I don't wish things could have been different with us? That I don't lie awake nights wishing you were there beside me? Or that nine years of my life hadn't just slipped by me unnoticed as my only son grew up under some other man's roof? But there are things that aren't meant to be, Carly. The timing's always been all wrong for us. It still is."

"*Timing?* Love isn't about timing, Rafe. Timing is how long you cook a turkey...or by how much you missed a bus. Nothing is ever perfect. If it were, this mare would have picked 3:00 p.m. instead of the middle of the night to foal. And that drunk who hit me would have stayed for another cup of coffee instead of skidding into me in the dark. And you and I wouldn't be standing here wondering why you're pushing me away.''

He raked a hand through his hair and slid his arms into the sleeves of his shirt. Fastening the buttons one by one, he shook his head. ''What do you want from me, Carly?''

She let out a long, shaky sigh. ''Nothing you're not willing to give.'' Reaching for her crutches, she eased up out of the straw. ''If you really believe that bad timing is what's kept us apart all these years, then you're welcome to your theory.'' She shrugged, disgusted, angry. ''Whatever makes it easier, Rafe.''

He grabbed her shoulders as she turned away and pulled her to him, his mouth angry, his eyes full of the frustration that crackled in the air between them. ''Nothing about this is easy, dammit. *Nothing.*''

Crushing her to him, he dropped his mouth down on hers in a savage kiss that said everything he could not. His lips slanted against hers devouringly, demanding to be met. His hot tongue plumbed her mouth, and angrily she answered him in kind. Because, though he kissed her until her knees went weak with wanting and his lips softened against hers, they both knew the truth—that this would change nothing. This unvarnished moment between them was simply another in a long string of goodbyes.

She gasped when he shoved her away to arm's length and scoured her face with a look that sent shivers down her spine. Breathing hard, his voice a raspy whisper, he said, ''Never try to tell me what I feel, Carly. You'd be wrong.''

And with that, he was gone.

Chapter 12

In Monday's mail, a packet arrived addressed to Carly from the law firm of Maynard, Barnes and Griffith. The envelope was contract-size and thick. It disappeared, unopened, into Carly's possession soon after, and Rafe tried to put it from his mind. He also tried to block out the phone call that came shortly afterward for her, the one she took in the other room.

By twelve, he was sitting in the outer room of the doctor's office, listening to the whine of the saw removing Carly's bulky cast for the slimmer walking cast that would replace it.

Even that sounded final to him, as if her cast were the last flimsy piece holding them together and when it was removed, even that excuse was gone. He stuck a finger under the knot of his tie and yanked, feeling like he was being slowly strangled.

She'd called for a truce as they drove into town today. "Let's just be together today," she'd said, "with no past and no tomorrow. We won't talk about us, or who's to

blame for what. We'll just—be." He'd agreed to it—in
theory—but that didn't stop his brain from working on
overdrive. It seemed that all he could think about was the
future and what it would be like without her and
Evan...and about the appointment he had in exactly forty-
five minutes.

"How's it feel?" he asked as Carly walked tentatively
out of the doctor's office, using her crutches more for balance than for support.

"A little odd to be on all twos again," she admitted.
"But great. He said I'm healing faster than he thought I
would."

"Terrific," he said, forcing a smile.

She tried for one, too. "Yeah."

"Hungry?"

"Starved."

He held open the outer door for her. "There's a place
just down the street."

They made small talk over lunch—stuck to safe topics,
like the weather and Evan's progress on Tampico. Rafe
did his damnedest to keep his eyes off her, frankly afraid
that she'd glimpse the growing panic in his if he didn't.
His heartbeat slammed against his chest as the minutes
passed and he glanced at his watch repeatedly.

"Hot date?" she asked casually over the rim of her
coffee cup. He looked up from his watch guiltily, and she
explained, "You don't usually wear a tie to town."

"Ah," he said, adjusting the knot. "No. Appointment."
He pushed his chair back and stood. "You okay here for
a couple of minutes?"

"Sure," she said, sounding puzzled. "I'm fine. You go
on."

"I'll be right back. This won't take long."

Through the window, she watched him cross the street
and disappear behind a hedge of greenery. Whatever his
appointment, he looked as happy about it as a gladiator

facing Caesar's lions. For a few minutes, she sipped her coffee, staring out at the cobalt blue of the sky through the café window.

"Rafe shouldn't leave a pretty lady like you all alone," came a voice from the other side of her table. She looked up.

A good-looking cowboy with a charming dimple and pale hazel eyes stared down at her with a friendly grin. "Mel Stratton," he said, extending a hand to her. "I'm a friend of Rafe's."

"Oh," she said, taking his hand briefly. "Nice to meet you."

"Mind if I sit down?"

"Uh—"

"I don't bite. Promise."

She glanced out the window to see no sign of Rafe. Not that she should worry. Rafe had hardly noticed she was along for the ride today. "Sure," she told Mel. "Rafe will be back in a minute. You can say hello."

Mel's solitary dimple deepened as he took Rafe's chair. "You're Carly, right?"

"Right," she answered, wondering how he knew.

"Chicky Green told me all about you. She wasn't exaggerating."

Carly smiled, remembering the flamboyant redhead. "I only met her the other night. She's wonderful."

"She said you were a lawyer?"

"Yes. Criminal law. You said you're a friend of Rafe's?"

"An old friend. We used to compete against each other. That's kinda what I wanted to talk to you about. I was hopin' you might have some influence over him."

Shock settled over her. "Influence? *Me?*"

Mel folded his hands in front of him. "He's entering the Durango pro rodeo competition. I saw him turn in his entry fee on Saturday."

Carly felt the blood drain from her face. "I know he intended to ride. I didn't know he'd actually entered."

Mel frowned, staring out the window in the direction Rafe had gone. "He's in no shape to ride, Carly. Even if he was all in one piece—which he's not—he's been away from it too long. He knows that, too. I know it's none o' my business, but I can't just stand by without sayin' something. And he won't listen to me."

Carly sipped her coffee. "You're not alone. If you know Rafe, then you know how stubborn he can be."

"I just thought—knowin' that you're special to him— you might be able to talk him out of it."

Carly blushed. "Special? Who told you that?"

"Nobody had to tell me," Mel said, folding his arms in front of him and leaning on the table. "It's written all over his face."

She swallowed hard, wishing it was true. The only thing obvious to her was that Rafe couldn't wait to get on with his life and usher her back out. "I'm afraid you're mistaken, Mr. Stratton."

"It's Mel. And I don't think so."

"Be that as it may, nothing I've said so far has deterred him from riding. And I'm afraid nothing will."

"Well," Mel said, "if a lady like you can't sway him, nothin' can."

She set her coffee cup down carefully. "There may be one thing." Her enigmatic statement drew a puzzled stare from Mel, but before he could say anything, Rafe appeared behind him.

"Didn't take you long, did it, Mel?" he asked with a bite of sarcasm, reaching for Carly's crutches.

Mel shot to his feet with a guilty look. "Rafe! We were just talkin' about you."

Rafe's gaze swung to Carly, and he smiled tightly. "I bet you were."

Carly couldn't miss the grimness in his voice.

"Is…everything all right?" she asked.

"Just perfect," he snapped. "Ready to go?"

"Hey, Rafe," Mel said, slapping him on the shoulder. "I'm serious, man, we were just talkin'."

"Sure. Carly?"

Mel stared at his boots, thumbs tucked into the back of his jeans, while Carly slid the crutches under her arms.

When Rafe turned to go, Mel pressed a business card into her hand.

"Chicky asked me to say goodbye to you for her, too. Good luck to you," he said. "You'll need it."

"Thanks," she replied, ignoring Rafe's hostile glare. So much for truces. "Goodbye, Mel."

As they walked to Rafe's car, the silence between them was thick enough to cut. Rafe walked two strides ahead of her and waited with the truck door open until she caught up.

"You're wrong about Mel," she said as she climbed into the seat.

"Am I?"

Then it struck her. "You're *jealous*," she said, staring at him in surprise.

Rafe slammed the door and stomped to the other side. "I am *not* jealous," he said deliberately. "I just don't like a guy like Mel putting moves on you. He's a *cowboy*, Carly. Even you can see that."

"So are you," she retorted.

"My point exactly. You've got no business with a guy like that."

She didn't *even* want to go there. "He's worried about you, Rafe."

"Oh, that's rich." He let out a bark of laughter. "Is that what he told you?"

"Yes."

Rafe slammed the transmission into first and peeled down the street.

Carly hung on. "What's really wrong, Rafe? It's not Mel who's got you so upset."

His jaw tightened, and he gripped the wheel harder. "The last bank turned me down."

"Ohhh…" She felt her heart drop. "Rafe. I'm sorry."

"So were they. Sorry the drought's put me behind on profits. Sorry I spent most of what profit I did make drilling for water that wasn't there. Sorry my future is looking dim. Just…goddamn sorry."

She started to speak, but bit back what she was about to suggest. If she told him what she was considering, he'd flatly refuse. If she didn't tell him, she risked losing everything.

Carly stared at the road whizzing by, wondering how everything had gotten so out of control. The card Mel had pressed into her hand was still there. She uncurled her clenched fingers and looked at it. It held the name and address of a law office in Durango, Lindsey, Burkholt and Associates, Attorneys-at-Law. Below that, Chicky had handwritten her own number.

How curious, she thought, slipping it into her pocket. Why would Chicky send her a business card? And why through Mel Stratton?

Five miles out of town, a colorful roadside sign slid into view, with just enough time for her to read it. She chewed on her lower lip, thinking. It was an inspired idea, she decided, and it couldn't have come at a better time. He needed some fun, today of all days. Their time together was almost over. She owed him something for all he'd done for her—and she needed a memory to hold on to when she left.

"Hey," she said. "I'm having a scathingly brilliant idea."

He slid a wary look toward her. "Good, 'cause I'm fresh out."

"See that road up there to the right?"

He frowned. "Yeah? What about it?"

"Take it."

He looked at her as if she were crazy. "What?"

"Go on," she told him.

"I gotta get back," he said, gripping the wheel tighter.

"And you will, right after my scathingly brilliant idea. There! Turn there."

"You're crazy, you know that?" he said, sounding convinced, yet pulling the wheel to the right.

"I know." She leaned back with a satisfied grin. "But that's not a bad thing once in a while, you know?"

The road looked innocuous, like a gravel path to nowhere. Rafe followed it with obedient reluctance as it wound through swelling hills and a sharp walled canyon of deep red rock. Midafternoon sun played against the landscape, casting it in shades of lavender and rose and crisply defined shadow. Carly drummed her fingers against the door frame, praying that this direction was right. It was farther than she'd imagined.

"You know where you're going?" he asked ten minutes into the drive.

"This way," she said, pointing straight ahead.

He sent her a wry smile. "Funny. I want you to know that I'm only humoring you because I've never gone down this road before. And now you've got me curious. Where the heck are we going?"

She just smiled.

Gravel spit against the bottom of the truck as the canyon opened onto a grassy, rolling plain. It was as if someone had unfurled a rolled carpet through a doorway. Below, nestled in a flattened expanse of green, sat a small visitor's center and parking lot, looking completely out of place here in the middle of nowhere. To the left, like so many mushrooms sprouting from the grass, stood a handful of anchored hot-air balloons, their colorful tops tugged by the breeze. Three hundred feet up against a starkly blue sky, another was scudding along on a high breeze like a wind-blown leaf.

Rafe stepped on the brakes, and the truck skidded to a stop. "You gotta be kidding."

She shook her head, feeling like a kid at Christmas. "Aren't they wonderful?"

"You wanna go up in a balloon?" he said disbelievingly.

"Yes, and you're going with me."

His eyes narrowed with suspicion. "Oh—I don't know. I've never gone up in one of those things before."

Yes, this was exactly what he needed, she decided wickedly. A little adventure, a dash of romance, a guaranteed rush of adrenaline. Yes, he needed this in more ways than he knew. "You know what they say? There's a first time for everything. C'mon," she said. "It'll be fun. My treat."

The deluxe package included a private flight with a picnic lunch of bread, cheese, fruit and champagne. Neither of them had eaten much for lunch. After paying for the package by credit card, she turned to find Rafe staring at the balloons, as if half expecting them to fall over.

"You pick," she said, indicating the balloons. Four equally striking ones stood waiting for customers.

His grin told her he was starting to warm up to the idea. "This is a hijacking, you know that, don't you?"

"Absolutely." She threaded her arm playfully into his. "Everyone needs to be hijacked now and then, just to keep things in perspective."

He shook his head. "Perspective, huh? I kinda like the perspective from down here on the ground."

"Chicken," she taunted. "Bwawk-bwaawk-bwaa-awk—"

Rafe's eyes darkened at the challenge. "Chicken, huh?"

She tucked her hands under her armpits and flapped them, backing toward the balloons. "Bwaaawk-bwaaawk—"

"Oh, you're gonna regret that, Jamison," he warned starting toward her.

"Bwaaawk! Bwawk!!" Shrieking with laughter, she hobbled toward the balloons. He chased her down and wrestled her into his arms until she was completely helpless and flat up against him.

Their laughter faded slowly as Rafe's gaze traveled over her face with a smile like she hadn't seen on him in years. "Okay," he said, his mouth only inches away from hers. "I pick the cardinal."

She glanced up at the bird-shaped balloon behind them. "Good choice, cowboy. Any particular reason?"

"Yeah," he murmured. "You look great in red."

It was so much more than she'd expected. The exhilarating feeling of floating, unfettered by the confinement of a plane. They stood together, staring over the precipice of the rich woven basket that held them, listening to the intermittent hiss of the flame burner as they lifted into the sky. The air was cool and smelled sharply of the pines that lined the hillsides below.

The earth seemed to slip away as they rose steadily upward. Like a patchwork of green and brown and lavender, the landscape spread out below them, but everything lost its distinctness. It all seemed to flow together—the rocks, the grass, the hills—as if no one thing were more important than the rest.

A red-tailed hawk sailed near them in lazy circles against the impossibly blue sky. As the pilot quieted the flame burner, she and Rafe watched the majestic bird in awed silence.

They floated to the east, tumbling past the Durango and Silverton Narrow Gauge Railroad, where the steel tracks etched a path across the foothills and disappeared into the mountains.

Rafe pointed east to the sprawling range tucked under the San Juans. "There's my place." His words were low and filled with pride, yet tinged by sadness. They both knew how perilously close he was to losing it.

"It's so beautiful, Rafe. I can see why you love it here." She threaded her fingers through his and, to her surprise, he allowed her touch. "It'll work out. You'll see."

"You have more faith than I do," he said, surveying his cattle, which dotted the landscape below.

"How's it going with Red-Eye?" she asked, broaching the forbidden topic.

Surprised, he grinned and rolled a stiff shoulder. "I'm wearin' him down. Don't worry. I'll be fine."

She didn't want to think about what riding in the rodeo might do to him, or how a serious injury could steal him away for good this time. Perhaps she was just being over-protective. He was a grown man, after all. He knew what he wanted. But it was about more than the two of them now. Evan needed a father. More than that, he needed Rafe.

For a long time, they stood gazing at the world below from a hawk's vantage point. A companionable silence stretched between them. What they were sharing required no words.

"Hey, folks—" the pilot called from behind them. As one, they turned toward him, hands still linked, lazy smiles still lingering on their mouths. The pilot snapped a Polaroid of them against the backdrop of the cobalt sky, then handed it to them. "A little memento of the afternoon."

Together, Rafe and Carly watched as the photo swam into focus on the film. When it did, what they saw sent a ripple of awareness through them both. For there, unburdened for that millisecond by the future or the past or the gnawing reality that awaited them back on the ground, they looked…happy.

With his head tucked under the truck's hood, Gus stood fiddling with Rafe's starter, alternately revving the engine and cursing under his breath. Carly walked toward the truck, enjoying the feel of the morning sun as she composed her thoughts.

Rafe and Evan had left an hour ago on horseback, with a pair of fishing poles tied to their saddles. Rafe knew as well as Carly that their time was growing short. He had needed an excuse to spend time with Evan, and she had welcomed it. She had something to do this morning, and she needed time alone to do it.

"Hi, Gus," she called. Gus straightened in surprise, and whacked his head on the truck's hood.

"Ow!" he grumbled, rubbing the spot with his hand. He frowned at the offending metal. "Confound it!"

"Sorry, I didn't mean to startle you," she said, reaching the truck and handing him the glass of lemonade she'd made for him. "You okay?"

"I'd be more okay if I could make this danged starter work the way it's supposed to. I guess it's gonna need a new one."

As she offered him the lemonade, his gaze traveled over the smart-looking navy business suit she'd put on this morning. Wariness crept into his eyes. "Goin' someplace?"

"If I can beg a favor," she said hopefully. "I need wheels."

"Sure. I got my car. Gotta go to the parts store, anyway. Where to?"

"Not too far. But..." She hesitated.

"But what?" Gus asked with a curious frown.

"I'm afraid I'll have to ask you to keep my destination a secret for now." She bit her lower lip. "I don't want Rafe to know until—"

"Until—?" He rubbed his stubbled chin and narrowed his eyes.

"Later."

"Why do I get the feelin' you're up to somethin'?"

"Probably because…I am?" she suggested with a guilty lift of her eyebrows.

"Oh-oh."

"I know, I know." She squeezed her eyes shut. She'd agonized over this for days now, and with her decision made, she had to go through with it before she lost her nerve. "Promise me, Gus?"

Gus sighed with resignation. "Why don't you tell me what you've got in mind while I get my keys?"

Gus was quiet when she'd finished. Thoughtful. He heaved a long sigh and shook his head. "You're sure you wanna do this? We both know how he's gonna react."

"I know." *And it wasn't going to be pretty.*

"Not that I'm tryin' to talk you out of it, mind you…" Gus said, visibly torn.

"I know. And it's too late, anyway. I've made up my mind. I've gone over all the pros and cons. I know what I'm doing. But I owe him, Gus, and more importantly, I *love* him. And, frankly, I can't think of a better reason than that."

Gus swallowed visibly, emotion swimming in his eyes. "Neither can I, missy," he said flatly. "Neither can I."

Rafe held Evan's wrist in one hand and Evan's fingers on the thick fly line in the other, sweeping the rod forward and back, forward and back, in the three-stroke rhythm of fly fishing. In one easy motion, they pitched the line forward, and Rafe whispered, "Now!"

Evan released the line and watched it sail out over the wide creek pool. The fly landed with a satisfying pop on the water. A smile lit his eyes. "I did it!"

"You sure did, pard," Rafe told him, standing back proudly. "That was exactly it. Timing was perfect."

Evan grinned, wide-eyed with pride, and watched his fly drift lazily downstream. "Think we'll catch anything?"

"This is a good pool," Rafe told him, sending his own

line sailing over the water. "I rarely walk away empty-handed. But you've got to be prepared. Sometimes the fish just aren't in the mood to get caught. That's it, now reel it in and send it out over the water again. You don't want things getting stagnant."

"What's stagnant?" Evan asked, spinning his line in.

Rafe stared out over the water. *My life before you came,* he thought. But he said, "It's when things get too quiet, and the water's too still. Trout like their breakfast moving."

Evan giggled. "Rafe?"

"Hmm?"

"This is better than ocean fishing."

"Yeah? I've never been ocean fishing," he said.

Evan tilted his head in thought. "It's kinda...stagnant."

Rafe grinned and reached out to ruffle his hair. Macky, who was lying beside Evan, leaped up to chase after a passing butterfly. Evan giggled and watched him disappear into a thicket of bushes.

"Hey," Rafe said, "you hungry? Your mom packed us some sandwiches...candy bars...apples..."

Evan sent his line sailing halfway as far as Rafe's. "Nah. I wanna catch a fish. Hey, Rafe?"

"Yeah?"

"Can we do this again sometime?"

"You bet." Rafe regarded his boy standing in the morning sun. Evan's hair shone, and his freckles seemed to have multiplied in geometric proportion since he arrived. He even looked as if he'd grown. Such a short time. Rafe wondered what he'd look like the next time he saw him, and how much of his life he would have missed by then.

Rafe's heart gave a twist, and he focused on sending his line back out.

"Mom says we're leaving soon," Evan said, trying to sound casual.

Forward, back. Forward, back. "That's what I hear."

A long silence stretched between them. Finally, Evan said quietly, "I don't wanna go. I wanna stay here."

Rafe's fly faltered halfway through its cast and plopped sadly into the water. He looked at his son. "I wish you could."

"Why can't I? Can't you and my mom make up?"

If it were only that easy. "We're not fighting, Evan," Rafe said, shrugging the tension out of one shoulder.

"Then how come you act so funny with each other?" Evan asked. "Like the way she looks at you when you're not looking and then looks away really fast. And when you and her get near each other, you try not to bump into her or anything, like you're scared of touching her. Are you? 'Cause her broken leg isn't contagious or anything."

Rafe stifled a laugh and focused on the fly skipping across the water. He attributed his ignorance about the inherent intuitiveness of children to his lack of direct experience with them. But even that couldn't account for Evan's handle on the body language that was apparently doing their talking for them.

"When you're older, maybe you'll understand this better," he said carefully, although twenty-some years hadn't yet earned him insight. "Your mom and I...we...well, we want what's best for you. And what's probably best for you is to go to Ohio with your mom, where there are lots of kids and a great school. And your mom said she was going to get you a dog."

At that moment, Macky came bounding back out of the bushes, tongue lolling with exuberance as he nosed his silky head beneath Evan's hand for a rub.

"I don't want another dog," Evan told Rafe firmly. "I just want Macky."

Rafe had no answer for that. He watched the boy and the dog, knowing Macky would be just as lost as Evan when the boy left. Rafe tossed his line back out and stared at the sun glinting on the water. "You could take him."

"*What?*" Evan's head swiveled toward Rafe in surprise.

"You could take Macky with you, if you want."

"But…but he's your dog."

Macky's goofy expression slid expectantly back and forth between the two of them, as if he knew he was being talked about. "He's crazy about you, Ev. Hardly leaves your side."

Evan gazed at the water thoughtfully. Finally, he looked back at Rafe. "He'd miss it here, wouldn't he? If he went, I mean."

Rafe didn't reply, just reeled in his line.

Evan looked out over the vast countryside surrounding the stream. "He's used to running around here with all this space. Chasin' birds and stuff. He wouldn't like living in an apartment." His fingers disappeared in Macky's thick fur. "No, I have to come visit him, is all."

Rafe swallowed thickly—around the lump that had formed in his throat. "He'll be right here waiting for you. So will I. We'll see you again real soon."

"Promise?" The boy's eyes entreated him.

"I promise, Evan. I'll make it happen."

"Rafe?"

He swallowed thickly. "Yeah?"

His fly drifted downstream, unheeded. "You won't forget, will you?"

Their eyes met and held over their fly rods. "Never," Rafe swore. "I'll never forget, Evan."

Rafe slid the sizzling pan-fried trout out of the skillet onto Carly's plate.

"I want you to know," she said, staring at the perfectly cooked fish, "I'm wildly impressed. I thought you said you couldn't cook."

"I can't. Except trout. When the streams are really running, either you end up with a freezer full of fish, or you learn to make it edible. Or," he said with a grin at Laurie who was passing the fried potatoes to Jake, "you make trout pâté."

The boys made retching noises and broke into a fit of giggles.

"I'll have you know," Laurie said briskly, "my trout pâté was the sensation of Jefferson Cader's end-of-the-season party up at Purgatory, just last week."

Jake leaned over to Evan. "Yeah, but what kind of a sensation was it?"

"I heard that," Laurie said, slapping an overly generous portion of potatoes onto Jake's plate. "Hmm. I guess that means none of you boys wants the crumble-top apple pie I baked specially for tonight, either."

"Yes, we do!" the three boys chorused.

"Ah," Laurie said with a satisfied smile. "Then, no dissing the cook."

"Yeah," Rafe agreed, sitting down between Carly and Evan. "I second that." Elbows touching, he and Carly glanced at one another and flickered a smile. She'd seemed nervous as a cat all night, Rafe thought. He supposed it was because of the two first-class airline tickets that had come for her today by express mail. He'd seen them lying on her bed, though she hadn't mentioned them.

Wide-eyed, Jordan gulped. "I think...I swallowed a bone."

"A big one?" Laurie asked with concern.

He shook his head, holding his throat. "A little one."

Tearing off a piece of bread, she handed it to him. "Eat this and—chew more *carefully*." When he seemed better, she turned to Carly. "Dad says you two went to town today. Shopping spree?"

Carly flushed deeply, glancing at Rafe, who was suddenly looking at her. "Uh, no. I— We—"

"Had a couple errands," Gus put in, clearing his throat. He stabbed at his fish and avoided Rafe's look.

"Errands?" Rafe said to Carly, taking a bite of fish.

She shrugged. "You know…a few cosmetics, a truck starter. That sort of thing." Her gaze flicked to Gus.

"Got your truck working just fine, Rafe. That old starter was bad as they get."

"Great," he said, narrowing his eyes. Something was going on here, but he couldn't imagine what it was—unless she'd gone to town to make plans for her departure. No big secret there.

"Chicky says hi," Carly added.

"You went to the feed store?" he asked in astonishment.

Carly let out a nervous laugh. "No! No…I—I didn't go to the feed store. Why would I go there?" She rolled a look at Gus. "No, I saw her at the, uh,—"

"Pharmacy," Gus finished. "Buyin' a bottle of pills."

Rafe nodded. "Pills."

"Yes. Uh-huh. Pills."

Laurie exchanged a sideways look with Rafe and went back to her fish.

"Anyway," Carly said, clearing her throat, "she told me to tell you the feed you ordered came in. So…I'm telling you."

"Is somethin' going on here?" Rafe asked, setting his fork down.

A wildly innocent look flattened Carly's expression. "Going on?"

"Going on?" Gus echoed with equal fervor.

"Yeah," Rafe said. "Going on." By now, they had the boys' attention too. The three boys were following the conversation as if it were a Ping-Pong ball, back and forth across the table.

"Nothing's going on." Carly lifted her water glass high. "Except that I think the fishermen deserve a toast for this incredible meal." She gestured with her water glass, and everyone else followed suit. "Here's to fishing partners extraordinaire!"

Evan chinked his glass against Rafe's with a bittersweet smile that nearly broke his heart. "And many more expeditions to come," Rafe added quietly.

Laurie glanced at Jordan, who was still cautiously chewing the piece of bread she'd given him. "Jordan, honey, I meant chew the fish carefully, not the bread."

"Oh," he said with a sheepish grin, and swallowed.

The phone rang amid the chaos of conversation that buzzed around the table, and Rafe got up to get it.

"Kellard?" said the voice on the other end. "Stivers here."

Rafe felt his jaw tighten. There was no one who could spoil his appetite faster than Jed Stivers. "Jed, look, I'm just sitting down to dinner. This is a bad time."

"A bad time? Hell, is there ever a bad time for congratulations?"

He looked at the receiver as if it had gone haywire. "*Excuse* me?"

Jed made an impatient sound on the other end of the line. "I said I'm callin' to congratulate you, son! Hellfire, it isn't every day I get to deal with such a savvy and, I must say, beautiful lady."

"What beautiful lady?" Rafe asked, swinging his gaze to Carly, who was looking at him as though she'd forgotten how to breathe.

"Ms. Jamison. Your attorney. She drives a hard bargain, Rafe. Didn't miss a trick. But how could I turn down hard cash?"

"Cash?" Rafe echoed dully, turning fully now to Carly, an island of silence amid a tableful of noise. Gus was staring at his half-eaten fish, pushing it around his plate. Rafe's stomach turned with a sickening thud.

"You don't know how glad I was to be able to call those fellas from Sunimoto and tell them that the deal was off. I never wanted to sell there, Rafe. I hope you know that. I was just in a bind. It's all yours now, free and clear.

My attorneys will be sending over the papers within the week. But listen, that girl of yours? She's sharp as a tack. You oughta keep her around.''

Rafe's fingers tightened painfully on the receiver.

"Kellard?"

Rafe heard the voice echo in the earpiece. "Yeah," he said, his voice flat as a skipping stone. "Sharp as a tack. Thanks for the call, Jed. I gotta go."

"Sure, sure, Rafe. I'll be talking to you real—"

He slammed the receiver down, making Carly jump and the rest simply turn toward him in surprise. He was just standing there, staring at her in disbelief, as if she'd suddenly grown green horns or sprouted purple polka dots. Damn, damn, damn, she thought.

Rafe slid one hand against his forehead and laughed without an shred of humor. "And here I'm thinking that you and Gus and Chicky are cooking up some kind of party or something."

Slowly, Carly stood, bracing one hand against the back of her chair. Her legs felt weak, incapable of holding her up. "Rafe—"

"But it turns out I wasn't even invited to this one, was I, Carly?"

Chapter 13

The look on his face frightened her. A cold knot tightened in her stomach. "Rafe, if you'll just let me explain—"

He looked around the room aimlessly, dragging both hands through his hair. "Explain?" He looked at the children, who were watching him with collective trepidation.

"What's the matter, Mom?" Evan asked in a small voice.

Carly swallowed heavily, unable to take her eyes off Rafe, a caged animal looking for escape.

Gus's thick gray eyebrows pulled together in the center as he looked up at his boss. "Now, Rafe, if you'll just calm down and think about it—"

Astonished, Rafe impaled him with a killing look. "You too? You knew about this and let it *happen?*"

Gus nodded. "Yeah, I did. But it's not what you—"

"Of course you did. You drove her didn't you?" Rafe said accusingly. "A few errands, you said. A new starter and oh, ' the way...let's stop by Stivers's and buy that pesky piece of land for poor Rafe, who can't qualify for a loan of his own!''

Laurie, who had only now caught on, shifted her astonished gaze between Gus, Rafe and Carly. A whispered epithet escaped her lips.

"It wasn't like that," Carly said, her voice shaky as an aspen leaf in winter.

"Yes, it was. It was just like that." Rafe turned on his heel and slammed out the kitchen door, leaving in his wake a thick silence, broken only by the rattle of the door in its frame.

The sound her fork made as she set it down on her plate seemed overly loud to Carly. In fact, the silence was deafening. She looked up at the others, who were watching her expectantly, all but Gus. His gaze lingered on Rafe's empty chair.

Her eyes felt dry and tight, and her throat burned. "I—I'm sorry," she said, knowing that was hardly adequate. "That wasn't supposed to happen tonight. I thought I'd have a little more time before…"

"Wouldn'ta mattered," Gus said to no one in particular. "Damn-fool stubborn pride."

"No, it's not his fault. It's mine. I knew how he'd react. I'm just sorry it had to happen now. I wanted this night to be…" She faltered, her voice cracking with emotion.

"I'll go talk to him," Gus said, standing.

"No," Carly said. "It's my mess. I have to explain it."

Laurie covered Carly's hand with hers. "You only did what all of us wished we could have."

She wished she could take comfort from those words. But consensus of opinion would mean nothing to Rafe. The issues behind this were too old and too deeply etched on their fragile relationship. She'd done more than wound his pride—she'd yanked it out from under him. And that, she suspected, he would never forgive.

She found him in the barn, pitching hay, working up a

sweat that had already dampened his shirt between his shoulder blades. If he heard her approach, he pretended not to.

"Rafe."

The muscles in his back flexed and strained as he heaved a forkful of hay into the manger of a stall. Moisture gleamed on his forearms below the rolled-up sleeves of his shirt.

"Rafe?"

He straightened sharply and turned on her. His eyes were clouded with anger. "Who the hell gave you the right?"

"To help you? No one."

"*Help me?*" he shouted. "Who asked you? I never did."

"I don't recall asking for your help, either, when you flew to Nevada to rescue me and Evan, but you gave it to me anyway. How is this different?"

He regarded her darkly through a sweep of lashes.

"Honey," he growled, "if you can't see the difference—"

"Why don't you just spell it out for me, Rafe, because frankly, I don't see it. You needed help, I helped you. Why is that so wrong?"

His fists curled at his sides and a muscle worked in his jaw. "Because this is *my* ranch. *My* life. *My* problem."

"Yes, your problem," she said quietly, her voice thick and strained. "It's your problem that you'd rather risk killing yourself than accept help from someone who cares about you. It's your problem that you care more about your damned pride than you do about that little boy in there, who needs a daddy."

"Oh, this is about Evan now?"

Her eyes stung sharply. "Evan's part of everything now, Rafe, or haven't you realized that yet?"

"Oh, let me see," he said darkly. "Maybe I missed that

part of Parenting 101 sometime in those first eight years of his life.''

The barb hit its mark with stunning accuracy. Carly winced and looked away.

He stalked closer, crunching the hay beneath his boots. ''Don't try to tell me about parental responsibility, Carly. I grew up with a drunk for a father who couldn't hold on to a job, much less a piece of land. This place is mine. I carved it out of this damned valley with my own two hands. Every acre has soaked up my sweat, every fencepost has been drilled into the earth by my hand. It's what I am. It's all I have to give to Evan. But I'll be damned if I make it out of charity.''

''*Charity?*'' Her breath caught in her throat, and an ache centered itself in her chest. ''Is that what you think?''

''What would you call it?''

''You...you think I *pity* you?''

''Don't you?'' he snapped.

''Yes,'' she said, backing away from his intensity. ''Yes, if you really believe that. If you can't see past your own stupid ego for once—''

''Ego? How arrogant is it to go around behind my back and—''

''You would never have allowed me to do it any other way.''

''You're damned right!'' he shouted, shoving his pitchfork into the pile of hay. ''Jesus, Carly what are you trying to do, take every bit of pride I have left?''

''Pride?'' she repeated. ''Is that all that matters to you?''

''Don't try to turn this around. This is about you taking it upon yourself to fix my life. That's my job, dammit. Not yours. And where the hell did you get that kind of money, Carly? You don't just whip that kind of cash out of a back pocket.''

''What difference does it make?'' she asked, knowing it made all the difference.

His eyes, the color of an arctic icefloe, locked with hers. "Tell me."

"I had it wired from my bank in L.A."

He blinked twice. "Just like that?"

"Just like that."

He leaned back on his heels and regarded her with a Why-doesn't-that-surprise-me? look. "Not bad. Probably didn't even hurt the old pocketbook, did it? Even I didn't realize the Public defender's office paid that well."

The time for holding back was past. This was a moment for truth, no matter the consequences. "Tom left me some money," she said quietly. There, it was out.

His expression didn't change, but the blood drained from his face. "Better and better. You actually expected me to take money from your dead husband?"

Carly felt her heartbeat slow to a dull thud. "This isn't about Tom, Rafe."

He reached for the pitchfork and stabbed at the hay. "I won't sign the papers, Carly, so you might as well call Stivers up and tell him the deal is off."

She turned slightly until the moonlight shafting through the nearby window fell across her face. How cool and still the world seemed right now. The horses in the stalls stirred restively. From somewhere in the distance came the lonely sound of a whippoorwill. She had thought—imagined— that the end, when it came, would announce itself with a bang or a thump, or the awful sound of her heart breaking. The silence was a surprise.

"The contracts don't require your signature," she said quietly. "I purchased the land and quitclaimed it to you. It's done."

He turned slowly toward her in disbelief. She'd eradicated the last bit of control he might have had. And she could see he hated her for it.

She started to turn away, but stopped. She'd let him

have the last word for the last time. This time, she had nothing left to lose.

"You think this was all about money, don't you?"

He didn't answer, only watched the tears forming in her eyes.

"It wasn't, you know. It wasn't a bribe, or a token, or even a flaunt. It was a gift." She fisted her hand against her chest and choked back a sob. "A gift of the heart. Because I love you. I did it for you, and for Evan, and maybe even for us. But you can't see that, can you? You equate love with pity, faith with charity.

"You know the trouble with you, Rafe? You're afraid of love. It terrifies you, doesn't it? And you've never been able to accept it, especially from me. Well, I'm sorry for you. It must be lonely as hell where you are. I hope you're very happy there, because Evan and I are leaving tomorrow. But hey, there'll always be a rodeo somewhere to run to, won't there? Who knows? You might even win."

She turned again to go, only to turn back for one last parting shot. Tears were running down her cheeks now, unchecked. She didn't care. "You know, Rafe, Tom may not have been the love of my life, but I loved him. And he *loved* me. He trusted me. And you know what? I *deserve* that."

"Is that everything?" Gus asked, hefting Carly's suitcase off her bed and glancing around the bare room.

She nodded, having already looked twice everywhere. "I think so."

"Well," he muttered. "Well…"

She put a hand over his and gave him a squeeze. "I haven't said thank you."

"Fer what?" he asked with a frown. "Steerin' you wrong? Makin' you hope for—" His voice faltered, and he shook his head.

"You didn't steer me any way I didn't want to go. None of this is your fault, Gus. It's just what's meant to be."

"Well, gol dang it," he said, angry now, "somethin' went awry somewhere, 'cause it shouldn't oughta end like this."

She smiled sadly at him, grateful beyond words for his friendship. "We'd better get going."

"Right. Truck's around front. I'll meet you out there." After he left, Carly took one final look around the room. Something caught her eye on the edge of the dresser, and she reached down to pick it up. It was the picture of the two of them on the hot-air balloon.

Carly rubbed her thumb lightly across the image, as if trying to conjure up the moment that had been captured there. Impossible, of course. That moment and all the others were gone now. It was over. There would never be a dressertop full of pictures of them together, watching Evan grow up. And maybe it was all for the best.

But it sure as hell didn't feel that way.

Carefully she put the picture back and headed for Evan's room. She found him lying on the bed with his back firmly to the door.

"Ev? Time to go, honey. You all packed?"

Silence replied. His suitcase sat open, but haphazardly packed, at the foot of the bed. One sock lay forgotten near the end of his bed, and she picked it up and tossed it into the suitcase.

"Ev? I know you don't want to go, but—"

"Then why do we have to?" he grumbled, still facing the bank of windows, where the San Juans stood sentinel over the valley.

She sat on the bed beside him, her weight dipping his small body toward her. "We've already talked about this, Ev." She started to rub a hand across his back, but he shrugged it away and rolled off the bed.

"I know," he said.

"Gus said he'd buy us some ice cream in town. Jake and Jordan and Laurie are meeting us there. That'll be fun, right?"

Evan scowled at her, seeing right through her pathetic distraction ploy.

"Hey," she said, holding out her hand to him. "C'mere."

Reluctantly he came, sitting beside her as he had since he was a little tiny boy. "You're right," she told him gathering him to her in a hug. "It doesn't feel like fun, does it? But remember what Aunt Katherine used to say?" She pulled a regal face of quiet dignity that made Evan watch against his will. In her best imperious imitation of Katherine, she declared, "'When life hands you lemons, my dahlings, pull out your best crystal pitcher and squeeze!'"

Evan smiled grudgingly, and Carly gave him a hug. "But you remember, no matter what happens with me and Rafe, you'll come back here lots. I promise you that. Okay?"

Knowing he had no choice but to accept the inevitable, he nodded. "Okay."

"Let's go, champ."

Rafe was waiting beside the pickup, under the obvious guise of securing her things inside the bed of the truck. When she and Evan approached, he turned. He looked awful, as if he hadn't slept. Or shaved. Dark circles smudged the skin below his eyes and emphasized the anger she still read on his expression. He took Evan's suitcase from Carly, briefly touching her hand. For a moment, they stood frozen, hands linked, as if somehow, that touch could heal whatever was wrong with them. But he pulled away and slid the small suitcase onto the truck.

He turned back to Evan as a sage-scented breeze drifted around them. Rafe hunkered down before his son, touched the lapels on his jacket and brushed a hand through his soft blond hair. "You take care of your mom, now, you hear?"

Evan nodded solemnly.

"I'll see you again, real soon, pard. Promise. Okay?"

Evan nodded, then threw his arms around Rafe's neck and held on tight. Rafe closed his eyes, and hugged him back. They stayed like that for a full thirty seconds before Rafe broke the embrace, pulling Evan back to look at him. "I never told you," he said, "but I'm...I'm so proud of you, son. And I'll keep Tampico right here for you for the next time you come to visit. He's yours now."

Evan's teary eyes widened. "Really?"

Rafe crossed his chest. "You earned him."

Evan hugged him again. "Cool. *Thanks*...Dad."

Rafe's heart gave a squeeze.

This time, Evan pulled back and reached into his pocket. When he withdrew his small fingers, he held a shiny coin. "Here. You take this," Evan said, pressing the lucky dime into Rafe's hand.

"But that's yours now," Rafe said with a frown.

"You know how you said that you can share luck? Well, I thought maybe if you had it back you'd be lucky again. And maybe..." The last drifted off, unspoken.

Rafe's gaze flicked to Carly, who was watching her son through glittering eyes.

"Thanks, Ev," Rafe said, taking the dime. "I guess I could use a little luck at that. I'll take real good care of it. You go on now and hop in the truck, while I say goodbye to your mom."

One final hug for Macky, who wagged a disconsolate tail, and Evan climbed aboard beside Gus, who was already behind the wheel.

Rafe turned back to Carly, tucked his thumbs into the back of his waistband and let out a long breath.

"Thanks—for everything," she said, clutching a bag of Evan's things in front of her like a shield.

Rafe took it from her and settled it in the back with the rest of the things. He shoved his hands into his back pockets. "I'll, uh...pay you back when I get the money together," he said into the uncomfortable silence that stretched between them.

If he'd slapped her, it couldn't have stung more. "Whatever," she said stiffly.

He searched her face, and then his gaze drifted to the horizon just past her shoulder. "You'll...let me know how to reach you?"

"Of course. As soon as we settle." She opened the door of the truck. "Goodbye, Rafe."

"Carly?"

She froze, then tilted her head just enough to see him.

A muscle worked in his jaw as he met her eyes. "Take care."

She wouldn't cry. She wouldn't give that to him now. "You too," she said thickly.

Rafe stepped back with a nod and watched her get in the truck and pull the door shut. Then, without another word, she was gone.

He stood for long minutes watching the cloud of dust spit up by the vanishing truck. Then he went to the paddock, saddled Bogus, and tore out of the yard at a ground-eating gallop.

And though he worked the horse and himself into a lather, he soon discovered that he couldn't go fast enough or far enough to outrun the feeling that he'd just thrown away his last chance.

Chapter 14

Rafe lifted Bogus's bridle off its hook in the tack room and laid it over the worktable. He slapped a dab of saddle soap on his rag and attacked the hapless leather.

"You done that one already," Gus said. "Twice."

Rafe looked up absently past the naked lightbulb illuminating the night-shadowed barn. "What?"

"I said you done that one twice already. And all the other tack in here, too."

Rafe narrowed a glare at Gus, then glanced at the shiny, supple leather hanging neatly in a row on the far wall. He pursed his lips. "So? You got a problem with my cleaning the tack?"

"Nope. I ain't got a problem. Just makin' an observation."

"Thanks for sharing." He scrubbed the leather relentlessly until it gleamed. When he looked up, Gus was still standing there at the doorway, staring. "Haven't you got somewhere to go, old man?"

"Yeah," Gus said. "I'm headin' to Laurie's. She wanted me to invite you for supper."

"No...I've, uh, got too much to do here."

"Yeah," Gus said, arching one hairy brow. "I can see that."

"Tell her thanks for me, anyway."

Gus braced a gnarled hand against the door frame. "It's been more'n a week, Rafe. How long you gonna hole up here? You ain't been off this place once since Carly left. Laurie said to tell ya she's startin' to get a complex."

"A complex? Laurie? That'll be the day." He swirled his rag around and around in the saddle-soap jar. "And I'm not holed up. I've just been busy."

"Right. Polishin' tack that don't need polishin'. Mending fence that don't need mendin'. And bitin' everybody's head off in the process." Macky, who was lying on the floor near Rafe, lifted his head from his paws and yawned loudly. "See? Even the dog agrees."

"I've been preoccupied," Rafe said in his own defense.

Gus glanced at Rafe's workbench and caught sight of the picture of Rafe and Carly lying carelessly against the wood. He picked it up and looked at it. It was worn around the edges, as if Rafe had been keeping it in his pocket. "No kiddin'."

Rafe looked up at Gus pointedly. "She said she was gonna call. She hasn't called."

"Do ya blame her?" Gus asked. "Pret' near bit her head off before she left."

Rafe scrubbed the reins with unnecessary effort. "You think I was wrong, don't you?"

"Ain't my place to say, Rafe. That's between you an' her."

Rafe glanced up. "But you think so."

"I think there's a fine line between self-sufficiency and

pure obstinance," he said with uncharacteristic seriousness.

Dropping his rag, Rafe shrugged the tension from his shoulders. "Maybe I have to be able to live with myself."

Gus shook his head. "Yeah, but can you do it without her?"

By now, Carly was somewhere in Ohio, with a new job and a new life. And he had no one to blame but himself. "I guess I'll have to, won't I?"

Gus sent him an uninterpretable look. "I reckon that's up to you." He turned to go.

"I'm riding tomorrow," Rafe told him.

The blood siphoned from Gus's weathered face as he turned around. "You're *what?*"

"You heard me."

"At the rodeo in town? But I thought—"

Of course he had, Rafe thought. Everyone assumed he'd give it up, now that he had the land he needed. But it wasn't over. Far from it. Rafe shrugged. "I'm still riding. It's the only way I'm gonna earn enough to pay her back."

With a shake of his head, Gus stared at him in disbelief. "You are the stubbornest cuss this side of the Continental Divide, Kellard. She bought that land so's you wouldn't *have* to ride tomorrow. And last I heard, she wasn't requirin' no payback."

Rafe stared down at the gleaming leather in his hands. "*I* require it."

"Ya know, somewhere down the line," Gus said, "somebody convinced you that accepting help was the same thing as failure, Rafe. And it ain't. Or it don't have to be. But that's somethin' you'll have to discover on your own. I just hope it ain't too late when you finally do."

With a foul curse, Rafe swept the tin of saddle soap off the table and sent it clanking into the wall. Gus hardly flinched. "I'm gettin' goddamned sick of everybody treating me like an invalid. There was a time I was on top, when everybody knew me and what I was capable of. Now, suddenly, I've got a hundred mothers all tittering over me like I'm some kind of cripple! Well, I'm not, dammit! If I want to compete, I'll compete! If I want to risk it, then it's my business.''

"I never called you a cripple!" Gus practically shouted back. "Nobody with a lick of sense would. It's your priorities that need some attention. Take it from an old man who let his life slip by until it was almost too late—worryin' about things that meant nothin' in the end.

"Those things, they don't keep ya warm on a cold December night, Rafe. They don't sit on your lap and blow dandelion feathers into the air, or sing happy birthday to ya when even you forgot it was your birthday. And they don't come through for you in a pinch when the whole rest of the world lets you down."

He rubbed a hand against his grizzled chin. "You wanna ride? Nobody's gonna stop you. But you better be damned sure that your reasons for goin' backwards are worth it. 'Cause if they're not, you might regret it for the rest of your life."

Rafe tightened the leather rigging on the bareback strap circling the massive chest of his bronc, High Chaparral. He'd stayed up most of last night thinking about what Gus had said. Sometime around three, it had started to sound reasonable, but by five he'd been back to square one. Around and around his reasoning had taken him, until nothing seemed to make sense anymore, except to show up.

So he had.

High Chaparral—a scruffy-haired sorrel with a cropped mane and tail who'd been known to drag hung-up riders against the arena wall for pure fun—blew out his belly with air and sent a malevolent look back at him. In reply, Rafe brought his knee up under the horse's ribs and cinched the strap tight.

"I may have been gone awhile," he told the animal, "and I may be an idiot for comin' back, but I'm not fallin' for that one."

Nearby, a dozen other riders prepared for the bareback event. Mel Stratton had shaken his hand earlier and wished him luck. Rafe had watched him inspect the horse he was slated to ride—an awesomely muscled roan named Skoal.

Rafe looked up and scanned the full stands. Gus and Laurie hadn't come—not that he'd expected them to. But as he turned his head, someone else caught his eye: a woman with Carly's blond hair and willowy body, moving with the crowd near the arena rail with her back to him. A boy Evan's size bobbed along beside her.

His heartbeat tripled in a fraction of a second. His mouth went dry and his mind blank. Rafe took a step or two in her direction, willing her to turn around.

"Carly?" he called, but his voice was drowned out by the sound of the crowd.

"Carly!" he shouted again.

In the next moment, he found himself running after her, pushing through the crowd of surprised spectators, who alternately grunted and cursed him for shoving past. Apologies, explanations and lame excuses flashed through his consciousness as he gained on her. The words *moronic, ungrateful* and *ignoramus* leaped to mind, alongside the fear that if he caught her she might just keep walking. God knew, he deserved that.

His hand closed around her arm. "Carly—"

The attractive woman—who was definitely not Carly—whirled at the touch with an affronted expression. "Hey, what do you think you're—?"

Rafe released her arm as if he'd been jolted by electricity and held both hands up, palms open. "Hey, I'm sorry. I—I thought you were... I'm sorry."

Her gaze slid asessingly down him, then back up. With a sympathetic shrug, she said, "That makes two of us." Gathering her son to her, she turned and kept moving.

Shoulders collided with his as the crowd moved past him and the woman and boy vanished into the surging mass of people.

Idiot. Carly was two thousand miles away in Ohio. What right did he even have to hope that—?

Oh, hell.

He rubbed a hand down his face, shaken. He wondered if he'd be looking for Carly in crowds for the rest of his life? Would his heart pound whenever he saw a winsome blonde with a Grace Kelly walk? Or when he heard the sound of a laugh like hers, would his brain go numb, like it had just now?

Would he end up like Gus, with a lifetime full of regrets?

You know the trouble with you, Rafe? You're afraid of love. It terrifies you, doesn't it?

Was he? Hell, yes. He was afraid. Afraid he'd jump, only to find the floor gone below him. Afraid he wasn't up to it all if it was gone. His reasons weren't a mystery. He had a long and sordid history of snatched-up floors and hard falls.

Hell, he could ride a bull whose only goal was to stomp him to death, or a bronc who promised to bash his brains against the wall, given half a chance.

But ask himself to let Carly love him—to love her back—and he was suddenly a nuclear reactor in a meltdown. Why was that so damned hard?

This morning, he'd sat on the porch and watched the sun come up over his ranch, spilling over the mountains like a slow-moving wave. He'd watched the same scene a

thousand times from that spot, but never before had he felt
the clawing emptiness that was inside him today. Because
it had struck him that the land he'd worked so hard to
save—the life he'd struggled to build here—none of it
meant anything without Carly and Evan to share it. It was
an empty promise.

I did it for you, and for Evan and maybe even for us,
Carly's voice echoed. *I love you, Rafe.*

Rafe stood stock-still, staring at the arena and the
crowds, and the sounds around him became a blur of noise.

I love you, Rafe. Love you. Love you…

And Gus's voice: *Can you live without her?*

It's your priorities that need some attention.

Rafe blinked as the announcer on the loudspeaker began
announcing the next round.

The truth struck him between the eyes like a sledgeham-
mer. She'd loved him. *Loved* him! She hadn't snatched
any floors away. *He* had. He'd been the one this time, just
as he had been the last time. Carly was a constant. Like
the moon or that sun pouring over his mountains. Waiting.
Waiting for him to wake up and see her for who she really
was. Not a ladder-climbing attorney, or a woman with
great potential. Just a woman, a good woman who loved
him.

"…Ken Chernus on Wildfire," droned the announcer's
voice on the loudspeaker as he announced the upcoming
event. "Mel Stratton will be riding Skoal off the Angel
Blue ranch, and last but not least, we've got us a real treat
today, folks," the voice on the loudspeaker continued.
"Some of you will remember him. He's an old favorite
here, an all-around cowboy in 1992, NFR champion Bull
Rider in '93. And a list longer than my arm of other cham-
pionships in the Mountain State pro rodeo circuit and the
national finals rodeo. He's back after a long absence. Let's
hear it for Rafe Kellard, folks!"

A cheer went up in the stands, but Rafe hardly heard it. He was too busy pulling a slip of paper from his wallet with the names Maynard, Barnes and Griffith on it. It had found its way there late one night, when his hand hovered over the phone in his den. He hadn't used it then, but he wouldn't make that mistake again.

He headed for the pay phone at the end of the arena. Mel saw him go.

"Hey, Rafe! Where the hell you going? The event's about to start!"

"Something came up," he told him without stopping.

Mel grinned with a slow nod. "Yeah," he said to no one in particular. "It's about time somethin' did."

Rafe punched in the numbers on the keypad and waited until a scratchy-voiced secretary answered.

"Maynard, Barnes and Griffith. How may I help you?"

Rafe's mouth went dry. "Uh, hello. Can I...could you please connect me with Ms. Carly Jamison?"

"Jamison?" the woman repeated in a perplexed voice. "One moment please."

Rafe waited. The next voice belonged to a man.

"Jonathan Maynard here. Who's calling?"

"I think there's been a mistake," Rafe said. "I'm trying to reach Carly Jamison. She's a new attorney at your firm. This is a friend of hers, Rafe Kellard."

"Uh," Maynard hedged, "Mr. Kellard, Ms. Jamison's not here."

Rafe frowned and felt his heart skip a beat. "Not there? You mean...she hasn't started yet? But I thought—"

"Not here as in not here, Mr. Kellard. Ms. Jamison changed her mind about our offer. She never came to Cincinnati."

Behind him, the crowd roared in response to a good ride, and Rafe covered his free ear with his palm. "What the hell are you talking about, never came? Of course she came. That's where she was going. I saw her plane tickets.''

''Well, something changed her plans, Mr. Kellard.''

''Where is she? Did she tell you where she was going?''

''I'm afraid I have no forwarding address for her. I'm sorry. Believe me, we were all very sorry to lose her.''

Rafe hung up the phone and stared sightlessly at the straw-littered floor of the barn. His legs felt filled with lead. Not in Cincinnati?

Where the hell could she be?

Ten days.

She'd been gone ten days. Had she gone back to L.A., where her friends were? Or somewhere else altogether? And why hadn't she called him?

Bracing one hand on the wall for support, he cursed foully and considered his options. He could call the airline her tickets were on, find out which flight she took out of town. He could hire a private detective...or call the police.

In frustration, he lifted the receiver and banged it three times against the lever.

''Wrong number?'' came a female voice beside him.

Rafe whirled. ''Laurie!''

''Or are you angry with the phone company now, too?''

He grabbed her shoulders. ''It's Carly. She didn't go to Cincinnati.''

''I know.''

''That Maynard guy? The partner? He said she just changed her mind and that he had no idea where she'd—'' He stopped short. ''What?''

''I said, I know she didn't go to Cincinnati.''

He searched her face for a long, disbelieving moment. ''You *know?* Why the hell didn't you tell me?''

''You didn't ask, Sherlock. And I wasn't about to tell you until you got that giant Dorito off your shoulder. Jeez, Rafe, you can really be an—''

"Where is she?"

Laurie glanced at his hands, still bracketing her shoulders. He removed them gingerly. "Where is she, Laurie?"

"She asked me not to tell you, not yet anyway. But frankly, I think she could use a little groveling on your part. She's been pretty upset."

"*Where*, Laurie?"

"She's here in Durango." She glanced at her watch. "For at least another...two hours, that is. She found a job at a law office in town, but she's booked on a three-fifty-five flight to L.A. A business trip."

"She's here? She stayed in Durango?" Rafe repeated idiotically. He couldn't believe it.

"Yes," Laurie answered. "But I'll let her tell you why." Opening the flap on her purse, she withdrew a business card with the address of a law firm in town and handed it to him. "And if you've got half a brain in that thick head of yours, you'll go and grab her before she leaves, and tell her what a numbskull you've been!"

"Hey, Rafe!" called a cowboy from the standby area. "You're up in two."

Rafe turned to Laurie, his heart pounding against his ears. "Numbskull doesn't quite cover it, does it?" he said, and with a shake of her head, she agreed. He glanced at his watch and backed away from her, heading down the barn entryway. "Scratch my name with the announcer, will you?"

She nodded with a self-satisfied grin. "Be happy to. Anything else?"

"Yeah, wish me luck!"

"Good—" she called after him, but he was already gone. "Luck." A smile spread across her face.

Dan Burkholt passed a tray of freshly baked New York Bagel Company bagels around the conference table, past

Jonathan Lindsey, Kay Header and Errol Halstrom, to Carly.

"Best damned bagels in town," Dan told her. "Like lox?"

Errol made a comical face, and Carly suppressed a smile, slathering only cream cheese on hers.

"Best damned lox this side of the Divide, too."

"You'll have to forgive him, Carly," Jonathan told her in a paternal sort of way. "Dan's passionate about his bagels, which is why he's part owner of the shop these came from. A shameless self-promoter."

"They're delicious," she said around her first bite.

"Good answer," Errol said, loudly enough for the whole table to hear.

Dan sent Jonathan a See-there? look and smiled broadly at Carly. "I knew she was bright when I hired her."

"You hired her?" Jonathan said. "*I* hired her."

Kay held up the Hamilton lawsuit file, with a smile at Carly. "Now that we've established how clever we all are, can we talk about the Hamilton case, considering that Carly is out of here in exactly one hour and fifty-four minutes? I'm sorry this one fell on you, Carly, but with your experience with the L.A. courts, you're the obvious choice for this one. Have you got everything you need?"

Carly glanced through the file one last time, thinking not about the case, but about Evan, whom she'd left with Laurie for the three days she'd be gone. If all went well, she'd be back in two.

To say she was reluctant to travel so soon would have been an understatement, but she'd taken this job with the understanding that she would consult on cases that involved California plaintiffs. She had yet to find her own place in town. Laurie had graciously extended an invitation to stay with her until they could. The search would simply have to wait anther two days.

"There are one or two things in his deposition that I wanted to discuss—" she began, but a disturbance in the outer office drew all eyes toward the frosted-glass paneled door.

"You can't go in there," Dorothy Werner's voice could be heard saying. A man's voice answered, but the reply was unclear.

"Wait a minute, you can't just—!"

The door swung open, and Rafe burst through it.

Carly's eyes widened, and her mouth fell open in shock. "Rafe—"

He was breathing hard, as if he'd been running. His glance took in the others, and then, just as quickly, dismissed them. He looked for all the world like a cigarette ad, in his leather chaps and his open-necked workshirt, all hard muscle and intensity. But it was the look in his searing blue eyes that tightened the knot in her belly that had been there since last she saw him.

A buzzing started in her ears and drowned out the shocked gasps of the others. Dan was on his feet, as were Jonathan and Kay. Alarm filtered through the room like a pulse.

"What the hell is this?" Dan asked, starting around the table toward Rafe. "Do you know this guy, Carly?"

She nodded, her throat constricting. She never thought he'd come to her. Never.

Rafe was three feet away from her with the table standing between them. "I need to talk with you, Carly. Alone."

Carly's eyes flicked to her partners, who were watching her closely, trying to read the situation. She felt herself blush. "We're...we're in a meeting, Rafe."

"Fine," he said, digging in and leaning on the table with both hands. "I'll say it here, then. I've been an idiot, okay? A first-rate, flat-footed jerk. Don't ask me what I was thinking. I obviously wasn't. Because if I had been, I never would have let you go."

Dan, Jonathan and Errol shifted nervously in their places, uncertain whether to stay or go. Kay, on the other hand, seemed to be settling back to enjoy the show.

Rafe went on, his eyes only on Carly, as if none of the others were even on the same planet. He dipped his head and looked at her through a thick fringe of dark lashes. "I'm…sorry, Carly. You were right. You were right about all of it. I am stubborn and I'm full of pride and if I had half the sense God gave a flea, I wouldn't have let you go nine years ago, either.

"I'm not perfect and, dammit, I'm never gonna be. And all I have to offer you is myself and a place to start. I know that's not enough. Not nearly enough for a woman like you. But you see—" he swallowed back a lump in his throat "—I'm lookin' for you in crowds and hearing your voice in my head. And the ranch—it's lonely as hell without you and Evan on it. So I'm askin' you, Carly, to please come home."

Dorothy and Kay gave a collective sigh.

Her eyes brimming with tears, Carly slowly stood, her knees shaky and uncertain.

Dan cleared his throat. "Uh, we oughta… Um, I think it would be prudent if we gave them a little…"

Jonathan smiled wryly. "Prudent. Right. *Excellent* word choice." He wrapped an arm around Errol's shoulder as they followed the others from the room. "Ever been to L.A., Halstrom? I hear it's pretty nice this time of year.…"

The door closed behind them.

For ten heart-wrenching seconds, Carly and Rafe stood silent, with the table still between them.

Carly bit her lip, holding back the tears that were threatening to spill down her cheeks. She shook her head.

"Rafe, I—"

"Don't say no."

She closed her eyes. "It's not that simple."

"Maybe it is," he said, stepping around the corner of the table. "Why didn't you go to Cincinnati, Carly?"

"Who told you?"

"Your former boss, Maynard," he said, closing the distance between them. "He was real sorry you didn't show. I wasn't. Laurie told me the rest."

She braced her hand against the table and backed up a step. "I never thought you'd call."

"Why, Carly? Why'd you stay?"

He was close now. So close she could smell the oh-so-familiar masculine scent of him. "Because Evan needs you," she said, "and I...couldn't bear for him to lose yet another father."

"Is that the only reason?"

She hated that he could melt her with a look, sweep all her well-intentioned rationalizations under the carpet with that voice of his that sent shivers up and down her spine. She lifted her chin, refusing to be bent. "If you think I was *waiting* for you to come barging in here like some...some *caveman* and—"

He dragged her flush against him and dropped his mouth on hers in a calculated assault on her already dimming senses. His tongue slid insistently against her teeth until she surrendered to the onslaught. His lips, slanting against hers, first one way, then the other, silenced all pretense. She forgot what she'd been about to say as his hands traveled down her spine to cup her buttocks and lift her closer. A sound—a squeak, really—escaped her as she felt her knees give and her body sway against him.

Finally, he lifted his mouth but a heartbeat from hers. "Weren't you?" He stared down at her. "Waiting?"

"What if I was?" she managed to say. "I never thought you'd come."

"I'm here. Marry me, Carly."

"Wh-what?" she stammered, wondering where her wits had gone.

He dragged his thumb across her lips, still damp from his kiss. "Come home with me. I need you."

For two heartbeats, she could only stare at him. Then, slowly, she shook her head. "No, Rafe. I can't. I won't. That's not enough. Not for me."

With a frown, he searched her eyes. "Carly—"

Tears slid down her cheeks now as she felt the old nemesis rise between them again. She pulled away, forcing space between them, yet clutching the front of his shirt in a damningly contrary gesture.

"I *need* food and sunshine and air. I *need* to see the leaves change in the fall and feel the crisp cold of winter against my skin. But need alone isn't enough to build a relationship on. And it's not enough for me."

He stopped her from pulling completely away and forced her to look at him. "You're right. It's not. And that was my mistake nine years ago. I never said it, because I thought maybe if I didn't say the words, it would hurt less when you left. But it didn't work. Because it almost killed me anyway. I loved you then, and I love you still."

Her heart quaked at the words.

"Carly—" He cupped her face between his hands. "You're my heart, and you own a piece of my soul. You always have. I've done a lot of stupid things in my life, but losing you was the worst. And I won't let it happen again. I was so caught up in trying to be someone for you, I couldn't see what I had right in front of me.

"I thought I could prove something to you by making the ranch a success," he went on, "but without you and Evan there, it's just a piece of land—it means nothing to me." Brushing a strand of blond hair from her eyes, he came as close as she'd ever seen him come to tears. "I

love you, Carly. I swear I'll never give you cause to regret
it again. I want to be a real father to Evan and a husband
to you. Marry me. And if I ever get stupid and stubborn
and prideful again—kick me.''

"Oh, Rafe—" She kissed him fully, drinking in the
taste of him, threading her hands behind his neck. This
man she'd loved for so long had finally come home.
"Yes."

He grabbed her by the shoulders. "Yes, you'll kick me?
Or yes, you'll marry me?"

She laughed. "Yes, I'll marry you!"

Crushing her to him, he held her tightly, almost as if he
didn't dare let her go. She never wanted him to. But there
was one thing she had to know. "What about—" she hesitated.

"What?" he asked.

"What about my job here?"

The certainty in his gaze relieved the worry in hers.
"You'll be great at it." He grinned. "And I'll do my best
to rehabilitate my image with your partners. Can't have
'em thinking you're marrying a caveman, can we?"

"Oh, I dunno. I don't think Kay and Dorothy minded
much. The others? They'll get used to it. Think you can
handle being married to an attorney?"

A challenging smile tilted the corners of his mouth. "If
you can handle being married to a struggling rancher."

"An up-and-coming rancher with a big future," she corrected against his lips as he kissed her again.

"Mmm-mmm...I like the up-and-coming part," he
teased, smiling against her mouth. "And you never know
when an attorney in the family just might come in handy."

"Mmm," she mused, watching him closely, "all those
pesky run-ins with bulls and bareback broncs?"

Sliding his hands downward against her backside, he
lifted her against him. "That's over." He dropped his

mouth heatedly to the curve of her neck and tortured the spot with his tongue.

"You...sure?" Breathless, she dropped her forehead against his, hardly daring to believe him.

Transferring his attention to her mouth, he demonstrated just how certain he was. When he'd left not a trace of a doubt in her mind, he lifted his mouth from hers with a decadent smile.

"There's only one event that holds any interest for me now, Carly. And it involves you—" he kissed her cheek "—and me—" her temple "—and a ring." The last kiss he pressed against her forehead, like a vow. "And you can start the clock and keep it runnin' on that promise, darlin', 'cause I have a feelin' this is gonna be a very long ride."

* * * * *

Take 4 bestselling love stories FREE

Plus get a FREE surprise gift!

As seen on TV!
Free Gift Offer

With a Free Gift proof-of-purchase from any Silhouette® book,
you can receive a beautiful cubic zirconia pendant.

This gorgeous marquise-shaped stone is a genuine cubic
zirconia—accented by an 18" gold tone necklace.

(Approximate retail value $19.95)

Send for yours today...
compliments of ▼ *Silhouette*®

To receive your free gift, a cubic zirconia pendant, send us one original proof-of-purchase, photocopies not accepted, from the back of any Silhouette Romance™, Silhouette Desire®, Silhouette Special Edition®, Silhouette Intimate Moments® or Silhouette Yours Truly™ title available at your favorite retail outlet, together with the Free Gift Certificate, plus a check or money order for $1.65 U.S./$2.15 CAN. (do not send cash) to cover postage and handling, payable to Silhouette Free Gift Offer. We will send you the specified gift. Allow 6 to 8 weeks for delivery. Offer good until March 31, 1998, or while quantities last. Offer valid in the U.S. and Canada only.

Free Gift Certificate

Name: _____

Address: _____

City: _____ State/Province: _____ Zip/Postal Code: _____

Mail this certificate, one proof-of-purchase and a check or money order for postage and handling to: SILHOUETTE FREE GIFT OFFER 1998. In the U.S.: 3010 Walden Avenue, P.O. Box 9077, Buffalo, NY 14269-9077. In Canada: P.O. Box 613, Fort Erie, Ontario L2Z 5X3.

FREE GIFT OFFER   084-KFD
ONE PROOF-OF-PURCHASE
To collect your fabulous FREE GIFT, a cubic zirconia pendant, you must include this
original proof-of-purchase for each gift with the properly completed Free Gift Certificate.

084-KFDR2

SILHOUETTE WOMEN KNOW ROMANCE WHEN THEY SEE IT.

And they'll see it on **ROMANCE CLASSICS**, the new 24-hour TV channel devoted to romantic movies and original programs like the special **Romantically Speaking—Harlequin™ Goes Prime Time.**

Romantically Speaking—Harlequin™ Goes Prime Time introduces you to many of your favorite romance authors in a program developed exclusively for Harlequin® and Silhouette® readers.

Watch for **Romantically Speaking—Harlequin™ Goes Prime Time** beginning in the summer of 1997.

If you're not receiving ROMANCE CLASSICS, call your local cable operator or satellite provider and ask for it today!

Escape to the network of your dreams.

See Ingrid Bergman and Gregory Peck in *Spellbound* on Romance Classics.

©1997 American Movie Classics Co. "Romance Classics" is a service mark of American Movie Classics Co.
Harlequin is a trademark of Harlequin Enterprises Ltd.
Silhouette is a registered trademark of Harlequin Books, S.A.   RMCLS-S-R2

SUSAN MALLERY

Continues the twelve-book series—36 HOURS—in January 1998 with Book Seven

THE RANCHER AND THE RUNAWAY BRIDE

When Randi Howell fled the altar, she'd been running for her life! And she'd kept on running—straight into the arms of rugged rancher Brady Jones. She knew he had his suspicions, but how could she tell him the truth about her identity? Then again, if she ever wanted to approach the altar in earnest, how could she not?

For Brady and Randi and *all* the residents of Grand Springs, Colorado, the storm-induced blackout was just the beginning of 36 Hours that changed *everything!* You won't want to miss a single book.

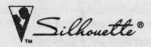

Available at your favorite retail outlet.

Look us up on-line at: http://www.romance.net

36HRS7

The Stars of Mithra

**Three gems,
three beauties,
three passions...
the adventure of a lifetime**

SILHOUETTE·INTIMATE·MOMENTS®
brings you a thrilling new series by
New York Times bestselling author

Nora Roberts

**Three mystical blue diamonds place three close
friends in jeopardy...and lead them to romance.**

In October
HIDDEN STAR (IM#811)
Bailey James can't remember a thing, but she knows
she's in big trouble. And she desperately needs private
investigator Cade Parris to help her live long enough to
find out just what kind.

In December
CAPTIVE STAR (IM#823)
Cynical bounty hunter Jack Dakota and spitfire
M. J. O'Leary are handcuffed together and on the run
from a pair of hired killers. And Jack wants to know
why—but M.J.'s not talking.

In February
SECRET STAR (IM#835)
Lieutenant Seth Buchanan's murder investigation takes
a strange turn when Grace Fontaine turns up alive. But
as the mystery unfolds, he soon discovers the notorious
heiress is the biggest mystery of all.

Available at your favorite retail outlet.